EZEKIEL'S OREGON

(EZEKIEL'S JOURNEY BOOK II)

JOHNNY GUNN

WOLFPACK
PUBLISHING
— EST 2013 —

Ezekiel's Oregon
(Ezekiel's Journey Book II)

Johnny Gunn

Paperback Edition
© Copyright 2018 Johnny Gunn

Wolfpack Publishing
6032 Wheat Penny Avenue
Las Vegas, NV 89122

ISBN: 978-1-62918-780-8

I

BOOK FIVE: THE JOURNEY
CONTINUES

Clive Newton was often described as a block of solid granite, standing about five feet and ten inches, with shoulders almost as wide, and sporting a massive chest. Newton weighed in at a hefty two hundred pounds, had mousey brown hair that hung straight, no waves or curls at all, and dull gray eyes. His square jaw and bold chin set off a neck about the same width as his shoulders. In other words, a block of granite.

Newton was a loud, pushy man who believed that because he was large and loud, he should get his way, and many a man found a simple argument ended by way of a fist to the jaw. He was part of a group known as Oregon Firsters. The Firsters were solidly against more immigrants coming in from back east. Newton was now in another rant on a late spring morning.

"Did you see that notice in the paper, Pritchett? That farmer Hawthorne is gonna run for the legislature. Another damn newcomer lookin' to tell us how to run our territory. Wish them fools would stay home where they belong. He's the one brought that Travis and Johnson with him, tryin' to run me out of business."

"You rant about this all the time, Newton, but let me ask you this. Were you born here? Of course, you weren't! You came here just like all the others, you don't want here. You came in as a mule-skinner for one of the first wagons, and think that makes you and those like you special. You ain't special, Newton," Pritchett said. Most of the time, Pritchett fended off Newton's rants with humor, but not that morning.

"I'll tell you, the first thing them newcomers say when they get here..." Newton continued. "This isn't the way we did it back home. Ain't I right? Well, I say, if you want to do it that way, go back where you came from and do it."

Newton had a small hauling business; two small wagons and half a dozen mules. He tried to keep two employees. He was sitting in the Salem Club with Paul Pritchett, the dentist/barber, whose shop was located next to the Salem Hotel and Salem Club. "Well, I've met Zeke Hawthorne a couple of times, Clive. He's a good man, and has a fine family. I think he might just be right for the job."

"The man's married to a damn injun, Paul; one of Travis's kids, and he wants more people to come to Oregon. He wants to bring more people, and we can't support the ones we already have."

"You're crossed up in your thinkin', Clive. Most companies can't keep employees because we have too many men who have come with no background in workin'. That's what's wrong, not the fact people are comin'. We just need educated people that will work for a living." Pritchett had been in this discussion many times and just shook his head knowing he wouldn't get through to the man. "We've got California miners that can't mine, we've got men that came with wagon trains with no training in any kind of employment, and we've got young men just looking for adventure..."

He took a breath and continued, "What we don't have are men looking to build a life for themselves in what will soon be the state of Oregon." Pritchett had come to Oregon before it became a part of the United States, owned a small patch of good ground that he'd claimed well before territorial status, and was a backer of the statehood movement.

"Stupid!" Clive Newton almost shouted. "I'm not educated and I own my own business. That Johnson is tryin' to run me out of business."

"If you're so good at runnin' your hauling company, how come it is that Johnson and Travis opened the hauling routes into California? Why didn't you open those roads, if you're so damn smart?" The argument was getting heated and Pritchett was losing patience with Newton. There were some in the saloon who started wondering if the good dentist was about to lose some teeth.

The Salem Hotel and attached Salem Club dated back enough years that the heavy timber and planking used in its building had a definite patina. Hanging kerosene lamps with crystal ornaments offered light, and the Club could best be described as rough-hewn. The long bar along one wall was heavy thick oak, and the back wall was roughly carved fir with a few shelves holding bottles.

The heat of conversation was increasing and the two men were joined by Harold (Bud) Best before it got too hot. Best was what he called a "laborer", which meant he only worked when he wanted to, never took a full-time job, and spent his money often faster than he earned it. "You boys sound a bit riled up this morning. Coffee got stingers in it?" He was laughing as he pulled up a chair to join them.

Bud Best had come to Oregon Territory by way of the California gold fields, grabbed one of the quarter sections offered by Sullivan's office and managed, after three years, to get a small cabin built on the land. A stream flowed into Mill Creek and salmon made their runs twice a year, allowing Best a chance to smoke several hundred pounds a year, which was his main dietary intake.

Best too, was an Oregon Firster and didn't have much use for the idea of statehood. He enjoyed his own brand of citizenship. That meant, no government to speak of, few laws of any kind, and like so many, Best did not have a great desire to succeed in anything more than survival.

"I was telling the Doc here about Zeke Hawthorne running for the legislature. He wants to bring in more people and wants Oregon to be a state. That's just wrong, I say." Clive Newton was about to say more when Ole Gunderson, a lumberjack and mill worker, slipped into the fourth chair at the table.

"Ja, I read that, too," Gunderson said, motioning the barman to bring a bottle and glass. The others were drinking coffee. "Oregon, I tink, is growin' up. By God, you got a job, Bud Best?"

"No, not lookin', neither. Did some swampin' down at Irene's for a couple of weeks, so no need to work for a while now. Besides, salmon are runnin'. I thought you

6

were going to take a job at Donaldson's Mill? Decided not to?"

"I helped 'em with that steam engine, and it's all in and workin', by God. I'm gonna go huntin' and fishin' now for a few weeks. That Travis, he wants me to stay, but why? I got enough money for a while, now."

"See?" Newton said. "It was Johnson's wagons that brought that mill down from Portland, not my company."

"For Pete's sake, Clive, Donaldson's partner is Moose Travis, the son of Johnson's partner. Of course, he got the job," Pritchett said. "The reason so many businesses in the territory are hard pressed to keep employees is there are not enough married men in the territory. If you had a wife, Bud Best, that place of yours would be a producing farm or you'd be working full time, and the same goes for you, Ole." He glared. "I think Hawthorne is the right man to lead Oregon into statehood and I'm going to support him."

"I'll not even give the man a nod," Clive Newton said. "I need to get back to the yards. Old Sam Banter quit this morning, so I gotta make a short run with one of the wagons. Hard to keep teamsters." Pritchett just shook his head, hearing that, and watched Newton walk out the door.

"There's an opportunity for a quick job," Pritchett said to Best and Gunderson. They just stared back at him as if he was talking to someone else. He got up, nodded to the men and slipped next door to open his barbershop. *Lazy fools,* he thought. *if they had a family to support they wouldn't be talking or acting that way. Maybe Sullivan should only offer these homesteads to married men.*

It was an angry Clive Newton that walked out of the

Salem Club. He was meeting with others in the Firsters group that evening, and he figured they would take things in hand; keep these newcomers out, and keep Oregon a territory where a man could be free of the eastern influences. Pritchett would have been alarmed if he knew what was really being planned.

2

"I'M GLAD WE GOT THE CORN IN BEFORE THE STORM, Hiram." Ezekiel Hawthorne laughed, standing under a shed with his adopted son, watching torrents of rain pelt the fields of his young farm. "They told me to come to Oregon! There's good ground and good water. They didn't tell me they never shut the water off."

It was March of 1853, and Zeke and his family had arrived in the Willamette Valley of Oregon Territory the summer before, looking to build their lives. Zeke Hawthorne left Missouri following the death of his wife and children, ventured across the great plains all by himself, except for his two mules, and found himself at Fort Bridger, along the Green River, late in 1851.

If the man hadn't had such a burning desire to build a large and successful farm, have a wonderful family, and feel fulfilled by all of that, Ezekiel Hawthorne would have been happy staying at Fort Bridger. He was enthralled by the Rocky Mountains, spent countless hours roaming the wild country, and fell in love with Sarah Travis, the half-Shoshone daughter of the trading post's sutler.

He grew up in the Ohio Valley hearing stories of Indian slaughter, and the terrible times of Daniel Boone. He was enchanted by stories of Lewis and Clark, and was amazed when he met his first Indians. He hunted with Shoshone warriors, fought battles against the Crow tribe, and was given the name Sharp Knife by a Shoshone leader following a battle.

He wanted to go to the Oregon Territory and a new life. Well educated, trained as both a journeyman cabinetmaker and blacksmith, he wanted a farm and family. At Bridger, he had met Sarah Travis, the daughter of the fort's trader and his Shoshone wife, Elaine.

"LOOK WHERE WE ARE, HIRAM," he said, spreading his arms wide, taking in the fertile fields of the long valley. There were rolling hills, filled with timber of every sort, advancing higher, step by step, into the massive Cascade Range.

"Last year we were still in snow this deep," and he pretended the snow was over his head, "waiting to leave Fort Bridger, and here we are, standing in mud this deep!" More exaggerated fun followed. "When this storm passes, we'll get the rest of the wheat in, and work on getting the hops properly planted and settled."

"You mean about a week from now, Papa?" Hiram was laughing right along with Zeke. He was thirteen years old and from a laugh to a frown took half a second. "Who were those men that rode by early this morning?"

"I don't think I saw them, Hi. What did you see?"

"I came out to milk and feed, Papa. It wasn't quite light, but I saw four men down at the end of our lane, on the main road to Salem. It looked to me like they had spent the night down there, and," he paused. Hiram was slowly shaking his head, and Zeke prodded him to continue.

"Well, they scared me, Papa. One rode up our lane, looked at me real hard, turned his horse and went back to the others. Then they rode off. I've never seen any of them before." He paused for a moment, thinking. "I was afraid they were part of that group called Oregon Firsters. You know they don't want you to run for the legislature, and they sure don't want more people coming to the territory. Mama says she is afraid of what might happen."

"Those men that call themselves "Firsters" are ignorant fools, Hiram, but I really don't think they are violent. They think just because they were here first, no one else should be allowed in. The problem is, there is no way they can keep anyone out. Oregon will be a state, a prosperous state, and I'm going to have something to do with that taking place."

He cuffed his adopted son lightly on the shoulder, adding, "Better get the team taken care of, then meet me at the blacksmith shop. We'll take a walk down there and see what happened."

Hiram took care of the animals and equipment and joined Zeke right away. They ventured out into the pouring rain for a walk down to the main road, their slickers flapping in the wind.

"Looks like you're right, son, that's definitely a cook

fire and they had a lean-to back in the trees there." Zeke and Hiram spent about ten minutes going through what was left of the overnight campsite, and headed back to the warmth of the blacksmith shop.

Zeke laughed, "You've got good eyes and good instincts, Hi. Thank you for telling me what you saw. I haven't wanted to put a gate across our lane down there, but maybe I need to rethink that. There is a lot of traffic on that main road, and I want all you guys safe."

Zeke hadn't realized just how observant Hiram was, and that the boy and his wife had discussed the threats posed by the Firsters. "There will always be those that don't feel comfortable with newcomers," he said. "Sometimes newcomers bring problems with them, sometimes they create problems just by showing up. What we're seeing, Hiram, is many people with a limited education trying to protect what they believe should be theirs alone.

Many of the newcomers left their homes because they feel there might be more to offer here in Oregon country. That's why we're here, but many of those coming aren't as lucky… or hard-working as we are. I know how to farm, I built our house, we have a great desire to be successful, and I feel a deep responsibility to my family and our new community."

He stared out the door at his new, hard-earned farm. "Do you understand how that affects the way we live and feel about Oregon, as compared, say, to Mr. Newton, who you've heard me talk about? That blow-hard who feels Travis and Johnson are running him out of business."

"When you explain it that way, I think I do," Hiram said. "I guess that's why you and Mama make me learn all this stuff. I want to be like you, Papa, not like those men that don't work."

SARAH WAS WATCHING the two splashing their way up the muddy lane. "Like two ten-year-old boys playing in the mud," she chuckled. The twins, Susanne and Joanne were sitting in special chairs designed by Zeke so Sarah could feed both. They were coming up on their first birthday in just a few months and growing fast. "You'll be out there, playing with your Papa pretty soon, girls."

They were born on the Oregon Trail, just a few weeks out of Fort Bridger, and were growing like little weeds. Both girls had learned how to pull themselves onto their feet and stand, so long as they could hold on to something. *Zeke and I went from meeting each other, falling in love, and having three children inside of a year. Life is just amazing.*

It didn't look like the rain was going to let up, so boy and man had to face it and go back to work in the wet. Hi, as he liked to be called, led the mules to their corral and put the harness' away. Zeke walked back to his blacksmith shop and got the fires lit. "At least I'll dry out in here," he laughed. He watched Hi work the mules and thought about how he'd ended up having such a wonderful son.

Just look at that kid, he marveled, *he eats like a grizzly bear, works as hard as those mules, and can't gain an ounce. He's as skinny now as he was when his pa gave him to us, but about ten times stronger.*

Hiram was the son of an old trapper and his Shoshone wife who had just about given up on life. When the fur trade ended in Fort Bridger, the man didn't have a trade to fall back on, had no desire to be a farmer, and to make things worse; didn't get along that well with Indians. The old trapper literally gave Hiram to Zeke and Sarah.

He's going to be a fine man soon, this son of mine. He was skinny, not very strong, and didn't know much about anything, and that was just a year ago, Zeke was thinking, knowing the boy could now read well, was writing well, and wanted to learn everything there was to know about life.

Zeke got the forge going, pumping just a bit on the bellows, added more hardwood charcoal, and slipped the coffee pot into the coals. "First things first," he mumbled, putting two cups on the workbench. *I left Missouri alone and didn't give a damn if I lived or not, and here I am now with a beautiful wife, twin daughters, an adopted son, and one hundred sixty acres of Oregon Territory farm.*

Hi came running into the little shop, shaking as much rain off as possible. "It's coming down harder, I think." He squalled and snorted, spotting the hot coffee being poured. "Are you going to Salem tomorrow? I know you talked about it. Can I give you a letter to give to Barbara? I told her I'd write her."

"You know you're too young to be thinking about running away with your aunt," Zeke laughed.

"I know," Hi said, his eyes lowered to the ground, his feet shuffling, "but she's the prettiest girl I've ever seen, and the nicest. I really like her, Papa."

"I know you do, son. I'll take the letter for you."

Barbara Travis was Sarah's baby sister who had arrived back at Fort Bridger just a few months before the family came west. She had been attending school in Boston. Instead of returning to the east, she came west with the family, intending to open a dress- making shop in the new territory.

Barbara was tiny, very attractive, and full of life. The word optimist didn't even come close to describing the young lady. For Hiram, it was love at first sight and he wasn't ready to concede that an age difference should interfere with his desires. Hiram was twelve, Barbara was twenty.

3

Oregon Territory in 1853 was sparsely populated, with most people spread along the Willamette Valley, and the rest along the Columbia River. The territory changed from rough and tumble fur traders of Canadian and American companies beginning with the opening of the Oregon Trail to emigrants flocking in around 1842. There was a fair sprinkling of Russians down from Alaska, and California's gold rush had brought even more immigrants.

The big change took place in 1848 when the area was officially declared Oregon Territory and became an integral part of the United States. Zeke reflected that this had happened just five years earlier, and he was now in a position to make the territory something very special, and hopefully help lead the way into statehood.

There were many, particularly those in business, that supported statehood, and there were many who didn't. Oregon Territory was huge, encompassing the lands from the Pacific Ocean to the continental divide, and north from Utah Territory almost to Canada. North of Oregon Territory was Washington country, still mostly British.

Those coming west for the adventure wanted the territory to remain wild, while those coming to build a new life by way of farming or business, wanted something more civilized.

"Employment seems to be one of the problems with almost everyone I talk to," Zeke explained to Sarah. They were sitting at the large kitchen table, mugs of hot coffee and a platter of warm biscuits available. "So many of the people who come don't seem to know what it means to give a full day's work to the man paying for it. We need to get skilled people, many with crafts in their background to move here. What we have been getting are the men who came to mine gold in California and failed at that, too."

"You're starting to sound like that horrid Farnsworth, in Oregon City," she said.

"I'm afraid you might be right," he joshed back at her. The large wood-burning cook stove spread warmth through the kitchen. Sarah refilled their coffee cups. Zeke added just a touch of rum to his, and grabbed another warm biscuit to spread with some of her strawberry jam. "Just look at us. In less than a year we are firmly established as citizens of the territory. How many are here and don't seem to understand the importance of building into statehood?"

"I think you're missing something in your reasoning about immigrants, Zeke," Sarah replied. "Look at us, as you said. Then look at O'Brien and his family, and Joshua Petersen's family. It isn't the lack of having a trade that's missing with so many of these men, it's a lack of having the responsibility of a family. The most successful people you know are married with a family."

Zeke was laughing out loud when he said, "You mean we should import a whole wagon train of lovely young single women?" She gave him a good swat, laughing with him, but she could see in his eyes that he agreed with what she was saying. "Responsibility; as in a marriage with family, maturity, and having a trade... there, my pretty, is what makes for a successful man," he said.

There were continuing problems with the local Indian tribes, with runaway slaves looking to be free, and disgruntled California forty-niners coming north. The runaway slaves and black free men were not well accepted in the new territory, and the Indians were often shunned because of what was referred to as the "Whitman" or "Walla Walla Massacre."

In 1847, just a year before territorial status, missionaries Marcus Whitman, his wife, and eleven others were killed by the Cayuse Indians along the Columbia River. The Indians believed that the missionaries poison had killed some two hundred of their tribe, while it was actually small pox and pneumonia that were responsible for the deaths. There was now much resentment among many of the long-time white residents.

Others in the territory were looking to the day of statehood and one of the burning questions dealt with slavery. Would Oregon be a slave state? There were those in favor of that, and many others not favoring the question. In Salem, as in other communities in the young territory, the debate sometimes became violent and physical.

One of Zeke's good friends, the man who had helped

him stake out his land claim, Territorial Land Commissioner, Roland Sullivan, was pushing Zeke to run for a seat in the territorial legislature. Zeke already sat on one of the committees that were developing future plans for Oregon.

"We only have a few issues that need to be addressed," the always optimistic Sullivan said at a recent meeting in the territory's new capital, Salem. "Our economic drivers are agriculture, timber, fishing, and transportation."

"I think you're right about that," Zeke said, "but without education facilities, bringing educated leaders to run those drivers, they won't operate to their fullest. We have markets inside the territory, but we need markets outside as well. The problems we've faced with those that feel immigration should not be allowed must be overcome.

"Some who are against the flood of people arriving are simply against change, but the group that has organized the Oregon Firsters, are becoming dangerous." Zeke sat back in a big leather chair and lit a cigar, staring out one of Sullivan's large office windows. "There have been reports of groups of men with clubs, axes, and knives threatening some of the families that are beginning to arrive. Also, wagon trains have departed from the east and will be arriving all summer, along with those who wintered in Salt Lake or around Green River. We need to protect these new people and stop the violence that's being threatened."

"We've got our work cut out, Zeke. Old Lewis and Clark got us here, now what do we do about it?"

ZEKE AND HI spent the rest of the day in the blacksmith shed, fixing plows that had hit rocks, building more plows and cultivators, getting the long poles ready for the hops that would go for Sullivan's planned brewery in Salem, and staying warm and dry.

Finally, Zeke called a halt. "Let's call it a day, son, and see what chores your mother has planned for us, eh?" He set a cultivator's disc down after mending a rock tear in the metal. "It's been a long day."

Hi helped bank the fire in the forge while his father put up his tongs, hammers, knippers, and swages. Zeke was slipping his hands out of heavy leather gloves, watching the rain pour down, and thinking about corn, wheat, oats, and hops... and, where his markets would be.

"Even if the rain quits tonight, we can't do anything until the fields dry out some," Hi said.

"You're right about that. I'm going to go into Salem in the morning. If Mama doesn't have too much for you to do, you might sneak off and find some fish in that creek of ours. Salmon will be running pretty soon, too, son."

"Sammy O'Brien said they are in the lower Willamette River now, so I'll keep a watch on the creek. I love salmon," Hi said. He was fascinated by the red meat, so tasty fresh or smoked, and had been from the first day their little wagon train reached the Columbia River last summer. "Are we gonna build a smoke house, Papa?"

They started to talk-up plans for that smoke house, and had it half built in their minds when they burst into the warm kitchen. They remembered to shuck their muddy boots before coming in, though and, of course, that was the first thing Sarah checked. "Good boys," she said. "you're learning."

Zeke gave her a quick kiss on the cheek and walked to the sink to wash his hands. "Looks like the girls are ready for some dinner," he said. Susanne and Joanne, born on the Oregon Trail last summer were squirming in the chairs Zeke had built for them, banging their little fists on the wooden trays, demanding attention and food. He gave each a hug and smooch, and settled in at the table.

"I have to go to Salem tomorrow, Sarah, and I'm afraid this rain isn't going to let up. I wanted all of you to come with me, but I don't think that would be a good idea. I'll take the farm wagon and the team, so make me up a good list of what you want and need. I hope to spend some time with Travis, and I'll pop in on Barbara. Moose will probably be at his mill."

"I really wanted to go with you, but it wouldn't be good for the girls and I can't leave them alone with Hi, that would be asking too much of the boy. I haven't seen Papa or Mama or Barbara, either, since Christmas. I miss them, and we're just a few miles apart."

"We'll plan a trip for the next break in these spring storms," Zeke promised. "I heard from a rider passing through last week, that Travis and old Johnson are making more plans for that business of theirs. I'll try to get more information, but it sounds like Johnson is going to close the warehouse in Oregon City and move everything to that mud hole they call Portland. They'll have a dockside warehouse, and that is a deep-water port.

"From what I see, they will have access to the ocean-going freighters and all the expected commercial traffic on the Willamette and Columbia rivers. With Travis and Snyder's operation in Salem and what Johnson is doing up north, they're gonna be very busy."

"I'm surrounded by my wonderful family, right here and right now," Sarah said. With just a hint of sadness in her voice, she continued. "But I miss my other family." Zeke got up from the table and walked around to her side, bent down, and kissed her gently.

He couldn't help remembering the horrible ache he felt when he'd lost his first wife, Elizabeth. *First the children, one at a time, buried and gone, and then dear Elizabeth. I howled with despair, and my sorrow is what drove me to give it up, traipse clear across this continent.* "I understand, Sarah," he said. "Family is the most important thing in the world, and we do have a large family." They laughed together as Sarah held Zeke's hand with one hand and tickled the twins with the other.

"The first decent weather to come our way, and we'll go to Salem, all of us," Zeke promised. He grabbed the coffee pot and filled cups for Sarah, Hi, and himself, teasingly offering some to the girls. "Right now," he said, gesturing to the rain splashing on the windows, "I think Hiram and I have to start on that ark we might just need."

"You better put in at least one extra bed, Papa," she said, lowering her eyes just a bit, teasingly. "We'll have at least one more at the table come winter." All Zeke could do was stand stock still with a little boy grin spreading across his broad face.

4

ONE THING ABOUT THE FRONTIER WEST; ONE COULD FIND
the most interesting people in some of the most obscure
locations. Four men arrived in Oregon City that March.
One came in on a wagon train; Shorty Duvall, a forty-
year-old who had never reached maturity. Angus Whitell,
about twenty-years-old, arrived on a schooner from
Boston. Johnny Loper, in his early twenties, came north
from California where he'd failed as a gold miner and was
wanted for robbing more than one merchant in Sacra-
mento. And fourth on the list, Quint Lopez who drifted
down to Fort Vancouver then across the river when some
Canadians discovered missing merchandise.

The Lion's Den, a rowdy saloon and dance hall on the
very outskirts of Oregon City served fine rum from the
West Indies, some fine bourbon from Kentucky, and even
vodka from the frozen, ice-fields of Siberia, simply
because Oregon City was home to those that craved fine
spirits from their original homes. Joaquim Van de
Klepfen, usually called Little Joe, owned the joint, was

often found behind the bar getting in the way of the busy barmen.

The Lion's Den was one of the first saloons to open in Oregon City. It started out as a tent, then came side walls made from good Oregon timber and finally, a real roof was added, taking out the canvas that had served its purpose. As the business grew, the building was added onto several times, and the structure now included a second floor for the business ladies, and a gambling den set aside and away from the noise of the music- makers and drinking crowd. It carried the flavor of the frontier with rough wood, scars on the bar, and the trappings of original settlers.

"Angus, you really did come all the way around the cape of South America? I came on a Dutch Man-o-War myself, through the India sea, up the length of Asia, and across to Fort Vancouver." Little Joe had spent many years at sea and loved to tell tales, some of which might even have been partly true. "As young as you are, was this your first voyage?"

"Naw," Angus Whitell said, betraying his Boston heritage. "I went to sea as a cabin boy when I was ten, on Whalers, mostly, but I drew this voyage to get me out of Boston and on out here to the west. I'm gonna get me a piece of this country and settle in some. Get me land-legs back," the youngster said. Humor spread across his face, his eyes dancing with it. "I'm still walkin' like a grogged-up deck mate." Whitell was jostled by Shorty Duval working his way to the bar.

"Easy mate, just say, 'scuse please', and I'll give you room."

"Damn right you'll give me room," the burly fellow

said. He shoved an elbow into Whitell's ribs, and the young sailor whirled around and planted a gnarly fist alongside the head of the newcomer who in turn fell back onto the patron on the other side.

"Watch what the hell you're doin'!" that fellow said. He shoved the newcomer off, right back into a second fist from Whitell. Duval crumpled onto the muck-filled floor of the Lion's Den, and another man walking by at the time, gave him a solid kick to the head, which allowed Duval to enjoy a fine sleep for a few minutes.

Whitell stood quietly for a minute, drained his glass, nodded, and said goodbye to Little Joe. He ambled out of the saloon and Little Joe noticed the seaman's rolling gait. "Man needs to remember his manners in public," Whitell snickered. He ambled toward the docks along the riverfront.

He planned to ride south toward Salem in the morning, having heard about jobs available in lumber mills down that way. At the stables, he bought a good horse and some tack, and rode toward a stand of trees about two miles out of town. "This country is beautiful," he mused. "I love the forests, so much like the dense forests in New England, but different trees. No so much hardwood, it seems. So much water, and so much open country, this is the place a man can build himself a life."

He had the horse in a gentle walk, sitting tall in the saddle, looking left, right, up, and down. "I want to see it all, feel the soil dripping from my fingers. First though," he added, "I need a good job. Then I need to acquire some land, and then I need a wife." He had a broad smile on his face, watching a beautiful steamboat churning its way up the Willamette, toward Salem.

"I'm glad I picked up some shirts and pants, instead of wearing these sailcloth britches," he said, "and looking at those clouds piling up, I'll surely need that slicker." He settled a fine wide-brimmed beaver hat on his long blonde locks and nudged the horse into a trot. "It's been a long time since I sat on a good horse." The ride to his little camp took just a few more minutes.

"You'll be a fine horse for me," Whitell said, stepping out of the saddle and tying the horse to a small tree near his camp. He looked around to make sure no one had come into his camp, what little there was of it. Nothing missing or moved about, so he unsaddled the horse and long-lined him between a couple of trees where he could get at some good grass. Then he gathered some wood, and got himself ready for supper and a good sleep. "Buffalo meat and smoked salmon. Didn't get this aboard ship."

SHORTY DUVAL, awakened by heavy boots to the ribs, regained consciousness slowly. "Git up, bummer," a gruff voice snarled. Duval saw the badge, felt the boot one more time and struggled to his feet. "Sleep it off somewhere else. And clean yourself up, man. You're a disgrace."

Duval mumbled something, still woozy from the beating he took and booze he'd drunk, and walked off down the muddy street toward the stables where he had his horse quartered. He had worked his way to Oregon as a drover on a wagon train out of St. Louis and found himself at the end of the line in Oregon City. He drew his pay, spent four days drinking it up, and had no idea what might happen tomorrow.

He saddled his tired horse, tied his bedroll on the back

of the saddle, tied off the saddlebags, and took the road south. Duval made about ten miles before the sun went down and found some trees to sleep under. He hobbled his horse in some grass, spread his blankets, and passed out, having consumed the next to last bottle of rum he had tucked in his bags.

WHITELL WAS UP EARLY, took a cold bath in the Willamette River, and worked over a pan full of buffalo meat, potatoes, and eggs along with a full pot of coffee. "That was brisk. That water's cold and clear as looking through glass. My ship must have gone aground in the rocks, I died in the wreck, and I'm in heaven." He was laughing out loud, finishing his breakfast.

It was a beautiful morning but he had that sailor's sense about him and could feel a storm working its way south. "I'll be a wet one before I get to Salem," he mused. He packed up his little camp and mounted his new horse for the day's ride toward Salem. Whitell wasn't sure just how far the ride would be, and he didn't really care. "Just to be here, is fine with me."

The rain arrived about noon and it was a whopper of a storm, with high wind and heavy precipitation. He kept a good pace and was joined by another rider, about half an hour out. "Mornin' to ya," Whitell said, friendly-like. He didn't recognize Shorty Duval, but did notice the black eye and split lip. "Headin' to Salem?"

"Wherever this road takes me," Duval snapped. The only time the two had been together was that spat at the saloon, and Duval didn't recognize the man that had belted him. "Don't much care for this country. Hope this road goes far enough south that I end up in California. Came in on a wagon train full of fool farmers. Just want my share of the gold in California." He reached back into his saddlebag and brought the last bottle of rum out, took a long pull, and offered some to Angus Whitell.

"A little early for me, thanks," Whitell said. "There's good work to be had in Salem, I'm told. A new big lumber mill going up, a couple of grist mills operating, and a brewery being built. Man can get a good job, easy."

"Don't know nothin' 'bout mills. I'm goin' for the gold."

The ride was quiet and the storm continued to blast the skies with streaks of lightning, and barrels of water cascaded to the ground. It was several hours later when Whitell and Duval rode up on a couple of men off to the side of the road, nursing a fire in the heavy rain. "You boys okay?" Whitell called as they reined up. "Hard to get a good fire in this rain."

"Damn hard," one of them laughed, and Whitell watched as the man sprinkled some kerosene on a rag, tucked it under some kindling, and put devil's flame to it. "She'll go this time or we be eatin' cold. Where you boys headin'?"

"Name's Angus Whitell, and I'm on my way to Salem. How about you?"

"Quint Lopez here," the man at the fire said. "That's my trail friend, Johnny Loper." Everyone nodded their hellos and Lopez continued. "I'm on my way to Salem, too, and Loper's headin' back to California, giving minin' another chance, he says. Who's your friend?"

"I ain't nobody's friend," Duval snarled. "Goin' south, hope it leads to California's gold. You say you been there?"

"Sure have," Loper said. "Climb down boys and join us.

Maybe if we all work at it we can get warm." Loper moved quickly, adding more wood to a fire that was now getting a good head to it. The busted-up windfall spit and popped, and gave it up, finally, bursting into hot flame.

"I'm goin' that way, but I probably won't be doin' much minin'" Loper said. "There's other ways to make gold in California," he gave a snide little smile. Duval thought he might understand that smile, and stepped off his horse to stand near the fire.

"Looks like a good place to make a little camp," Duval said, pulling the bottle of rum from his saddlebag. He took a full pull on it and offered the bottle to Loper who accepted with no problem. "Maybe the rain'll quit by tomorrow. I hate this country."

Whitell knew he couldn't make Salem before the sun went down and decided he might just as well join up with these men for the night. "I've got some buffalo meat, enough for us, I think, if one of you gents has some coffee we could boil."

They kept a good fire going, ate well, slept under tarps and after a quick morning meal, the four rode off toward Salem. Duval and Loper rode together, talking about some plans that could work when they reached California. "One thing we'll need," Loper said, "is some money to get us started, and I think I know how we can do that, too."

Whitell and Lopez didn't talk much on the ride into town.

"Seems like I'm the only one of this bunch that is looking to take a job and settle down," he mumbled. They were riding through a heavy rain that simply hadn't let up once since the afternoon before. *Little Joe told me about how* to get land, he called it homesteading, and that just about suits me fine. Man could raise a fine garden in this country, work seems plentiful, and I want all that. It was slow riding in the heavy storm, with winds blowing things about, the horses spooky as hell, and mud, mud, mud.

Whitell spent hours admiring the river, enjoying seeing the land spread out from the river in both directions toward high mountains. The Cascade Range to the east was magnificent, covered at the very top with snow, and all the flanks of the range covered in heavy timber.

The four spent one more night in a camp outside Salem and rode into town following breakfast the next day. They were nearing the Bank of Oregon when Whitell said, "I'll be leaving you gents, now. The mill I'm looking for is up Mill Creek a few miles. You all have a good trip into California."

Loper, Duval, and Lopez said goodbye to Whitell and let their horses meander down the road, looking for a saloon and a chance to do some serious planning for the future. Quint Lopez called to a burly man, asking where the nearest saloon might be.

"Turn to your left at the bank," Clive Newton called. "In fact, I could use a hit myself." He led them down the street, made the turn and waited for them to tie off their horses before entering the Salmon Head Saloon.

II

BOOK SIX: WILD WEST POLITICS

5

OREGON TERRITORY WAS GROWING AND SO WERE THE political factions that wanted to be heard, including both sides of the slavery issue, groups that wanted fewer immigrants, and those that wanted more. Unlike many of the other frontier territories, Oregon's background was a combination of mountain man/fur trapper and international sailor/explorer. Most of the Americans came by way of the fur trade. The British came by sea as traders, and by way of the fur trade.

The Russians came down from Alaska for trading, including the fur trade, mining, and fishing, while many Europeans arrived by sea as international traders. The west, north of California was complex in many ways. Relationships between white men and the women of various Indian tribes were considered normal during the fur trade period, but shunned by recent immigrants. Black free men and black runaway slaves were not always welcomed unless they had something to offer such as a trade or special ability.

Farming was extensive in the Willamette Valley and was primarily on the eastern side of the wide river. The western side of the valley had been mostly set aside for a local tribe of Indians, but logging interests and some farming interests were moving into that area as well, and relations with the Indians were brittle at best, with many of the white settlers always remembering the massacre following the Whitman flu epidemic. Wheat was the primary crop and there were a couple of mills already in operation with more being planned.

The vast Snake River area of eastern Oregon Territory was beginning to attract immigrants. Many ranches were being developed and a few small communities were popping up along the Oregon Trail.

"ZEKE," Travis bellowed his welcome. The voice came from deep inside an office behind the new mercantile store he and Hector Snyder had built. "Glad you could make it. Come in and sit." He stood to shake hands with his son-in-law, stuffed some more wood in a large pot belly stove, found rags to protect his hands from a boiling pot of coffee, and poured two cups, lacing both with healthy doses of rum.

"How's your spring-time planting coming?" he asked.

"We've got a lot of the wheat in, but more to go, and most of the corn. Just getting ready to plant the hops, but I'm not sure this rain will ever end. I could have come to town in a canoe faster than I made it with the wagon." Zeke laughed, enjoying the coffee. "Looks like you have this place less than organized." There were crates, boxes, objects, and stuff scattered everywhere, and Zeke was sure he just heard a wagon pulling up with more merchandise.

"I'm running this place just like I did the trading post up at Bridger." Travis laughed, "And driving old Snyder out of his mind. He's catching on to my madness, though, and we're moving a lot of merchandise."

"Is it true that Sullivan is building a brewery?" Zeke asked. "We talked about it during the winter, and that's part of the reason I'm in town today. He'll want my hops, but I won't plant them if he's not building."

"He's building," Travis said. "According to Johnson, a ship came in from the east coast with a load of copper and brass for him weeks ago. You need to take a break from the plows and come up to Portland and see what me and old Johnson are building. Damn me, Zeke, I'm having more fun than I thought I'd ever have, and turning a dime too."

"The last time I rode out of Oregon City and saw that mud swamp you're calling Portland, I wouldn't have given you a dime for it."

"It's a deep-water port, Zeke. It's gonna be as busy as San Francisco within two years, mark my words on that. They're putting steam engines in those big boats, and will challenge the amount of time it takes to get cargo from Boston to Portland with them. We'll still run our wagons on the Siskiyou trail from California, but that warehouse will be filled mostly by the boats coming from the east.

"There's even crazy talk about trading ships coming into port from China and other Asian areas. Yes sir, Zeke, things are poppin' around here."

"Sullivan wants me to stand for a seat in the Territorial Legislature but I'm pushing for Mike O'Brien to make a run for it," Zeke said. "What's the talk around Salem, Travis? Are the Whigs going to remain strong?"

"I think so. We'll have a new governor shortly if those in Washington learn to do their duty. Joe Lane doesn't want to be governor. He never wanted it but stood in when Grimes finally left. Now we need someone who's only thinking of Oregon in that office."

Zeke and Travis talked politics, transportation, warehousing, and farms for another hour, emptying the coffee pot and lowering the level in the rum bottle considerably. "I'm going down to see Barbara and then corral Sullivan," Zeke said. "Here's Sarah's shopping list if you can have your people fill my wagon while I'm gone. Is there a chance that Moose will be in town today?"

"No, afraid not. That's one frustrated young man, Zeke. He can't keep a crew. They get paid, get drunk, and don't come back. It will take him some time to come up with a seriously professional crew for that mill. He has good equipment, has the mill laid out just right. All he needs is some good lumbermen. He ran that mill at Fort Bridger and knows the business, but he needs people who are willing to work."

"That old fool in Oregon City that hated people moving to the territory sure didn't know what he was belly-aching about, did he? We need educated and willing to work immigrants, Travis. I'll see you before I leave for home," Zeke said. He shook hands and made his way through the chaos of the big store and out onto the main street of Salem.

He's right, Zeke chuckled to himself, *this place is just as jammed and stuffed as that old trading post of his was back at*

Fort Bridger. He was also quick to notice there were plenty of people in the store buying some of that merchandise.

THE RAIN HAD TURNED to a heavy mist as he made his way down the street toward the waterfront. He turned south for two blocks, and then continued westward, seeing more and more building in the capital city. Businesses were cropping up, highly specialized carpentry and cabinet shops, ironworking facilities were active and almost every business along the way had a sign-up offering employment.

"If that farm fails, I'll not have to worry about a job." He chuckled, but was also aware of just how important it was to bring in people who wanted to work. He thought often that Oregon Territory offered tremendous opportunity to those who were willing to work for it. "This isn't the country for a laggard," he mused. He was smiling as he walked near Barbara's enlarged shop.

He was passing the new Bank of Oregon building, solidly built of local rock and heavy timber, when the banker, Obediah Sinclair stepped out. "Mr. Hawthorne," he said. "How nice to see you. I understand you might be thinking of standing for election to the Territorial Legislature."

"It is being discussed," Zeke said. He and Sinclair were friends and shook hands. "I've not made up my mind, however. I'm on the commission we developed to work with the legislature, and that might be where I'll stay."

"If you do decide to make the stand, Hawthorne, I want you to know that the Bank of Oregon will back you all the way." They shook hands again, and Sinclair strode off down the street, finding a big cigar to chew on, on the way. Zeke wondered how on earth Sinclair could know that Sullivan had even asked Zeke to run for office. *It's certainly more than a pleasant thought. Assemblyman? Just might be.*

He continued his walk and noticed four rough-looking men riding their horses up from the waterfront. They weren't dressed as cowboys, none of the trappings of the California Vaqueros, and didn't seem to have much with them. "I wonder if these are the men Hiram saw near the farm? No pack animals, just bedrolls tied behind their saddles, and large saddle bags."

He also noted that each man had a side arm tucked in his pants, and there were rifles carried in their saddle scabbards. *Most of the men who work in the fur trade shun side arms, preferring knives and rifles*, he thought. He walked slowly, trying to see if there was any kind of recognition, and knew he had never seen any of them before. *These are the kinds of men that old Farnsworth hated with a passion. I hope they are seriously looking to stay and hold jobs.* It was a good thought, he chuckled, but didn't believe it for a minute.

BARBARA TRAVIS, Sarah's baby sister, had spent several years in Boston, first going to school, and then joining up with a brilliant engineer who designed a machine that would sew fabric. She worked with Zack Singer to create the Singer Sewing Machine and even brought one with her when she returned to Fort Bridger.

Along with seamstress work, Barbara found herself teaching a few of the women in Salem how to operate the machine. She had contacted Singer in New York and made arrangements to be his representative in Oregon Territory. Singer's patent suits were wrapping up, and Barbara was planning to sell many machines.

The Victorian age was in full view as far as women's fashion was concerned, and on full display as Zeke entered the shop. Mannequins were dressed to kill, elegant gowns and day-to-day wear vying for eager eyes, and off to the side, almost out of view, several tables with sets of men's outerwear were displayed.

A young lady unknown to Zeke came out from an inner room to greet him when he entered. She appeared to be Indian, which didn't surprise him at all. She was short, just a bit on the heavy side with flowing black hair and deep, dark eyes that sparkled when she welcomed him to the store. "Hello," she said. "May I help you?"

"What a beautiful shop," he said. "I believe you're holding a friend of mine hostage in the dark dungeon in the back. Her name is Barbara, and I'm paying the ransom."

The young clerk got a terrified look on her face and then heard loud laughter coming from the back room. "Zeke," Barbara cried, coming at a gallop from the back of the store, skirts flying one way, long hair flowing the other. "I haven't seen you since Christmas," and she flung herself at him, letting him whirl her around a time or two. Barbara wasn't quite as tall as the young Indian, and weighed considerably less.

"Cynthia, meet my brother-in-law, Ezekiel Hawthorne. This is the man I've told you about, who is father to the young boy I'm madly in love with. Zeke, meet Cynthia Morning Glory, from the Siskiyou tribe."

It took just a few minutes to get all the helloes taken care of, and Barbara asked Zeke about Hiram. "He's doing just fine, Barb. Here, I've brought you a letter from him. He's growing like a weed, gaining as much weight as he can and still's skinny as a rail. And, yes, he is still madly in love with you," he laughed. "Wouldn't happen to have a couple of shirts that might fit him, would you? He's outgrown most of his and isn't quite big enough to wear mine yet.

"From what I see, you've kept that machine of yours pretty busy. Is it still performing the way you thought it would?" he added.

"Definitely," she said. "Zack Singer is a genius in my mind, Zeke. Cynthia says she can smell smoke when I really get a long hem going." Cynthia giggled, trying to duck her head.

"I do have some shirts for you and Hiram, and that dress that I promised Sarah, too. I sent three complete sets of clothes up to the mill for Moose. He never gets into town anymore. That boy takes his work serious, but I'm afraid we might lose him to the tribe, Zeke. He's really worried about what we hear from folks coming in on the Oregon Trail.

"The Bannocks and Paiutes, along with the Western Shoshone are raising all kinds of problems through the Snake River areas, and we've heard some nasty stories about the Mormons and the Shoshone in the old Bridger area. Moose wants to go back, be with the people. We'll never see him again, if he does, Zeke."

"Well, I'm not sure about that, but you're right about some of the stories. Moose has very strong feelings about his people, was very close to the tribe, far more so than either Sarah or you, and he really didn't want to come with us in the first place. He only came to be our guide, and then fell in love with this country, and who wouldn't?"

Zeke and Barbara spent another hour talking about her business, his farm, and Moose and the mill, before Zeke took his packages of clothing and made his way down to the waterfront and Sullivan's offices. He found a large sign proclaiming "Willamette Beer, Made with pure Willamette River Water" welcoming visitors to the complex.

"Very nice, Mr. Sullivan," Zeke said. He shook hands with the always effervescent man. "It looks like I'll be growing an abundance of hops over the next several years."

"Decades, you mean," Sullivan said. He was laughing and offered his hand. "Come in, Zeke, come in. I have a contract all drawn up to buy every pound of hops you can grow, sir, and I have the plans laid out on my desk for you to see, as well."

Zeke stood over the desk admiring the brewery plans, read through the contract Sullivan offered, signed it, and sat down in a comfortable leather-covered wingback chair. "How does your shadow even keep up with you, Sullivan?"

6

ANGUS WHITELL RODE UP MILL CREEK THROUGH HEAVY timber, but on a well-used roadway, admiring the countryside. The rain had finally stopped and the sun was warming things nicely. If he could land a job at the lumber mill, he would then ride back to Salem, find that land office he'd been told about, and file on some property.

"There was so much talk about California and gold, back east," he mumbled. He was riding at a comfortable walk, having a grand conversation with his horse. "I also kept hearing about Oregon, and good ground and lots of water." He was laughing to himself about the water and the two days of rain he just rode through when he came over the top of a slight rise and saw the mill in the distance, alongside the creek.

They're using waterpower and steam power. They must be cutting the timber up higher in this range, bringing the logs down in the creek, and driving the saws with steam. Whitell had seen steam engines but never worked with or around them, and was fascinated by the idea.

"Mr. Travis," he said, walking into the manager's office. "My name's Angus Whitell and I'd like to apply for a job. I've been a sailor all my short life, don't know a thing about a lumber mill, but I am smart, can learn, and will work hard." He had practiced that little speech for half an hour riding up the mountain trail.

"That's the best news I've had in six months," Moose said. The big man stood up and grasped Whitell's hand. "Come in and sit down. Coffee?" he asked, getting a nod yes. "No one is born knowing how to work a lumber mill, everyone has to learn, so you would be starting like everyone else in this business.

"I'll give you a tour of the mill, tell you what I would expect of you, and if you are still interested, we'll get all the paperwork out of the way. Where are you staying?"

"I'm not, yet. I wanted to secure employment, file on some property, and then figure out where I would live."

"I've built a small bunkhouse for my single employees, and you can certainly stay there. I have a woman who provides two meals a day, which would be deducted from your pay each week, or you could pitch a tent and take care of yourself," Moose said. He moved to the stove and poured each of them another cup of good coffee.

"I think the bunkhouse is more my style, Mr. Travis. Is there provision for my horse, too?"

"Call me Moose, Angus, we're not very formal around here. We have a small stable, but you would be responsible for feeding and care of the animal. We try to work ten hour days and the pay is two dollars a day if you stay in the bunkhouse, two fifty if not. There is no charge for using the stables and corrals. Want to see the mill?"

"Yes, sir, I do," Angus Whitell said, jumping to his feet. *Two dollars a day and I get two hot meals a day, too? That's more money than I've ever made in my life, and I get a warm, dry bed to sleep in. I wish Mama was still alive so I could tell her about this.*

Moose caught the smile and twinkle in Angus's face. "Not quite the same as aboard a ship, eh?"

"No, sir," he said. "I might be rude in asking this, but are you an Indian?" Whitell had been in many foreign ports, had friends of many backgrounds, but could not ever remember one time in his life that he had had a conversation with an Indian.

"My father was a fur trader at Fort Bridger and my mother is a Shoshone lady, so I'm half Indian, although I feel more Shoshone than white. Is that a problem?" Moose had run into a few of the men looking to hire on that wouldn't because of his Indian blood, and it infuriated him.

"Not in the least," Whitell said. "I'll teach you ropes and knots and you teach me how to hunt. In between times, I'll learn how to run this mill." They laughed, shook hands, and became instant friends.

Moose gave Angus a grand tour of the mill, explained how the logs were moved onto tracks and fed into the blades, all driven by a steam engine. "It's a Rumely Stationary Steam Engine that was brought by sailing ship last year. We're all still learning how to run the thing properly. It's rugged and strong," he said, as they watched logs being fed into the massive cutting blade.

"I sure like the way it sounds," Whitell said. "They're

powering big ships with engines like this." He could feel the floor vibrate with the pounding of the engine, felt the enormous amount of energy generated by just boiling some water.

Moose explained the various stages the timber went through to create lumber for building, how the scrap from the logging was used to feed the steam engine's boiler, and how there was very little waste. "We need coal and hardwood charcoal, too, but we burn our waste wood every day."

Two hours later, they were back in Moose's office. "It's hard work, Angus, but you look like you're used to hard work. If you're willing to learn this business, work hard, there will always be a place for you here. My dad built the first lumber mill at Fort Bridger, and that's where I learned the business."

"I loved being at sea, Moose. I've been to places that many people have never even heard of, but for the last year, all I've been able to think about is having a place of my own, a home. I'm just twenty, if my numbers are right, and I've been at sea since I was ten. I want a home and a profession... a craft." He settled back in a bent cane chair, smiling broadly, sipping more coffee. "I want to be a lumber mill hand of the first order," he said. "Where do I sign?"

Moose had him fill out the paperwork, so he would get paid, and Angus Whitell took his horse to the corral. There, he unsaddled him, slipping him a nice fork full of fresh grass, and took his saddle bags and bedroll into the bunkhouse, making himself a nest at one of the bunk sites. "I'll go into town tomorrow and file on my home-stead, buy some things, and start work day after tomorrow," he muttered, putting his tack next to a comfortable-looking bed.

He walked into the mess hall attached to the bunkhouse to introduce himself to the woman in charge. "Hello," he said, finding her in the kitchen, carving a roast from a venison carcass. "I'm Angus Whitell, about to start work here." He was looking into bright, gray eyes fastened to an aging face that featured a grand smile.

"Hello, yourself, Angus Whitell," she chuckled. "I'm Beulah McCarthy. Welcome to our little piece of heaven. I was born in Boston and you sound like you were too."

"Aye, ya, that's so, Beulah McCarthy," he laughed. "I think we'll be fine friends. What are the rules of the house?"

She spent the next half hour explaining the meal procedure, how she took care of laundry, changed bedding once a week, and some of the things that weren't allowed. "I don't much care for strong language, me boy, and won't tolerate a drunk, but a wee nip before bed is just fine. I think we'll get along fine. There are two other men that will join you in the bunkhouse, and Moose usually joins us for our meals, as well.

"So, young Mr. Whitell, I'll see you at six this evening, and breakfast is at six as well. Get yourself settled now."

MOOSE SETTLED INTO HIS LARGE CHAIR BEHIND THE HEAVY oak desk, nursed a cup of coffee and stared for many minutes at the ceiling, watching a couple of flies' dance about, letting his mind simply wander where it would. Lately, that intense mind wandered back to the Rocky Mountains and the Shoshone village he missed. Those were his people, people he loved and right now, feared for their safety.

"I promised Mr. Donaldson I would build this mill and get it operating successfully, and I intend to do just that, but I see opportunity in Angus Whitell. He is the kind of man I've been hoping would walk in that door, young, aggressive, intelligent, and a man who appears to be as strong as I am," he muttered. "He has leadership written all over him, and I'll bet anyone that he would make a fine millwright."

Moose wrote down a list of objectives that he would lead Whitell through over the next several months; including how to operate the steam engine, build parts for the steam engine should it fail, in essence, be a steam engineer within a matter of weeks. "That has to be paramount because it's so essential to our operation." Operating the moving tracks that fed the saws, the saws themselves, and the maintenance of the equipment would be next, and would take another several weeks.

The steam engine, using belts, turned a long steel pole near the ceiling of the main mill building, and that pole had pulleys attached at various locations which drove belts that powered equipment. The long chain-driven tracks for the timber were driven by pulleys, the saws were driven by pulleys, cut lumber was moved on chain driven rails driven by pulleys. If that big Rumely steam engine failed, the mill would shut down.

"By this time next year, Mr. Angus Whitell, you will be able to run this operation and I'll be in a position to make a long visit with my people." Moose had a smile on his face thinking about Fort Bridger, his friends and relatives in the village, and living again in the old way. "When I get back I'm going to eat an entire buffalo," he said. He was still chuckling ten minutes later, as he put all his paperwork away.

The coffee had turned cold and he swished it out onto the mill floor and headed to his newly built cabin to look over some new clothing his sister Barbara had sent. Instead, he dressed in his old buckskins, grabbed his bow and a quiver full of arrows, and took a long walk into the deep forest around the mill.

"Sure wish Hiram was with me right now," he said, remembering how the youngster was able to shoot fish with his bow and arrow and take ducks from the water. Moose was considerably older than Hiram, but they were both half Shoshone and proud of it. "He put an arrow right through a deer's heart last fall when I was down at their farm." As with Moose, Hiram was named by his Shoshone mother. She called him Little Eagle.

Moose moved quietly through the leafy forest, a mix of evergreen and deciduous trees, huge, wide, and tall. His mill cut spruce, cedar, fir, pine, oak, and other trees in Oregon's vast forests.

He was thinking about Ezekiel, his sister, and their now large, growing family. *Other than my father, Zeke is the only white man I have ever allowed myself to trust. My tribe named him Sharp Knife, and I call him friend.* Thinking of Zeke, Sarah, and their family, made him think of his own situation.

I have my own business and I wonder if it's time to think about a wife and children. He was deep in thought and almost missed a large whitetail buck trying to sneak into some heavy brush. "Damn," he muttered, bringing his bow up. But he didn't shoot. Instead, he simply watched as the large animal worked its way through the brush with very little noise. "Shoot him and I'd have to quit for the day," he chuckled. He moved on a line toward a hummock that overlooked a long, heavily timbered valley.

"If our lumberjacks cut every fourth tree, there's enough timber in that valley to fill Oregon with buildings," he said. *I'm actually helping to bring more settlers into this country while worried sick that the settlers are going to ruin the lives of the tribe I love most. Is there such a thing as wrong, and right?* He took that moment to sit down on a large fallen tree and look around the countryside.

Those coming through the people's country never think of anything but themselves. They wantonly kill any animal they

53

see, just because they can. They hate the Indians because they've been told horror stories and have built up a fear that is unfounded. They don't seem to care about the misery they bring.

Moose Travis had so many questions and knew he had few answers. Hatred of the white settlers was building in the western plains, Rocky Mountains, and the Great Basin. The settlers, rude and selfish for the most part, felt it was their right to be there, to take what was there, and to demand the army keep them safe.

The Indian nations in the plains and the Rocky Mountains; in the area between the Rockies and the Cascades were just learning what the white invasion meant, just learning that their way of life was going to be jeopardized, and they were becoming fearful and resentful. The Crows, Sioux, Shoshone, and Bannock nations were just now starting to feel the encroachment.

New people coming to Oregon were carrying more and more stories of Indian attacks on their wagon trains, more and more stories of incursions by the settlers in lands that were held sacred by many tribes, and of the wanton killing of buffalo, deer, and elk. "Why won't the settlers recognize that they are moving through our land, killing our food supply just for fun, for sport? My people will need help and I have no idea how to help them," he murmured.

This is a good evening for this kind of thinking. Mama and I used to talk of these things. I talked with some of the old men often. Now, and he had to chuckle to himself at the thought, *I just wander around talking to the trees.*

He wandered aimlessly through the great forest, pulled his bow on two more deer, and slowly made his way back toward the mill. He was about half a mile from the compound when another large buck stepped into view. Moose slowly drew the bowstring back, let an arrow fly, notched a second, and watched the buck take ten or twelve steps. Blood flowed from a wound deep in its chest, it's front legs buckled, and it sagged to the ground, where it bled its final half pint onto the forest floor.

There Hiram, he snickered, *that's the way we do it.*

Half an hour later, Beulah McCarthy was interrupted in her cooking chores by a knock on the kitchen door. "Moose, what on earth are you doing?" She wasn't surprised to see the man dressed in his finest buckskins, that happened regularly, but she was surprised when he came into her kitchen and dropped a large, fresh liver into her sink.

"Oh, my, just look at that," she said. She had a huge smile covering her broad, freckled face. "I think I just changed the menu for tonight, Moose Travis, I do believe I did." She was laughing along with the big man and reached up to give him a kiss on the cheek and he gave her a hug back.

"I'll skin the deer, let it hang for a day or two, and then bone it out for you, Beulah," Moose said. "Sure wish there was buffalo in this country, but I guess we can't have everything, eh?" He went back to his kill, skinned the buck, and half carried, half dragged the carcass back to the mill site. He hung the carcass in a shed and covered it with a sheet to keep the flies off, salted and rolled the skin, and stored it with some others that he would tan and prepare for clothing for he and Hiram.

As he went back to his cabin he realized just how important Angus Whitell's visit was. "I needed his exuberance and that little venture through the forest to clear my mind." Dressed in canvas pants and wool shirt, his hair pulled back and braided tightly, Moose headed back to the bunkhouse mess hall and joined Beulah, Angus, and three others for a big supper of fresh venison liver and onions swimming in a hearty brown gravy, mashed potatoes, and fresh biscuits.

"Only thing missing is one of my sister's apple pies," he chortled to himself.

SUPPER WAS BEING EATEN at another camp, this one about a mile outside Salem by three men who were not pleased with what was on the menu. "This country ain't for me," Johnny Loper grumbled, stuffing a spoonful of beans into his mouth. "Too wet, and the pickin's is few.

"I'm headin' south in the morning and won't get off that horse until I'm in California. Coach runs in California carry gold, here, they carry farmers with no money. I'm goin' where the pickin's include gold."

"You been to California?" Quint Lopez asked.

"Yup, shore have," Loper said. "I had to light out kinda fast but I'm goin' back, tomorrow morning." He spooned in some more beans. "Wouldn't hurt to have some pocket money, though. A poke full of gold would make that trip smooth as honey."

"You thinkin' of that bank, ain't cha?" Lopez asked.

"Shore am," Loper said. "You in? Looked like an easy hit to me. What about you, Duval? You up to hittin' a bank?"

"Sounds like you bein' a criminal or something," Duval said. "Ain't never stole nothin', not sure I want to. I just like to eat and drink, some. You boys go ahead without me. I don't think I'd know what to do, anyways," he said, pouring another cup of coffee.

"It'd be easier if you sorta stood guard, you know, outside the bank to let us know if the law was comin' our way." Loper looked long and hard at Lopez, who returned the look, and the two of them slowly got to their feet and spread aways out from the fire.

"Ya see, Duval," Loper said, "we got us a little problem, now. You know what it is that old Quint and I have planned, and that makes you an accessory. You know what that means?" He had a mean glint in his eye as he walked slowly around Duval's back. "It means that you are part of the bank robbery whether you want to be or not. It means you know what me and old Quint here are plannin' to do."

"Well," Duval said, "you boys go ahead and do what you want, I might just mosey on back to Oregon City and do some swampin' for Little Joe, or somethin'."

The man was never quick with his mind, and he had no idea what Loper was planning, and never saw the skinnin' knife gleam in the moonlight. He only slightly felt the blade slash through all the cords and veins in his neck, and he slumped forward, dead.

"Didn't really want to do that," Loper said. "A simpleton like that might just tell the first person he met what the hell we're plannin, Quint. Well, help me drag him into the trees so's he won't be found for a few days, and figure out how the best way will be to take out that bank."

"I like your style, Loper," Lopez said. "Best thing for us is to give that bank a real good look, make sure we know where the most money is kept, how many people are working inside, and if they have guns. You got any clean clothes?"

"I see what you're agettin' to, Quint Lopez. I come north quick, some fools real close behind me, so didn't have time to pack a bag," he said. "I doubt Duval had much with him. Guess it is you who gets to do the spying on the bank, and I can take a ride around town and make sure I know how to lead us out with the least difficulty."

"We're a good team, Johnny Loper," Quint Lopez said. "We'll head back to town right after a good breakfast. Don't think we should hit the bank tomorrow, though. We'll need to work out all of everything we learned, and get every dollar we can. We'll go to California in style, Partner," he cried, throwing another large piece of wood on their fire.

8

SULLIVAN LIVED IN A GRACIOUS HOME BACK ABOUT TWO
blocks from the Willamette River and the busy riverside
district of Salem. His home was on the corner of
Commercial and Second Streets and his territorial office
was on State Street, near the new capitol building
complex. As large as Sullivan was, he often walked to his
offices.

He lived alone, had no hired help, and many of his
friends would testify that the man was an exceptional
housekeeper. Sullivan loved life, almost felt a calling to
spread good tidings at every opportunity, and seemed to
be a success at anything he attempted. One would not be
wrong to say that Roland Sullivan tended to hold those
that shirked work in contempt, and in Salem, with
hundreds of businesses advertising for help, he refused to
help anyone who simply wouldn't hold a job.

"Old Ben Franklyn got it wrong," he said to Travis at
the store one morning. "It should be 'Early to rise and late
to bed', to make that man healthy, wealthy, and wise. I'm

almost ready to start the actual building of my brewery, Travis, and I need more help. Thousands of people coming to Oregon for the good life and most won't work. Bah!" He spat the word out.

Travis beckoned to a young man standing at the counter with an armload of items to come join them. "Mr. Sullivan, meet Angus Whitell. Angus, this gentleman is opening a brewery here in Salem, do you think those two men you told me about would be interested in working at a brewery?

"Angus worked his way here on a schooner out of Boston, arrived in Salem day before yesterday and hired on with Moose at Donaldson's Mill."

"No," Angus said, shaking his head. "No, those two might want to visit a brewery, but certainly not work in one. Or work anywhere. They are bums, I'm afraid. I didn't ride down here with them, they joined me on the trail and spent most of the time drinking and complaining." His eyes lit up. "You say your name is Sullivan? Are you the Territorial Land Commissioner?"

"Why, yes, I am that Mr. Whitell. Are you looking to file a claim on some of our fine Oregon land?" Salesman Sullivan came to the front immediately, despite how important it was for him to hire some help for the brewery. "We have some fine quarter sections in those rolling hills near Donaldson's Mill. Come by the office when you leave here and I'll show you some properties on the map that are available."

"I will, sir. If those men that rode with me do show up, I would suggest you hide whatever it is you value. One of them, Johnny Loper by name, actually bragged about being chased out of California by those he stole from."

Sullivan shook hands with Whitell, said goodbye to Travis and worked his way out of the crowded trading post, found his horse, and made his way to the Bank of Oregon for a meeting with Obediah Sinclair. The sun was shining on this spring morning and people were out and about despite the early hour. It was a quick ride from Mill Street over to Center and 12th.

"It's mornings like this that make life worthwhile, eh Mr. Sinclair?" Sullivan said, stepping off his high stepping trotter. "Even old Peppy here wants to run with the wind. Jack Summers caught a beautiful salmon this morning, O.B., so the run must be on its way."

"Come in, Sullivan, and let's talk brewery and distillery, shall we, before you start selling more Oregon Territory to those of us who've already bought." He laughed, ushering the large man inside the ornate bank. The floors were highly polished Oregon hardwood with wool runners, and the walls were woods that had been carved into extraordinary motifs of Oregon life. Great forests, wild animals, rivers, and people were carved and shone with natural wood oils.

Italian marble columns appeared to hold up the front of the building, and that marble was also apparent in the cashiers' cages, and along the walls as wainscoting. Sinclair's office featured every conceivable type of Oregon hardwood, with carvings to depict life in the territory, from fishing to farming to trapping and everything in between.

"As you know, Sullivan, there is a strong temperance movement, especially from the women of the territory, and I wonder about your idea of a distillery in Salem. As you know, this bank already backs your brewery completely, but there are questions about too much hard whiskey being available already."

"I rather doubt that whatever alcoholic beverages I should distill would add to the current supply. I believe I would simply be replacing the inferior and expensive stuff that is now imported. There are some foul liquors brought in from the east, sir, and my distillery would offer a much better brand at a much lower cost.' He sat still for a moment, thinking hard. "No, I don't see that I would be adding, but rather, replacing. The temperance ladies will always be with us just as the imbibers of liquor will be standing at the rail."

Sullivan took a cigar offered by Sinclair and sat back in a large leather wingback chair studying a portrait of Sinclair that hung behind the banker's desk.

"The bank intends to back your plan, Sullivan. I just wanted you to be aware of what some of the town's ladies were discussing." He reached into the top drawer of his desk and brought out a large document for Sullivan to sign. "This is the contract we discussed. Read it carefully, Sullivan. You know, I might sneak something in on you." They both laughed at the statement. "You can bring it back as soon as you can. Say, are you still having problems with help?" he asked, reaching into a lower drawer of his massive oak desk and producing a bottle of fine brandy, he poured each of them a healthy snifter full.

"It just beats all, Sinclair, that we have so many men unwilling to work for a living. I'm offering more than a fair wage to get those buildings up and get the brewery operating. You remember how old Farnsworth used to rail against immigrants? He said they took jobs from Oregon men, but he was dead wrong, sir. We need men to come to this territory who are looking to build empires, to work hard, to be successful" He sighed.

"Well, you know me, I could speak on the subject for a week and not repeat myself, but I hope there are hundreds of wagon trains on the Oregon Trail this year, and that every wagon has four men ready to go to work."

"I wish I had an answer," Sinclair said. "I spoke with Hawthorne briefly and he isn't sure he will stand for the legislature. We need that man in the legislature, Sullivan. Work on him some, for all of our sake."

"He's a natural leader, OB. Smart as a whip and with a beautiful family. I'll talk to him some more."

Sinclair was still chuckling to himself after walking Sullivan out to his horse. "You've done as much for this territory as the old mountain men did opening the Oregon Trail, Sullivan. You must be very tired when you finally retire at night."

Sullivan was laughing heartily as he rode off, even doffing his hat at two riders coming up the street. "Good day, gentlemen," he said, putting his gelding into a nice trot, heading for his office.

"STRANGE OLD BIRD," Quint Lopez said. He and Loper rode into town to survey the bank and the streets of Salem. "Let's meet at that saloon near where the steamboat is docked in an hour, Loper. We can compare notes and make our plans."

Johnny Loper nodded his agreement and rode off as Lopez dismounted and tied off his horse. "We will want to ride south but the main streets seem to run east and west," Loper murmured, giving a shake of his head to Lopez and nudging his horse forward. He rode east for three blocks or so, not finding what he considered a main road south. He skirted over north a block and found himself next to Travis's trading post building on Mill Street.

"That's a big store," he muttered, slowing his horse and looking at the building that had been added onto several times. "If the bank doesn't work out, we gotta give this a good look."

He turned back west and rode slowly along Mill Creek Street toward the Willamette River, coming to the main road south just a block from the river. He rode back to the trading post, turned his horse around and rode fast, back to the river. "That's a long ride through the middle of a busy section of town," he muttered, turning his horse around again.

This time, he rode east right on past the trading post and kept going for another couple of miles, looking for trails off Mill Creek Road. "If we ride hard this way, ditch whoever might try to follow, and hideout for a short time, we could make our way out of town late at night, and head south."

The forest was thick and the possibility of simply traveling cross-country seemed out of the question. Loper knew they would have to stay on existing trails and use the main road south along the river to escape. "That bank looks like an easy mark, but we'll have to work hard to get out of town." He muttered some more, pulled a chunk of tobacco out for a chew, and turned the horse back to town.

He had it set in his mind when he rode back into Salem and down to the dock areas, tied off his horst, and slipped into Irene's Dockside Saloon. "Bottle," he snarled at the barman, and took a table near the front windows, watching for Quint Lopez. He was on his second glass of whiskey when Lopez walked in. "Have any luck at the bank?" he asked, pouring whiskey for the man.

"Yeah, but it would help if we had a third man. There's the manager, just a puff of a man, and two clerks behind the cages. There's a locked door between the lobby and back where the clerks, vault, and money are. It would be best if we had someone outside. That street is really busy."

"Yeah, and our idea of simply running hell bent for California isn't gonna be in the plans, either. We'll need to get out of town, into the mountains to the east, and hideout for some time before sneaking onto the road south. I was on one road that simply ended," he said, pouring each of them another glass of whiskey. "We'd need to stay in those mountains for about a week, I think, give things a chance to quiet down, and then slip out at night."

"All right, then, let's go find a place to hide, and plan on taking out that bank in the morning, soon as they open," Quint Lopez said.

"Actually, Quint, I think later in the day would be better. Remember how much traffic there was this morning when we rode by, and quite a few people in the bank or coming to the bank. I'd hit 'em right about one or two."

"You're probably right," Lopez said. "We'll need food at our new camp."

"MR. WHITELL." Sullivan beamed, welcoming Angus to his

office. "Have you had a chance to look over any of the land up Mill Creek?"

"I rode up yesterday to find the mill and then came back down this morning. It's beautiful country, and the rolling hills remind me somewhat of New England. Let's take a look at those maps you were talking about."

Sullivan walked him over to the large conference table where maps were laid out, showing the various sections of land available in that area of the Willamette Valley. "Here's 12th Street, where we met this morning, and up here, on this other map is Donaldson's Mill. The quarter sections, that is one hundred sixty acre plots, that are not shaded are available."

Angus was looking at mountainous country laid flat on the maps and trying to remember what he had seen on his two trips along Mill Creek. "This section back here," and he pointed at a couple of plots a mile or so north of the creek and probably two miles from the mill, "I think is where I was most interested riding through, and this particular piece," and he put his finger in the middle of a property, "is especially nice. What's our procedure?"

Before Sullivan could get started, Whitell strode to large windows that looked out on State Street. "Look, Mr. Sullivan. Those two men riding by? They are the ones I was telling you about. That's Loper and Lopez. There was a third, Duval, but he must have ridden on.

"Those two are dangerous and shifty, sir," Whitell said, coming back to the map table. "I wouldn't trust either one with a dollar."

"I saw them at the bank when I stopped in this morning. I nodded hello to them and they simply rode right on by. Most rude gentlemen. So, let's get started on the paperwork, shouldn't take too long, and you can go back to the mill owning a fine piece of Oregon Territory."

The paperwork was done in half an hour and Sullivan suggested a lunch and cold beer at Sadie's Salmon House on Commercial Street, just up from the river. "The salmon run has started and if anyone has salmon steaks, it will be Sadie. She grills them over an open fire right behind the bar," Sullivan said, almost drooling thinking about it.

It was a short five block walk down from the capitol complex and a beautiful spring day to make the walk with a gentle breeze blowing up from the river, trees exploding in color and fragrance, and the quiet bedlam of activity in the young, growing city. As they crossed Third Street, Sullivan was hailed by a man coming out of a shop.

"I've been looking for you, Sullivan. The salmon are running, my friend. Let's give them a welcome this evening, shall we?"

"Hello, Sheriff. It would be a fine evening to catch a salmon, I'm sure. Fred, I want you to meet Oregon Territory's newest land owner, Angus Whitell. Angus, this is Salem Sheriff Fred Sharp, one of the finest men in the territory."

The two sized each other up, smiled warmly, and shook hands. "We're on our way to Sadie's for lunch, Fred. Will you join us?"

"Most happy to, Sullivan. Have you found work, Mr. Whitell? If not, a man of your size would be welcome as a deputy in my office."

Angus laughed gently and said, "I start tomorrow morning at Donaldson's Mill, Sheriff, but I thank you for the offer."

Commercial Street was just that, filled with every conceivable type of business, from general merchandise to groceries, from lumber to petticoats, and Sadie's little café was right in the middle of all the action. As the men turned north off State Street, they heard a ruckus stirring up the dust about a block up the street. "There goes lunch," Sharp said. "I'll catch up with you a little later. Duty calls."

9

SARAH WATCHED ZEKE AND HIRAM MAKING THEIR WAY through the muddy pathway to the kitchen door for their noonday meal. She stood ready to remind them about their boots and found a nice surprise when they slipped them off without being told. "You boys are getting better every day," she smiled, holding the door open. "Dinner is almost ready to put on the table, so wash up, but quietly. The girls just went down for their nap."

"We won't be going back out this afternoon, Sarah. Sullivan, O'Brien, and the sheriff are coming out for a little pow-wow with me. They're still trying to convince me to make that run for the territorial legislature."

"I wish you'd listen to them, Zeke. You're the right man for the job. We came to Oregon Territory because of good land and good water, and now, my dearest friend, you have a chance to make Oregon an even better place to live. Oregon needs men like you. It's what you preach every day of the week, Zeke Hawthorne, so follow up on your own words."

"Well, now, I just got a fine dressing down, eh, Hiram?"

"You always tell me to listen to Mama. I think you should too."

"Two against one," he harrumphed, but with a smile. "Have the girl's votes been tallied yet?"

Smiles and laughter joined a venison joint, boiled potatoes, and early green peas at the kitchen table. "The things you're most concerned with are the things that will bring Oregon to statehood, Zeke, and you're in a position to do something about that."

"I know I am, Sarah, but I haven't even built the farm up, this is our first year of planting, and I've signed contracts for a crop that isn't even up yet. How can I possibly take the time to run for political office?"

"I think you'll find that you won't have to do much more than give the same speeches that you give to the mules every day," she laughed. "I've heard you out there, telling the mules about the need for education, demanding that they understand the need for trade schools, emphasizing how important transportation facilities are."

"He does, too, Mama," Hiram said.

"With Sullivan and the bank talking about you all over the southern end of the territory, with you and O'Brien talking about you to the farms up and down the Willamette River, and with Johnson talking about you in Portland, Oregon City, and up the Columbia River, you're a shoe-in for the legislature."

"With a campaign chairman like you, I can't lose," Zeke laughed. "Let's see what Sullivan has to say when they get here. You have a mighty strong argument, though. Maybe you should be the one running."

"That would stir it up, wouldn't it?" she laughed. "Finish up boys, so I can clean up. I suppose all you men will gather in the kitchen, as usual?" she shook her head walking toward the big stove. "Why did you even build a living room?"

Zeke was looking forward to this meeting with Sullivan and Sharp, wanting to hear all the gossip from the capital, and their interpretation of it. He knew his plans, knew how much work had to be done on the farm every day of the week, and worried about his own limitations. "I've never been in a position of leadership like this would be," he mused. "I have my ideas of what Oregon should grow to, how I would like to find a life in this wonderful territory, but am I capable of suggesting these things to other people? Just who do I think I am to think I might have answers like that?"

On reflection, he knew the answer to the first question was a resounding yes. He could almost feel people respond to him when he spoke and knew people listened and understood his thoughts on statehood. "All of this since I stepped into the saddle on Ruth that day back in Missouri and rode off into the great unknown." He walked out onto the porch, watching the rain pelt the verdant ground he called home, and felt inadequate to what he already knew he was going to do.

There has never really been a question, has there? I've been unwilling to come right out with it while inside I've known that I want to be in that legislature, I want to be a part of bringing this little piece of heaven into the union.

MIKE O'BRIEN ARRIVED first and was welcomed by Hiram.

"Did your son tell you about the salmon I caught, Mr. O'Brien?"

"Sure did, Hi. It sounded like a fine fish. Your Papa expecting me?"

"He's in the kitchen, sir. I'll put your horse up for you. Mr. Sullivan and the sheriff aren't here yet. Go right in." Hiram hurried off with O'Brien's stud horse while the burly cattleman headed for the kitchen door of the large farmhouse. O'Brien had been in the territory for several years and was operating a cattle ranch just a few miles north of the Hawthorne farm.

O'Brien had a wife and two sons, worked with several Mexican hired hands that he brought up from a previous California cattle operation. O'Brien's next neighbor to the north was Joshua Petersen who was growing wheat and corn, along with plentiful amounts of beans. He too was married, but there were no children in the family, yet.

"Afternoon, Zeke. Looks like we're getting a good break in the weather for a while. How's your planting coming?"

"Howdy, Mike, come on in. You call this a break in the weather?" Zeke was pointing out the window as sheets of rain splashed down. "We've got just about everything in now. We'll be working on the hops for another week if the weather holds." He had to chuckle over O'Brien's comment and his comeback. "Coffee's hot if you'd like a cup."

O'Brien took a cup, laced it with some rum that was sitting on the table. "I guess you know we're not going to let up on you until you tell us you're going to stand for the legislature. We're a mean bunch, Zeke."

"You're pikers compared to Sarah and Hiram. Those

two have been on me for weeks, and I can't find any solid arguments to use," he laughed.

"You know you're the man, Zeke," O'Brien said. "Just settle back and let Sullivan and I escort you to your proper seat. Did you see the letter in the *Oregon Statesman* that Obediah Sinclair wrote about you?"

"Sarah put the newspaper on my dinner plate instead of pork chops the other night, Mike, that's how much pressure I'm getting around here." He stood up when Hiram stuck his head in the door to say that Sullivan and Sheriff Fred Sharp were coming up the long drive. "Good, Hiram. Take care of their horses for them, and then come in and join us."

From the time Hiram had become a part of the family, he was treated as if he was already a grown man. He worked side-by-side with Zeke in the fields and shops, was expected to take part in all family discussions, and his opinion was listened to. Sarah was a trained teacher and Hiram's education was always an important part of his day. He could barely understand the language when he became part of the family, and now he was reading as if he had started at five-years-old.

Sullivan was full of excited thoughts on the fine weather that filled the Oregon Territorial skies, the sheriff was blunt and quiet, and the group settled around the kitchen table. Sarah had a large pot of fresh coffee made in minutes, a bottle of rum sat in the middle of the table, and she excused herself.

"No, Sarah, I wish you would sit with us," Zeke said. "With the Sullivan gang over there," and he spread his arms to take in the sheriff, Sullivan, and O'Brien, it would only be right that you and Hiram join their gang, and press me into service." In most cases, with politics being the subject at hand, a woman would not be welcomed, but with Zeke Hawthorne, those at the table expected Sarah to be with them.

Zeke had a smile on his face as each person at the table took his or her turn to explain how important it was for him to represent this section of the territory in the legislature. He listened quietly, sipped on his well-laced coffee, and when they were all through, he reached in his coat pocket and read from a sheet of paper.

"I sent this to the *Oregon Statesman* day before yesterday, and asked that it be published in the next edition," he said. "Dear Sir, I said, It is with some trepidation that I now offer myself to the citizens of Oregon Territory, to represent the Willamette District in the Territorial Legislature. I will always be available to answer any and all questions, and will be pleased to discuss the many problems that need to be taken care of. I stand for statehood and will defend the constitution of these United States of America always. I will appreciate your vote."

He sat back in his chair, just a touch of smugness splashed across his face, and let a grand smile slowly make itself obvious. "Gotcha," is all he said, reaching for the coffee pot and filling his cup.

"Well, you old rascal," Sullivan laughed. "You just sat there and let us talk and talk and talk. Did you know about this, Sarah?"

"No, Mr. Sullivan, I did not. Zeke, you let me talk for half an hour today at dinner, and never opened your mouth."

"Actually, I made up my mind last week, and the only person that I discussed it with was Mr. Sinclair at the bank. He gave me his full blessing, and I wanted to hear again just how I was going to drive this territory into statehood. I can't possibly put into words just how I feel about your support, and you must know, I'll be calling on you constantly for help."

"How does the election work, Papa?" Hiram asked the question that Sarah wanted to ask as well.

"I can answer that," Roland Sullivan said. "There are representatives from each county, and they are elected by the legal residents of that county. The more people there are in a county, the more representatives they have in the House of Representatives. The other half of the legislature is called the Council, and there is one member from each county."

"I think that's one of the things I'm very much in favor of," Zeke said. "I believe it is best if the citizens of Oregon pick their representatives through the ballot box. I've talked with other members of the legislature, I've talked with Governor John Gaines, and I think it's something that's needed. Among many other things."

"How do we do something about the employment situation?" Sullivan asked. "It's getting to the point that some merchants in Salem are worried about continuing in business."

"Sullivan, you're a one man walking advertisement for Oregon Territory, and it would be my suggestion that you begin a writing campaign to the major newspapers in this country, talking about opportunity for craftsmen and those willing to work. San Francisco, Chicago, St. Louis, New York, New Orleans," Zeke said. "Flood the editor's desks with Oregon's bounty, sir."

"Oh, my," is all Sullivan could stammer for several

moments. "What a splendid idea. I've got so many things to bring to their attention. With our splendid weather, soil so rich things grow on their own…" and the group bellowed at him to save it for his letter campaign.

"One thing, Mr. Sullivan," Sarah said. "Emphasize the importance of family. A woman is what makes a man great, and don't ever forget that. A man with a family will be far more likely to want to be a successful farmer, rancher, or businessman."

"Oh, I just thought," Sullivan said, nodding in agreement with Sarah. "Sheriff, tell Zeke about that little fracas you broke up the other day."

Sharp didn't much care to talk about what he did as sheriff, didn't much care to talk about much of anything, really. He could sit and listen to other people talk all day, and seldom contributed to a conversation.

"Just a couple of stupid rowdies," he said. "That's what this meeting is all about, I think. I've heard you say a thousand times, Zeke, that you came to Oregon Territory because you heard good things about our soil and water. But why are so many people coming who have no idea of why they're coming?" Sharp shook his head, pondering his own question before continuing with Sullivan's story.

"Those two ruffians, and I'm sure they're wanted wherever they're from, were stealing food from Simpson's Fresh Market. Stealing food, with guns drawn, and probably fifty signs in stores all over Salem begging for workers. One of them, Johnny Loper, a real smart Alec, dared me to shoot him."

"Did you?" O'Brien asked.

"Sure as I'm sittin' here, I did, Michael O'Brien," Sheriff Sharp laughed. "But seriously, why was he even in

Oregon? I didn't kill the fool, and he's sitting in my jail right now, worrying some bandages on his arm. I asked him why he was in Salem. He told me it was because they didn't want him in California.

"Gentlemen, Mrs. Hawthorne, that's a sad commentary on our territory." The sheriff sat back and took a long drink of hot coffee.

"I don't think you've talked that much in five years, Sharp," Sullivan laughed. "But you sure as all get out are right. And, Zeke, you're right, too. As soon as I get back to Salem I'm going to start that letter writing campaign and blanket the big cities. Yes, sir, that's what I'm going to do."

"If I could bring up one more suggestion," Sarah said, quietly. The men all stopped talking and gave her their attention. "Starting about ten years ago, the Methodists in the territory opened the Oregon Institute, an education facility that I've made myself aware of. Zeke, if you and some of the other men who are fine craftsmen offered your services, say once a week each, you could teach such crafts as cabinet making, glass making, iron work and blacksmithing.

"There is need of harness and saddle makers, carpenters, sail makers, and let's not forget these new steam engines that are coming into use. Somebody builds them. Somebody works on them, fixes them when they break. Others need to be taught all of this.

"I know those that run that fine institute, and they would welcome you. One blacksmith class a week. One carpentry class a week. One cabinet making class a week, and within a year, you would have, maybe not journeyman status craftsmen, but well trained people for jobs."

"What a splendid idea," Sullivan all but jumped out of his chair. "I have just the man to put that together, Sarah. You met Slick Snyder when you came into Salem one time during the winter, I think."

"He's Hector Snyder's son? At the Trading Post? I remember," she said. "He's about twenty and joined his father last year after going to school in St. Louis."

"Introduce him to the people at the Oregon Institute. He's a trained educator, like you, and I would bet Slick could have that idea of yours in operation before the summer is well underway."

"Interesting," Zeke said. "Are you aware that the legislature meets in the Oregon Institute Building? They finished the 1851-52 session at the end of February and will meet next in December." He paused for a minute, contemplating something. "All this seems to mesh somehow, and all of us sitting here are a big part of it."

The afternoon was slowly slipping toward early evening and Sullivan and Sheriff Sharp had to get back to Salem and Mike O'Brien had to return to his ranch. Zeke pretty much summed up the meeting when he said, "Now that we have Oregon's problems solved, all we need is a delegation to head to Washington and plead for statehood."

III

BOOK SEVEN: ROAD TO THE
LEGISLATURE

ZEKE, SARAH, AND THE CHILDREN RODE INTO SALEM several weeks after his big announcement in the newspaper, for a day of shopping and mingling; meaning electioneering. Zeke drove the wagon, but he had his saddle horse tied to the back of the wagon and planned to stay in town later than Sarah and the children. Hiram would drive the wagon, filled with supplies back to the farm.

He tied off the mule team in front of the Salem Trading Post and walked in to find Travis. Sarah held one of the twins and he the other, with Hiram following along behind, as they made their way through aisles jammed with every conceivable item known to man or beast.

"Look at that," Hiram said, pointing at a set of snowshoes. "I remember those, Papa. They were made by Wolf Dog and Travis had them hanging in the store at Fort Bridger."

"He said he was bringing everything from that trading post when we left," Zeke answered. "I don't think he'll find a buyer down here for a while." Hiram's eyes were dancing, looking at hundreds of items spread about on shelves, hanging from the ceiling, and tacked to the walls.

"Sarah," Travis boomed from his office tucked in the back of the store. "How did you wedge this old dirt farmer off the mud-covered plain?" He threw his arms around his oldest child and hugged her tight. "Just look at these girls. They'll be marrying off soon, I believe," he laughed. "Hiram, me lad, you're as tall as your Mama, and gaining a little weight, finally.

"Mr. Assemblyman, welcome to my palace of fine merchandise," Travis quipped to Zeke. "Looking for votes, are we? Well, you've certainly got mine and Hector's."

"Yup, vote gettin' time," Zeke chuckled. "Got a letter from Paul Pritchett, the barber. Do you know him?"

"Sure, but I never go to him. Haven't cut these locks since I married Elaine, and that's been more than twenty-five years. He's a bit rough as a dentist, I've heard, but honest and enjoys talking. I guess all barbers are that way. Was he looking for something special?"

"Offered his support, Travis. He's one of my stops today, along with Sullivan, and many of the businesses down along Commercial Street. Sarah wants to spend some time with you, if you're not too busy, and then slip down to Barbara's store, too. Hiram's going to stay with Sarah, supposedly to help with the twins, but mostly to moon over Barbara."

"Papa," Hiram said. "It's just that she's so pretty." He got quiet when both men simply gave him the big look, smiling, shaking their heads. "Well, she is," he whispered, and walked out into the store to find a stick of candy. He had both hands stuck down deep in his pockets, giving the hardwood floor a solid look-see. He could hear the chuckles all the way out. Heck Snyder was behind the counter, talking with another man as Hiram walked up.

"Hiram, good morning to you," Snyder said. "I'll be with you in just a minute." He turned his attention back to his customer. "So, Clive Newton, it looks like this comes to seven dollars and a quarter. Do you want one of the boys to load you up?"

Newton paid his bill and snarled, "No, I can do that myself." He looked over at Hiram, scowling. "You're one of the half-breeds Hawthorne brought with him, are you?"

Hiram had never been spoken to that way and was slightly confused for just a moment, then angry. "I am Hiram Hawthorne, sir. I don't appreciate your insult, and I expect an apology." There were few men in Salem that would talk in that tone of voice to Newton, but Hiram had been taught to respect himself, and had been taught good manners. And was not about to be treated in such a rude manner.

"Half-breed bastard," Newton said. He took a swipe at Hiram who danced out of the way and came up standing tall, with a large skinning knife in his hand. Heck Snyder leaped across the counter and stood between Hi and Newton.

"Get out of the store, Clive Newton, and don't come back. You're not welcome here."

"That little bastard pulled a knife on me!" He was screaming angry, trying to shove Snyder out of the way, while Hiram was standing, crouched, ready to take on the burley muleskinner. "Get out of my way, Snyder," Newton screamed.

"What's going on here?" Zeke said. He ran to the front,

taking in the tableau: His son, knife drawn, a teamster fighting off Heck Snyder, screaming obscenities at Hiram, Snyder howling at Newton to get out. Zeke slipped an arm around Hiram, got him to ease the knife back in its scabbard, and told him to go back to his mother.

"No, Papa," Hiram replied. "That man has to apologize to me, to you, and to grandpa."

"That man is an ignorant fool, Hiram. Keep the knife put away, and stay out of the way for just a minute." He was smiling proud, seeing his son stand up to a bully of a man, three or four times his size.

Zeke stepped around Heck Snyder and looked Clive Newton up and down. "You have insulted my family, sir. Step outside with me," he said. He pushed Newton hard, forcing him out of the store and off the porch. The two men were standing in the muddy street, glaring at each other.

"I'll kill you, Hawthorne," Newton said, opening his heavy buffalo coat and reaching for a large skinning knife. In two moves, Zeke had the man turned, tripped, and face down in the mud. Zeke had a knee between the man's legs, prodding enough that Newton was more than aware of it. Zeke had his own knife out and was pricking the man's neck.

"My son said he wants an apology, Newton. Now would be a good time to offer that." He let the knife tip jab just a little bit. "My son is waiting." Newton could feel a trickle of blood run down his neck.

Hiram had jumped off the porch and was standing facing Newton and his father, his legs spread, his coat opened so Newton could see his knife as well. "My father's name with the tribe is Sharp Knife, Mr. Newton. I'm the son of Sharp Knife, and I want an apology now."

Newton felt another prick of that pointed blade and coughed out some words. "Don't speak that language, Mr. Newton," Hiram said. "Say it in English so we all understand."

Newton coughed out "I'm sorry," and Zeke let him get to his feet. "If you're ever rude to any member of my family again, Mr. Newton, I will slice your body into side meat for the dogs." Zeke held that knife at the ready, and slipped an arm around Hiram's shoulder, giving him a good squeeze. "Better move off, Newton, before I turn this boy loose."

Newton stumbled to his horse, tethered nearby, and rode off, spouting foul language all the way down Mill Creek Road. "That was a very brave move, Hiram, but it was also not the smartest you could have made. If you pull a weapon, you must be ready to use it. Would you have been able to take that man's life?"

Hiram wanted to immediately say yes, he would have, but he also realized just exactly what that meant. Could he take a man's life? He would spend a great deal of time thinking about what he had done and the biggest question of his young life, asked by his father.

A crowd had gathered, watched the near death of a man, and moved aside as Zeke and Hiram climbed back up on the porch and went into the Salem Trading Post. "That's quite a boy you have, Mr. Hawthorne," a man standing just inside the store said. "I'm Slick Snyder, Heck's son.

"Some of these men that call themselves Oregon

Firsters are not going to appreciate what just happened. Newton is an ignorant fool, but he does have friends."

Zeke shook the offered hand and nudged Hiram to do the same. "I've always said that an ignorant person can learn, Slick, while a stupid person simply won't. I'm afraid our Clive Newton is probably just a stupid person.

"Have you had a chance to talk with my wife? She has plans for you, my young friend," Zeke said.

"She just invited me to come to your farm in the next few days to lay out these plans for industrial education in Oregon. I'm looking forward to the opportunity."

It took Zeke more time to calm Sarah down than it did to curtail Newton's outrage, and with help from Travis he was finally able to get the story out. "Our boy is more man than boy, Sarah. We've taught him the importance of good manners and the importance of self-respect. He simply stood up for himself, just as we have taught him to do.

"He'll spend the day with you and the girls and you, my dear lady, will know that you are being escorted by a real man." He wanted to believe that Sarah understood, and he saw the glint in Travis's eyes, saying that he did, for certain.

"You've got a fine lad, there, Sarah. This old grandpa is proud of him."

Sarah understood that, like herself, Hiram was half Shoshone, and she understood she had been in a similar situation and had acted very much as her son did. She also remembered how Zeke had stood up to ignorant men at Fort Bridger, and how proud of him she was. "Thank you, Hiram," she said, putting her arms around the boy and hugging him tight. "You're a fine young man."

It was more than half an hour before Zeke could finally get out of the store and make his way to Salem's downtown. He spent the first two blocks brushing dried mud from the fracas from his clothing, doffing his hat to the ladies, and saying hello to many friendly faces.

SARAH CALMED down after Travis made coffee and they were able to talk about something other than what had happened. Hiram sat alongside his mother, holding her hand and telling her it was okay. After several cups of hot coffee, Sarah said it was time to visit Barbara, and Hiram helped get her and the girls settled in the wagon. It was a short drive to Barbara's shop.

"I'm so glad you came," Barbara gushed when they walked in. She had a small office in the back of the store and escorted the group in. "Just look at you, Hiram," she said, seeing that the boy was taller than she. "My goodness, but you're a fine young man, aren't you?"

Hi blushed crimson, stood with his face looking at the floor, terrified at what he might say if he opened his mouth. Barbara put her arms around him and hugged him tight and he knew he was going to pass out. "If you keep growing you'll be as big as Moose pretty soon. Aren't you going to say hello?" She asked in that teasing way of hers, and gave him a peck on the cheek to add to his misery.

"Anything interesting going on since your last visit, Sarah?" Barbara had a small wood stove in her office and had water boiling in a pot. "Want some tea?"

Sarah had no intentions of talking about the events at the trading post. They drank tea and talked about the farm, about planting, about Zeke running for the legislature, and of course, about the new baby that would be born later in the year. "You must be so excited about another baby," Barbara said. "You don't think it would be twins again, do you?"

"My God, I hope not," Sarah laughed. "From the looks of your shop, you've been busy. Anything new on the romance front?"

"Busy, busy in the shop, and I don't want to even think about anything like romance. I don't think I'm the marrying kind."

"I'll marry you," Hiram said, then realized what he'd done, turned beet red once more, and got up from his chair and walked out onto the street for some fresh air. *That was certainly stupid. She's so pretty.*

Barbara and Sarah tried not to giggle, but knew that Hi had to have heard them when he left. "That boy loves you dearly," Sarah said.

"I know, and I shouldn't tease him. He's not really a boy, anymore. He's thirteen years old, Sarah, and doing man's work at the farm. I'm very proud to be his first love," she giggled.

"I better get back up to the trading post and get the supplies loaded. It's a long ride back and we'll still have to unload when we get there. Have you seen Moose at all? He never gets out to the farm."

"He's got that mill cranking out lumber by the ton, Sarah. He was in a couple of days ago for some supplies and we had lunch. He's hired a new man that he's very happy with. I'm looking forward to meeting him. His name is Angus Whitell, and he's from Boston. Moose says he's really a good hand."

"Boston." Sarah said. "Well, you two will have lots to talk about, eh? Tell that brother of ours I love him and he better find time to visit." It took just a short time to get loaded in the wagon for the quick trip back to the trading post. Hi never said a word, just drove the team and smiled. Barbara, of course, gave him a long hug goodbye along with another peck on the cheek.

"MR. PRITCHETT? I'M ZEKE HAWTHORNE," Zeke said, walking into Pritchett's barbershop. "I got your letter and wanted to stop in and introduce myself, and to answer any questions you might have."

Pritchett's shop was clean with the swiveling barber's chair front and center. The floor was polished hardwood, and there were mounted salmon, deer heads, and artwork hanging on the walls, including a portrait of the barber. Pritchett was always dressed in a starched white shirt and string tie, and wore a white apron as well. He pushed his eyeglasses up on his nose and smiled at Zeke.

"It's a pleasure to meet you, Mr. Hawthorne. I have fresh coffee if you'll join me?" he said. "Or, we could sneak next door to the Salem Club and be more comfortable." Zeke thought Pritchett would prefer that, and they walked to the club after the barber put up a notice that he would return as soon as possible.

They got a mug of beer each and found a table by the front window and settled in. "I've had several talks with Mr. Sullivan and Mr. Sinclair, and they've had nothing but good things to say about you, Hawthorne. I'm also aware that another group of men, the ones that call themselves Oregon Firsters, are very much opposed to your election."

"They are, indeed, sir, but I firmly believe that Oregon is growing up and needs to be prepared to become a state. The frontier status was necessary, but growth in population, economy, and education are what will drive Oregon into the future. You've been in Oregon for some time, I believe."

"Yes, I've been here longer than most of those that call themselves Firsters," he laughed. "I came west with the American Fur Company, worked my way here with those Frenchies, and fell in love with this country. Like Mr. Sullivan, I believe in the future of Oregon, and I support what you're working for."

They were on their second mug of cold beer when they were interrupted by Clive Newton screaming obscenities as he charged through the batwing doors of the saloon. Zeke stood up and faced the angry, drunken teamster, but did not pull his knife. "Don't do something you'll regret, Newton," he said. "I whipped you when you were sober, I'll have no trouble with a drunk."

Newton's language was as foul as any muleskinners could be, and he charged at Zeke from fifteen feet away. Zeke used the man's own fury, stepped slightly to the side, grabbed Newton's heavy coat, and spun with him, letting go on the back side of the spin. Newton slammed into the far wall, headfirst, and slowly sank to the floor, almost unconscious.

Zeke stood quietly watching as Newton tried to get back on his feet. "Go home and sleep it off, Newton. Don't make this worse. So far, all you've done is embarrass yourself, don't be stupid."

The words meant nothing to the man in his drunken stupor. He gained his feet, opened that heavy coat, and drew a large skinning knife that gleamed. "I'll kill you, Hawthorne, you injun lovin' sumbitch, I'll kill you. I'll kill your filthy squaw and those half-breed bastards you brought here with you."

There was deadly silence in the saloon and those nearby slowly moved away from what was sure to be a deadly encounter. Zeke didn't pull his knife but he did slip out of his jacket, and everyone saw his weapon in its well decorated scabbard, at his side. "You're drunk, Newton. Put the knife away and go home. You're a rude, stupid, obnoxious man, Newton, and I don't want to kill you, but I will. Go home."

Instead, Newton lunged at Zeke, the knife thrust at Zeke's middle, and the big man grasped Newton's arm, lifted it high, brought his knee up, and drove the arm down. The sound of Newton's elbow splintering from the impact filled the saloon, followed by the sound of the knife clattering to the floor.

Zeke stood Newton up, and before the man even had time to scream his pain, Zeke slammed a fist square into his face, driving him onto the floor. Zeke picked the knife up and handed it to the bartender, and suggested that someone should call the doctor and maybe the sheriff, too.

"I'm sorry you had to see that, Pritchett. I could have killed him, maybe I should have, but he definitely had intentions to kill me."

"You did what you had to do, Hawthorne. I have to say, though, there may be repercussions from his friends in the Firsters."

"I'm afraid you're right about that." He looked out the front window and saw Fred Sharp hurrying across the street. "Here comes the sheriff, now." He watched Sharp come in the door and saw another man hurrying along as well. "Must be the doctor, coming in, too."

Jonah Smith had his offices on the second floor of the Oregon City Mercantile and was stoking his wood stove in preparation for the meeting of Oregon City Firsters. Smith was among the first non-trappers to set up shop in the area, well before it became a U.S. possession. The territory was shared by Great Britain and the U.S. prior to territorial status, which began in 1848. There had been a shared provisional government beginning in about 1843.

Smith had studied law in New Orleans, managed to take the life of a well-known gambler, and fled west with a group that followed what became the Santa Fe Trail.

He continued west into California, arriving in 1840 and setting himself up in a law business in the rich ranching areas near Santa Barbara. His knowledge of Mexican law was limited at best and he became well known as a schemer and known friend to the criminal element. He left California before the gold rush, moving north into the Columbia River area where he continued working various schemes and conspiracies. He moved to Oregon City when the British suggested he leave Fort Vancouver.

"Ah, Ted, I'm glad you could make it," Smith said as Ted Newcomb came into the office. "I expect Charles to be here any minute. Coffee?"

Ted Newcomb had settled on property along the north end of the Willamette Valley and operated one of the first working ranches in the area. He was a large, robust man with long dark hair he kept tied back in a braid, often wore buckskins, and had a hatred for all the easterners coming into the valley. There had been considerable talk among the Firsters that he should be a candidate for the territorial legislature.

The legislature was bicameral, and met every year, usually from December into February. The upper house was called the Council while the lower was the House of Representatives. The lower house was the larger, and its size depended mostly on population. Members chosen to represent individual counties. The upper chamber was also elected by county.

On the maps in Sullivan's office, Newcomb's property included about two thousand acres of prime Willamette Valley land extending up into the heavily forested Cascade Range. In reality, Newcomb didn't believe in property lines and ran his livestock, cut timber, and planted wherever he felt like it, and if someone complained, they faced an angry frontiersman with a loaded musket.

In general terms, it would be safe to say the majority of those calling themselves Firsters had limited education, were not craftsmen, and had little use for laws that limited their actions. Most would find it difficult to make a living along the east coast, particularly in heavily populated areas.

"Hold the coffee, Jonah, I've brought my flask. So, I see that upstart Hawthorne is making headway in his campaign. I've just about made up my mind to give him a run for that office and then run him right out of the territory. With Hawthorne bringing that Travis and Johnson in with him, they're taking lots of jobs and business from men that built this territory.

"Yes, sir, Jonah, spread the word that I'm running for a Willamette Valley seat in the legislature." He took a long pull on the flask and handed it to Smith to pour some in Smith's coffee. Newcomb was about to say something more when Charley Florin walked in.

"So, you finally made up your mind, Newcomb. You've got my backing all the way." Florin opened a meat market as Oregon City started to come together as a community, leaving the trapping life behind him. He always had beef, lamb, goat, and plenty of fresh fish on hand. Much of his meat was salted or smoked, with fresh being available for short periods during butchering.

"Is this why you called this meeting, Jonah?" Florin was rail thin, with a weathered, thin face that was long and sad-looking. His eyes were gray as was his beard and hair, and he always looked as if he might burst into tears at any moment. His spindly legs were slightly bowed, his shoulders hunched, and he walked with a slight limp that came from a tussle with an ornery mule many years before.

"This territory only exists because of men like us," Florin said. "We need to see to it that the frontier spirit continues, that we keep this place just the way we found it. All these new people are destroying our way of life. They're gonna try to tell us we can't hunt or fish unless they give us permission. I'll give them permission to leave, anytime they want. We can win this election, Ted. You can win this election, and then, we'll not let them railroad us into statehood."

"Say, Newcomb," Jonah Smith said. "Have you met George Belknap? He's also against Hawthorne's positions."

"I've heard the name but never met the man."

"He lives in Salem City and supports statehood as long as Oregon is a pro-slavery state. Hawthorne is against slavery."

"Slavery? That's just a natural way of life for most people. The church in California held most of the Indians as slaves, Indians capture slaves from each other, Europeans have held slaves for thousands of years. If I could afford one I'd have a slave or two myself. To hell with Belknap and slavery, it's statehood that I'm against and will fight Hawthorne to the bloody end."

Smith and Florin voiced their agreement with Newcomb in loud hoorays and stomping feet. "Statehood would ruin Oregon," Newcomb said. He put some more chunks of hardwood in the stove and took another long pull from his flask. "I guess being a territory of the states is okay, I don't get along that well with the Britishers and Frenchies, but statehood would destroy our way of life. Let's make a serious campaign out of this. Let's destroy Hawthorne; kill him if we have to."

The three men spent the next several hours planning Newcomb's campaign. They would write letters to the newspapers in Oregon City and Salem, and send riders up and down the Willamette River, Columbia River, and into the Snake River country. "We'll run these injun lovin' easterners right back where they came from," Newcomb bawled to Smith's and Florin's delight.

"ARE YOU SURE OF THAT?" Jonah Smith was in Harkin's Mercantile, campaigning for Ted Newcomb.

"Sure as the day I was born," Stephan Harkin said. "Hawthorne and that Indian half-breed he calls his wife weren't never married proper and legal-like. Those children are all half-breed bastards, I'll guarantee."

Jonah Smith was rubbing his hands in delight at the news. "I've got to spread the word on this. Hawthorne will never sit in that legislature after the good people of Oregon hear this. I've got to ride to Newcomb's ranch right now. Thank you, Stephan. Thank you."

Harkin, Smith, Newcomb, and Florin spread the word as quickly as they could up and down the three major districts in the territory. There were obscene letters to editors in every community, posters calling Hawthorne's children bastards appeared regularly. It was just a week before the election that Rutherford Johnson and Jeremiah Travis were holding a rally for Ezekiel Hawthorne at their warehouse in Oregon City. It came about as a direct result of the Newcomb promotion and campaigning.

"That fool has just about got all the way into my craw," Travis exploded one morning, and sent a message to Johnson to plan some kind of large rally for Zeke. He said that he should also plan to have some security on hand. "I don't trust these ignorant Firsters for half a second.

They'll try something stupid, you can place money on that!"

Johnson organized the rally and Travis made the long trek north to Oregon City to attend. Travis was about to speak when Jonah Smith stood up and yelled at him. "How do you answer, Mr. Travis, that your man Hawthorne isn't legally married to your half-breed daughter?"

Many of Hawthorne's supporters started yelling for Smith to get out, Firsters were cheering and clapping at Smith's remarks, and Travis held up his hands, asking for quiet. "I'll be more than glad to answer that question, Mr. Smith. I'll answer to Mr. Smith, not lawyer Smith, since you don't have a single document testifying to you being a lawyer."

The Hawthorne crowd cheered, and Travis continued. "I came west with the original trappers, as many of you know, and there was no law in that country. Today, thirty years later, there is still no law in much of that country, including where Fort Bridger stood.

"We lived by a creed based on a combination of the good book, tribal customs, and what worked to keep us alive. Under the mountain man's creed, I married my beautiful wife, Elaine, and Zeke Hawthorne married my daughter, Sarah. My children, sir, are not bastards and neither are Zeke's." Travis was as angry as anyone had ever seen him, but it was a controlled anger, and he was shaking his massive fist at the man as he spoke.

There was pandemonium in the large Johnson warehouse as Zeke Hawthorne's supporters were standing and cheering for their man. Travis allowed them to continue their demonstrating for a time before waving his arms and calling for quiet. The quiet was slow in coming and Travis took his time before continuing his own tirade. "If you do not apologize to my family this moment, then I call you a liar and demand that you meet me outside this building this moment."

Travis was angrier than Johnson had ever seen the man, the crowd was screaming their support for what he had said, and Smith found himself about to face an old Indian fighting mountain man who had killed more men than Smith had ever even argued with. "Now, Mr. Smith!" Travis howled, rambling down from the podium.

The crowd parted, allowing the old Fort Bridger trader free passage to where Jonah Smith was standing. Just as Travis was ten feet from the man, Smith turned and ran from the building. Cheers and jeers followed him out of the warehouse and onto the muddy streets of Oregon City.

It was all people could talk about for days; that Travis ran Smith off, that Travis, this old man who once was a mountain man, who once trapped with Bridger and Bent and Carson, scared the pants off the upstart attorney. Newspapers in Oregon City, in the building community of Portland, and in the capital city of Salem, carried variations on the story in issue after issue.

Then, newspaper after newspaper called for the election of Hawthorne, condemned the actions of the Firsters, and followed up with stories of coming statehood, of Oregon pride, and called for some of the same things that Hawthorne and his supporters were calling for; such as increased education, better transportation, and building markets for Oregon produce and commerce.

In many minds, Ezekiel Hawthorne was already a

winner even if the election hadn't been held just yet. Not in the mind of George Belknap, however, who was steaming angry because of the stupid mistakes made by the Firsters.

"I tell you, McCaskill, what Jonah Smith did was tantamount to electing Hawthorne. We need to silence the ignorant Firsters to stop Hawthorne from being elected. By attempting to sully the man they instead made him a damn hero. I tell you, we're going to lose this election because of Jonah Smith and that fool, Newcomb."

George Belknap was a member of the Oregon Assembly, representing the southern Snake River district. Originally from Virginia, Belknap came west during the California gold fever era and moved north to ranch in the vast high desert west of Fort Boise. "I tell you, Geoff, this country needs to be proslavery and needs to retain its frontier openness. I have to hire riff-raff instead of bringing in hard working slaves."

Geoff McCaskill and Peter Flowers nodded in agreement, and McCaskill continued from where Belknap left off. "Assuming that loss," he said, "we must then force the issue of Oregon being admitted to the union as a proslavery state. Fight Hawthorne and his crowd on purely legal and political grounds. Newcomb is calling for Hawthorne's death. That would simply make the man a martyr and end anything we could do."

Geoff McCaskill was a trader with operations in the far northeast and northern areas of the vast Oregon Territory. His trading pack trains were filled with goods that arrived in the territory by way of ocean going vessels from the east coast and from Asia. His posts were along the western Rocky Mountains from Utah north and west into the Yellowstone.

Peter Flowers operated a ranch along the northern Willamette and, like Belknap, was originally from Virginia. His family worked tobacco, cane, and cotton plantations and held many slaves. He fully supported Oregon becoming a proslavery state.

"Let's spread the word and have a general meeting of our people before the next session of the legislature," Belknap agreed. "Maybe the first week of December would be a good time. We're all well-educated southern gentlemen and we need to eliminate Hawthorne's arguments, not the man."

"We do have help, remember, from our congressional representative." Peter Flowers had been rather quiet up to that point. "We can call on his resources before the session and during."

"All right, then," Belknap said. "We do what we can to keep the Firsters from making things worse, meet before the session, and work with Joe Gaines. I think we're on firm ground, men."

The meeting ended with some fine Virginia rum being passed around along with Virginia cigars in ample supply.

"I'D SAY YOU'VE HAD YOURSELF QUITE A DAY, EZEKIEL Hawthorne," Sullivan laughed, motioning for Zeke to take a chair. "The buzz around this old town is that you bested one of Salem's angriest men twice, and in public. What does our good sheriff have to say about all this?"

"Clive Newton is a very stupid man, Sullivan, and Sharp says the fool is lucky to be alive. I tend to agree with that statement. Doc Preston is sure he will have to amputate what's left of his arm. Maybe he would have been better off if I had killed him.

"No, I don't mean that. I had a long talk with Fred and he spoke with most of the men that were in the Salem Club. They all insisted that I was simply defending myself from a dangerous drunk. I have no idea, though, how this will affect my campaign, Sullivan."

"What happened tells me that you are a real man, Zeke, and I want a real man representing me in the territorial legislature. Your son was abused and then threatened and you defended him as a good man would. Then you were threatened and you defended yourself. You did the right thing, Zeke, and I'm the one to tell everyone in Oregon Territory." They both laughed at that comment, knowing that was precisely what Sullivan would do.

"Before we go on, have you read this morning's paper? Seems as though your father-in-law was up in Oregon City last week campaigning for you. Didn't he tell you what happened?" He handed a copy of *The Oregon Statesman* to Zeke.

Zeke took the paper and started reading the front-page article, his brow furrowing just a bit, and then a smile came on strong. "He never said a word about this," Zeke said. Amazement crossed the big man's face as he continued to read the report from Oregon City. "I haven't heard a word about this, Sullivan. My God, between that and now me getting all rowdy with Newton, I'm gonna have a terrible reputation."

"No, Zeke, you will have the reputation you deserve. You and your family stand up for what's right, and defend your position. You're a lucky man to have a father-in-law like Travis, and even luckier having a wife like Sarah. You'll win this election, my friend, and you'll be good for Oregon."

Zeke wanted to believe Sullivan. He knew Travis was right, and was proud of what Travis did. *I just wonder if I'm proud of how I handled the situation with Clive Newton. Did I go too far?* Then he remembered the fight with a drunken Indian back along the banks of the Green River and thought, *He would have killed both me and Sarah.*

"For your information, sir, I sent packages of information about our territory to newspapers all along the east coast, the Ohio Valley, and Great Lakes. Of course, with the slowness of communication in those areas, we won't know if anything will be published for some time, but the deed is done." Sullivan stood a bit taller and in his mind, could already see wagon trains filled with journeymen craftsmen plowing across the wide prairie.

"That's our first step and it's a good one. I'm going to ride back to the farm before I wear out my welcome in Salem." There was a touch of irony in Zeke's chuckle. "The election is upon us and all this nonsense right now might have an impact.

We'll just have to live with it."

Zeke walked out to where he had his horse tied off, mounted, and rode down to Commercial Street, heading north along the Willamette River Road. A steamboat was just getting underway for the trip north to the Columbia River. Zeke watched the beautiful boat for about half an hour as he made his way north.

"This is the future," he muttered. "I can almost feel the changes that are coming. Are they as frightening as some imagine, or as magnificent as others see them? Engines powered by boiling water, amazing. Moose is using a steam engine at the lumber mill; that boat is powered by a steam engine; and there are stories about the large ocean going ships that move across the oceans without the benefit of sails. What an age we live in."

FOR THE NEXT SEVERAL DAYS, Zeke stayed at the farm while Sullivan, O'Brien, and many others spread his word up and down the Willamette River Valley. The newspapers were inundated with letters and notes from the citizens of the valley, most supporting Zeke.

Zeke didn't fret about the election, but some of the things he heard, even filtered by his friends, did bother him a bit. Following his serious altercations with Clive Newton, at least one newspaper in Oregon City insisted on referring to him as Sharp Knife Hawthorne.

"Here I am trying my best to bring Oregon Territory out of the frontier era and into this modern age of civilized society, and they call me Sharp Knife Hawthorne. Bah."

"I consider it an honor to call you Sharp Knife," Sarah said. "Remember, oh husband of mine, you got that name defending me. The newspaper in Salem called you Sharp Knife too, and you weren't upset."

"Well, they did it to tell how I jumped at Newton when he threatened Hiram. That's different." He harrumphed a time or two and went back to his blacksmith shop to take out his frustrations on some pieces of steel. Sarah tended to remind him often how Travis had stood up for him and the family when that lawyer made those crude remarks.

"You'll always be Sharp Knife to me, Zeke. And my Papa is very proud of you." She smiled and gave him a hug. "My territorial representative in the House of Representative is Sharp Knife Hawthorne, and I'm willing to tell the world that I love him."

"Did you see that group of wagons that passed through this morning?" Hiram was getting ready to harness the mules for his afternoon work in the cornfields. "I counted five large wagons and three smaller ones. There were a lot of people, and it looked like many families."

"That's what this territory needs is families, Hi. Single men without obligations or responsibilities will not build us to statehood."

"I believe you, Papa," Hi said. "You've convinced me, but I can't vote yet." He ducked a chunk of hardwood thrown at him halfway in jest. "When will the results of the election be known?"

"It'll take a week to ten days to get all the ballots in. Each county will certify their vote, then the territorial secretary must certify the count. Probably at least another two weeks, son. I'm sure Mr. Sullivan will see to it that we get the word just as quickly as possible.

"When you finish the corn this afternoon, let's spend some time checking on the hops. All I have to go by is what the seed catalog talked about. I've never grown hops and I don't know anyone that has. Sullivan wants hops for his beer but said he also wants wheat for his beer. I've never made beer either, so all this is new to me."

"Everything I've done since I met you is new to me," Hiram laughed, getting the team moving toward the corn patch.

BARBARA TRAVIS HAD her horse harnessed and hitched to her little buggy for the ride to the Travis home for Sunday supper. "I wish Sarah and her family could join us on these Sundays," she whispered, urging the team forward. "I hope Moose comes down from the mill."

Barbara spent many years away from the family, first attending school in Boston, and then working for Zack

Singer. She had all the family instincts of the Shoshone tribe, and treasured being close with hers. Travis had built a large, rustic home on the very outskirts of Salem, at least a mile up Mill Creek Road from the Trading Post, and Barbara drove her team onto the property, immediately recognizing Moose's horse in a corral. "I wonder who that other horse belongs to?"

As she tied off the team, Travis rambled onto the porch with a welcoming bellow, and helped her unhitch. He walked with her and the horses to the corral, never once being silent. "You amaze me, Papa. It's as if I've been gone for a year and it's been a week since I was here."

"My family is more important to me than life itself, Barbara." He put his huge arms around his tiny daughter, and hugged her. "Let's go in. There's someone new for you to meet. He's working for Moose at the mill, and is going to settle on some fine property."

"Moose told me about him, Papa. He's from Boston, so maybe we know some of the same people."

The Travis home was filled with warmth and love, just as Barbara remembered growing up at Fort Bridger. A lot of the furniture was from their old post home, and there was new built by Zeke. Animal skins, Shoshone decoration, and frontier strength filled the rough-hewn log home.

There were hugs around, and Barbara couldn't take her eyes off the friendly visitor. Angus Whitell wasn't so much a tall man as a very sturdy man, compact, strong, and fine looking with his longish hair handing in curls and waves. "Barbara." Moose said, "I want you to meet my newest employee and friend, Angus Whitell. Angus, my sister, Barbara.

"Angus is from Boston, so you two should have something to talk about." He looked at Angus and said, "Barbara went to school in Boston for several years."

"I'm pleased to meet you, Miss Travis," Angus said, taking her small hand in his large one. "I was raised in Boston and sailed out of there for many years."

She didn't think he looked old enough to have sailed out of Boston for many years, but didn't say anything other than, "My pleasure, sir." She found his eyes fascinating, bright, and full of humor. "What brought you to Oregon?"

"I went to sea when I was ten," he said, "and I've traveled the seven seas, seen many lands, but what I've wanted for years is a home and farm of my own. When my last voyage brought me to Oregon, I found myself beached," he laughed. There was a lilt to his speech that Barbara could remember hearing from those along the docks in Boston, and she smiled at the memories.

They spent considerable time talking about Boston, discovered that between them they didn't have a single shared friend. "How can we have been there so long and not known the same people?" she asked.

"I don't believe the dock crowd that I knew would be the kind of person you might want to know," he quipped. She didn't believe that, and wanted to spend a lot more time with this friendly man with the wonderful sense of humor. And then it was time for supper.

Sunday supper was filled with family talk, talk about the Donaldson Mill, about the Salem Trading Post, and about Barbara's busy little business. "I wish Zeke and Sarah could be here," Barbara said as Elaine served apple pie and coffee. "That farm must keep them awfully busy."

"Do you think Zeke won that election?" Moose asked. "Those people sure said some ugly things about our family. I beat that one man at the mill that spouted off about all us being bastards. Angus had to pull me off before I killed the fool. I wonder how Zeke could stand hearing that foul talk."

"Papa did a good job on that one man up in Oregon City," Barbara said. "Zeke beat up that man that made crude remarks and threatened Hiram. I think old Sharp Knife will be a fighting legislator."

Moose and Angus said they had to get back to the mill, and Barbara wanted to get back down to her little home behind her shop. "Will I get a tour of your mill if I show up some day?" Barbara asked, getting her team harnessed. Angus stepped up and helped her with the heavy leather.

"If Moose won't show you around, I will," Angus said. He showed just the hint of a blush when Moose chuckled some.

"You come up anytime you want," Moose said. "Maybe Angus will even give you a tour of his new property," he jibed. Angus turned bright red and got busy throwing a saddle on his horse. Moose winked at Barbara who also blushed just a bit.

I think I might just like that tour, she thought several times on the way back down Mill Creek Road and into Salem City. *I like a man who seems to know where he's going and why he's going there.* She shook herself out of a bit of a reverie remembering the only time she ever felt comfortable with a man.

Zack Singer was married and a philanderer, she knew from the moment she started working with the man, but he had a way about him. *I wonder if this Angus Whitell has more to offer than a pretty face and strong body. Sarah was so lucky finding Zeke when she did, and just look at them,* she sighed.

She pulled her team up in front of her shop to find some vile notices pinned to the door, naming her a bastard child of Jeremiah Travis, a half-breed, and calling for her and the Travis and Hawthorne families to leave Oregon at the next opportunity. There was a threat of serious violence coupled with the comments.

Barbara Travis may have been a tiny woman, not quite five feet tall and very thin, but she had the make-up of a buffalo bull in the springtime, and turned the team back onto the street and drove straight to the Sheriff's office. It was near sunset on a Sunday evening, but Barbara was ready for a fight.

"As a member of the business community of Salem City, I want to see some action," she said to Tommy Prescott, Fred Sharp's chief deputy. Prescott was in his early twenties, single, and had a bright smile for Barbara Travis.

"I'll follow you back to your shop, Miss Travis," he said, slipping into a heavy coat for the late spring evening. "You should not have to face such rude postings. These Firsters are getting out of line, Ma'am, and the sheriff won't tolerate it."

He mounted his horse and she followed in the buggy back to her shop. "This is disgraceful," Prescott said. He took the posters down, carefully, hoping that something on them might point he and the sheriff at specific people. "Do you feel you need special protection? I can have one of the deputies stay close-by tonight." His smile and bright green eyes said it might even be him staying.

"I'm not afraid of much of anything, Tommy," she said. "I'll be fine and I'll keep all my windows and doors locked tight. Do you think you might find out who did this? The election is over, even if we don't know who's won, so this is just pure hate coming from crude people. My father will explode when he finds out who did this."

"Sheriff Sharp and I will find out who and take care of them. I know I wouldn't want to be on the wrong side of Travis or Zeke Hawthorne. Believe me, Miss Travis, we'll work hard to find out who did this. You have a good night," he said, offering his hand. She took his hand and held it tight for just a moment.

She took care of the team and buggy with a smile splashed across her pretty face. "My goodness," she muttered. "Two men smiling their friendship at me tonight." She made sure her home was locked tight and fell asleep with romantic dreams dancing in her head.

13

THE RESULTS OF THE ELECTION LEFT NO DOUBT THAT MOST
of the people in Oregon favored the idea of statehood,
and wanted to move forward from frontier status to
modern civilization. Ezekiel won his seat with a comfortable margin but it was obvious that there were also many
people who were not in favor of moving rapidly toward
statehood. Zeke was left with the idea that it might take
several years, even several sessions of the territorial legislature before the question could be raised with
Washington.

Life on the Hawthorne farm continued to be hectic
with Zeke's new obligations. He didn't have to leave very
often, but there were considerable communications by
post, and Sarah was sure there was never a day that
someone didn't stop in to have a chat with the assemblyman. "Do I need to make an appointment, Sharp Knife, if I
want a quiet conversation with you?" She teased
him often.

Moose had his lumber mill at full capacity for the first

time. Whitell was a fast learn and fine hand, had the steam engine working at capacity, and became adept at keeping it in running order. Spring along the Willamette Valley became summer and crops were growing strong.

"We have to make one more change, Zeke, now that you're a full-fledged member of the Oregon Territorial Legislature," Sarah said. "You must start holding your meetings in the living room and not my kitchen. We had five men in here yesterday afternoon while I was busy with the twins, making our supper, and helping Hiram with his language studies.

"They ate the biscuits before they cooled, drank three full pots of coffee, and made themselves at home with the apple pie I had planned for supper." She was shaking her finger at Zeke, but laughing through her entire speech.

"You've made this room the most comfortable, friendly, and warm place in all of central Oregon, Mrs. Hawthorne," Zeke said. "People say what's on their mind because they're comfortable."

"I think I'm even more fat right now than I was just before I gave birth to those twins," Sarah grumped. She changed the subject because she knew that Zeke was right. The family was sitting at the kitchen table enjoying a late Sunday morning breakfast. Zeke and Hiram had already been hard at work for several hours and were ready to eat anything and everything offered.

"You've got a couple of more months, don't you?" Zeke was sure she said that she would deliver in the fall. "You don't suppose you're carrying twins again?" His question got an immediate response.

"No!" The word emphatic wasn't strong enough for her. "No, no, no," she said, again. The twins were energetic, strong, and doing everything they could to learn to walk. It was a madhouse every day and although Sarah loved it, she knew that another set of twins would be far more than she would be able to handle. "One bouncing boy, Zeke. That's all I'm bringing you."

"Alright, then," Zeke said, "with that settled, I'll see what I can do to build a little add-on office or den to our almost too formal living room. You're right, though. Holding my little sessions in here must make it difficult for you."

Turning to his son, Zeke said, "Hiram, you and I have some work to do, designing the new offices of Ezekiel Hawthorne, Member of the Oregon Territory Assembly."

"I'm sure we're going to need hired help, Papa, and pretty soon. The corn, beans, and wheat are almost more than I can handle. Keeping them cultivated and getting the weeds under control keeps me and those mules going every day. The hops are coming along fast, and they need considerable work as well."

He shrugged. "Between the two of us, Papa, we're not keeping up. There's a lot of blacksmith work that needs to be done, we're building those cabins for visitors, and now you want to build a set of offices, too," and he just hunched his shoulders and didn't finish the statement. The boy had blossomed during this spring and summer finally putting on the weight that was needed for his height. He stood a full head taller that Sarah, and for his almost fourteen years, was still growing daily.

"You're right, Hi," Zeke said. "Those little cabins for visitors might end up being a bunkhouse for farm workers. I have to be in Salem next week for a visit with Governor Gaines. I'll make the rounds with Sullivan,

Travis, and the banker, and see what I can do about that."

"HAD any more trouble from those Firsters, Zeke?" Sullivan was pacing about his large office, going from window to window and back to his table full of maps. "Old Ted Newcomb didn't get very many votes after Travis chased Smith out of the warehouse that night."

"They're pretty much shut down, Sullivan. There's a lot of talk about trying to get the statehood movement underway in this next session of the legislature. There is support, but I think it's way too early. Those in the north are not convinced, I'm sure. I think it's too early, but Governor Gaines is the one pushing for it, and I find that rather strange since he fought so hard to keep the capital in Oregon City."

"He's never been a big supporter of statehood in the past." Sullivan was still pacing about.

"What's bothering you, Sullivan?"

"I can't get my brewery finished, Zeke. There just aren't any workers. Moose is shorthanded, the steamboat crew is shorthanded, businesses up and down the streets here, in Oregon City, even in Portland, are screaming for help."

"That's part of my visit to Salem today. I need to hire at least one, probably two full time hands for the farm. Hiram and I are at capacity, I do believe."

"I had a long talk with Slick Snyder about the industrial school he's trying to get put together, and he's having trouble getting men interested in learning a solid trade."

"We simply have too many frontiersmen, Sullivan.

Civilization has caught up with us and we aren't ready. Johnson is still running his wagons into California, on a regular schedule, isn't he?"

"Well, yes, of course, but he has teamsters that have been with him from the start."

"I wasn't wondering about his help, I was thinking more along the lines of getting the word into California about our lack of good help."

Sullivan picked up on what Zeke was aiming at. "Yes," he said. "Yes, we can certainly spread the word that good paying jobs are available in this land of opportunity and honey we call Oregon. I'll have posters printed and Johnson and his teamsters can spread them throughout the central valley of California."

"Make sure the concept is jobs and work. We don't need more lazy single men looking for easy pickin's. Families looking for a better life should be the theme."

"I will, and I'll also send out another batch of letters to the newspapers in the east. We won't know if that's going to work for months, maybe years, but this California idea, we might get results right away."

"Joe Lane arrived back in town yesterday, I'm told, and I want to drop in on him before I head back to the farm. Keep me posted on how the brewery is coming along. I'll have a fine crop of hops for you, according to Hiram."

"I know you can't hold them off," Sullivan said, "and I know we have a contract, but I may not have a brewery. This is frustrating as all get out, Zeke. I have customers with money in their hands and no product." Neither man had an answer and just left the questions hanging.

"HELLO, Joe, it's good to see you again. How was your voyage?" Zeke asked.

Joseph Lane was the Oregon Territorial representative in congress and had just returned to the territory for a visit. Lane fought in the Mexican war, reaching the rank of general and was appointed Oregon Territory's first governor. He resigned from that position to take the office of Territorial Congressional Representative.

"It's a long voyage, Zeke. A long voyage from New York to Oregon. The only good that comes from being at sea for months is the time that can be used for reading. I understand there are congratulations coming your way. You'll be good for Oregon, Mr. Hawthorne."

"Thank you. Is the word from Washington filled with hope and economic strength for this country of ours?"

"Hardly," Lane said. "The slavery question has everyone in an uproar and it's sure to have an impact on whether Oregon reaches statehood. Those people in New England simply don't understand the necessity of having slave labor on the large southern plantations. You can't run farms of that size without a tremendous labor force, and slavery is the answer for that."

"I'm afraid we'll disagree on that point, sir. I'll never understand the concept of one human being actually owning another human being. I'm sure when we reach the point where we can actually petition for statehood, Oregon will be a free state."

The conversation turned to other matters Lane wanted to pass on, and Zeke also needed to understand more about what the east coast was thinking, past the slavery question. Steam engines were being used on boats and ships, and railroads were talked about, with some being built.

Transportation would build the west, but there were many questions that had to be addressed well before transportation could even take place. "The large immigration numbers are going to help Oregon," Zeke said. "One problem, though, is how these groups of people treat the people that live on the land they pass through. Wanton killing of Indians, the outright slaughter of buffalo, and disregard for local customs will surely lead to problems."

These were the same questions that could lead Moose Travis to give up his partnership in the Donaldson Lumber Mill and return to his Shoshone tribe near the Green River. "What is Washington's response to these problems?" Zeke asked.

"Damn Indians need to learn their place. This is our country. It is manifest destiny, Zeke, and the Indians better get used to it. The president, with congressional backing is ordering the army to offer full protection to the large groups moving west, and one way of doing that is to move the Indians onto reservations. If they won't move peacefully, the president believes it might be necessary to move them forcefully," he barked, and took a deep breath.

Cheeks red, Lane continued, "One way is to decimate those vast herds of buffalo. That will force the Indians to move to the reservations where they would learn to farm. If needed, the government will then provide cattle to raise."

Ezekiel Hawthorne left his meeting with representative Lane, disheartened and angry, and rode hard for home. *Everything we've heard is true, I guess. The government is behind the immigrant's behavior toward the local populations, the game animals, and the destruction of the Indian way of life. This will lead to a long and bitter war between the American invaders and the Indian nations, and the Indians will lose. They would be overwhelmed by numbers, alone.*

"I TELL YOU, Sarah, it's going to be a hard fight for this territory to become a state with the likes of Joe Lane being our representative in Washington. The fight isn't going to be one of economics and transportation, it's going to be the question of whether Oregon will be a free state or a slave state."

Zeke and Sarah spent hours at the kitchen table that night talking about slavery, about manifest destiny, and about Washington's answer to westward migration. Hiram sat in on the discussion, as always, and asked some excellent questions. Zeke knew that Hiram had a vigorous mind, was very intelligent, and wanted to learn everything he could. This night proved him right.

"What you're saying, Papa, and what I'm starting to believe makes me wonder why so many people are allowing this to happen. Are all the white people involved simply doing it because of greed?"

"You just hit an old square nail on the head, son. The plains they are crossing are vast lands to be cultivated, to be used for raising animals. There are great mountains filled with gold and silver that make some men's minds boil with desire. There are incredibly long, wide, deep rivers through which large boats can move goods and people.

"Yes, son, it is greed that will make these people justify

their actions. They will take the land, take the gold, demand ownership of the waters, and those that live there now will be forced off. Thousands of people, Indian and White, will die before this great migration is over."

And I'm now a part of the problem, Zeke thought. He was alone now, sitting in a large leather chair in their living room. A fire was blazing on this cool summer evening, and he was nursing a snifter of brandy. *I'm asking people to move to Oregon. To join one of those long wagon trains across the vast plains and through the Rocky Mountains. I'm asking those people to make their way through traditional Indian lands and come to Oregon, to become a part of the problem.*

It was very late that night when Zeke finally crawled into bed, to feel the warmth of Sarah, and fully understand what an insignificant little speck he was in the scheme of life. He let his hand move across Sarah's extended belly and felt the movement of his child, and held back the tears that wanted to break through.

14

ZEKE AND HI CAME INTO THE KITCHEN FROM THEIR EARLY morning chores to find Sarah sitting at the large table, bent double and moaning slightly. Zeke hurried to her side. "Sarah, what's wrong?"

"I think today is a good day to have my child," she said, trying her best to smile. "Help me back to bed and send Hiram to fetch Mrs. O'Brien. He needs to hurry, Zeke."

Hiram was out the door and had a horse saddled before Zeke could get Sarah upstairs and into bed. "The girls need to be woke up and fed, Zeke. Take care of them and then worry about me. I wish Mama was here." She was crying and smiling at the same time, and then moaning and gripping his hand with the strength of a man.

"He's squirming and kicking, Zeke, and the contractions are almost as strong as he is," she said. "Hurry with the girls."

Zeke didn't want to leave her but knew he had to. "I wish your Mama was here too," he said softly, kissing her on the forehead. He laid his hand on her tummy, felt the little rascal moving about, bent down and kissed her very gently. "I love you, Sarah."

Susanne and Joanne were already awake and he got them dressed and downstairs, got some breakfast in them, and put them in their little playroom next to the kitchen. It was filled with blankets, toys, balls, and dolls, and nothing that could jab or stab. "They are trying so hard to learn to walk, I could stand here and watch for hours," he muttered, and heard Sarah moan.

He was on his way back to Sarah's room when he heard horses coming up the long drive at a fast clip. He ran back down, through the kitchen and helped Mrs. O'Brien down from her horse. "Hurry," he said, leading her up to Sarah.

"You and Hiram have work to do, Zeke. I'll call if I need anything. Me and Sarah can take care of what needs to be done here," and she scooted the men out of the room. Zeke tried to tell her that he had pumped extra water and it was in pails and buckets, but she shushed him and waved him out the door.

"Just like on the trail," Zeke snorted. "Do you remember? Your grandmother kicked all of us out of the wagon. Made us go fishing." He laughed, remembering that day more than a year ago.

Back on the Oregon Trail everyone seemed to know that Sarah would have twins, but today was another day. *Such immense changes from my life in Missouri with so much death and illness and sorrow. Now, I have an incredible life with a wife and three children on a farm thousands of miles from Missouri, and about to have a fourth child. I am truly blessed.*

He and Hi walked to the little blacksmith shop. "Will you have a brother or a sister?" he asked.

"It would be nice to have a brother, but it doesn't matter to me. I sure like my sisters. Susanne is trying to walk and Joanne just scoots. But Joanne can eat with a spoon better than Susanne. They'll be fishing with me before the summer's over."

Zeke laughed at that, but also agreed with him. "Did you see either Sam or Skinny this morning? I hope they're out in the corn."

Zeke had hired the two Saunders boys to work full time on the farm. They didn't want to eat with the family, instead setting up housekeeping in what was to be guest quarters. Zeke had installed a fine wood-burning cook stove, and the cabin had a rock fireplace as well. "Those boys have been taught how to take care of themselves," Zeke said. "Life isn't always good to you, and the survivors are the ones that roll with what life offers instead of fighting it or complaining about it." Zeke was tickled when Hiram repeated his little homilies back to him, sometimes days later.

Sam was sixteen and Skinny was eighteen, and their widowed mother lived in Salem, taking in laundry and keeping house for a couple with four children. The boys had been on their own for a couple of years.

Skinny was about five feet eight and didn't weigh more than a hundred ten pounds while Sam stood almost six feet and weighed a solid one ninety. "I wonder if they're really brothers?" Hiram asked after meeting them.

"Same mother, different fathers," is all Zeke said. He hoped he wouldn't have to explain past that point, but Hiram did ask how that was.

"How come they have the same last name?"

Zeke had the coffee boiling by that point and poured two cups. "Let's just sit for a few minutes, Hi, and I'll try to explain how things happen sometimes in this life we live." Hiram was thirteen or fourteen, no one could be sure, and he understood, as any farm boy would, all about the birds and the bees, but maybe not so much about how life twists things around sometimes.

"Mrs. Saunders isn't really a widow, Hi," Zeke said. "She used to be what is referred to as a working girl, and she got pregnant a couple of times. Sam and Skinny were lucky that Mary Saunders was their mother. She raised those boys to be gentlemen, to be self-reliant, and to be responsible men. They're good hands and I hope they stay with us for a long time."

"Is that why some of the people in Salem don't like her or her sons? Because she was a whore?"

"Yup. She was from a dirt-poor family, was thrown out when she was very young, and had to make her way the best she could. She's a very strong woman, Hi, and did what she had to do just to live. She raised those boys proper. She worked hard to put food on the table and clothes on their backs. It had to have been terribly difficult and often embarrassing.

"Some people think they are just too righteous to see the good in others. Mary is a good woman and I'm glad to have her boys working for us."

"I kinda like the idea that I'm much younger than Skinny but I'm much bigger than he is."

"He had a bad start in life, Hiram. He's lucky just to be alive, but he is a good worker. You want to go check on them while I go check on your Mama? It's too early to harvest the corn or wheat, but the crops need to be checked.

"While you're out, look at the beans. I'm sure they're ready to start picking. We'll need to pick once a week from now on. And take a look at the hops, too."

Hiram said, "Yes, Papa," as if saying, *what did you think I was going to do?* He was growing up fast. Hiram walked over to his still-saddled horse and rode off toward the corn fields. Zeke made tracks for the big house, listening hard for a baby crying. He remembered to shuck his boots on the weather porch and looked in on the twins before heading upstairs. They were wrapped in blankets fast asleep.

He took the stairs quietly and stuck his head in the door and found Sarah holding a beet red child close to her. She looked up and her smile made Zeke's heart pound for several beats. "You have a son, Sharp Knife."

Zeke looked at Mrs. O'Brien and she gave him a strong nod of approval and he sat down on the bed, a broad smile splashed across his ruddy face. Then he bent down slowly, and kissed Sarah. "I want you to say hello to Mr. Travis Ezekiel Hawthorne," Sarah said. He took the blanket-wrapped baby in his gnarly hands and saw a pair of bright hazel eyes staring back at him.

"How do you do?" He kissed the baby's forehead, scratched a finger under his chin, and continued to just sit and smile. "You are going to be one big boy." He hefted the child up, and laid him carefully back in Sarah's arms. "Travis Hawthorne. That's a perfect name for that boy. Your grandpa is going to spoil you rotten, young man."

He wanted to stay but Sarah and Mrs. O'Brien shooed him out, told him to go to work, that they had work to do, and besides, Sarah wanted a nap. His smile would have lit half of Oregon if the sun went dark, and he did a little jig on the way to his shop.

"That corn's lookin' good, Skinny," Hiram said. He rode around one of the large plots of corn looking for the two Saunders boys. "Where's Sam?"

"He's about twenty feet down the row, there. I'll get him." Skinny trotted down a row of corn that stood well over the top of his head and emerged in a couple of minutes with Sam alongside.

"We'll start picking the fresh corn next week, I think," Hiram said. Zeke was planning to save back a considerable amount of corn for winter feed for the animals. "Right now, we need to start on the beans. We'll pick beans for the next two days on those north fields, then pick the south fields. I'll go back and hitch the team and get the empty bushel baskets while you guys head over to the fields."

"You been farmin' a long time, Hi?" Skinny asked.

"No. This is my first year. But Papa had a big farm in Missouri, so he knows all about farms."

"He can't be your Papa. You're an Indian." Skinny was scowling some when he said that, and Hi didn't take kindly to the attitude.

"I'm half-Shoshone, Skinny. My real mother is Shoshone and my real father is an American trapper. Papa adopted me when we left Fort Bridger so he and Mama are my parents now. I'm Hiram Hawthorne." He was as forceful as a teenage boy could be.

"You're a half-breed," Skinny said with contempt.

"That's very rude, Skinny. I think you'd better take that back right now!" Hiram was considerably larger than Skinny Saunders, and felt certain that with all the fun wrestling he'd done with Moose, he would be able to take the older boy down, but he also was fully aware that the younger but much larger Sam Saunders was standing right there.

"You're working for the Hawthorne family farm, Skinny, and we don't tolerate rudeness from those who work for us. When I bring the wagon and baskets back I will expect an apology." Hiram stepped into the saddle and rode his horse back to the barn to harness the team.

Papa told me there would be people that would talk to me that way, and to call me names because I'm half- Shoshone, and he also said I don't have to accept that kind of attitude. I won't be talked down to. I won't. Just like that foul-mouthed man in Salem that Papa whipped.

He had the team almost hitched to the wagon filled with bushel baskets when Zeke came bounding into the barn. "Well, son, you got your wish. You now have a new brother, and he's a big boy." Zeke hugged Hi close to him, almost singing a song as he danced about. "We named him Travis after your grandpa, how about that?"

"Wow," Hi said. "Now I have two sisters and a brother, and I'm the oldest." He was excited, but the run-in with Skinny was still simmering and he knew he had to say something.

"You headed out to the bean fields? That's good. I guess the boys will meet you out there."

"They are on their way now," Hi said. "We'll pick for the rest of the day. Will you come out?"

"I want to work on the cradle for Travis and then I'll

be out. Is there something on your mind, Hi? You look a bit worried about something."

Hiram spent the next few minutes telling Zeke about the problem he had with Skinny and the fact that he was demanding an apology. "I didn't lose my temper or make any threats, Papa, but I'm sure Skinny knows I'm angry about what he said."

"This is awkward, Hi, but I want you to make sure you do get that apology. At the same time, we don't want to lose those boys. We have promised many bushels of fresh green beans to the markets in Salem and Oregon City, and we can't afford to lose those sales."

"I won't do anything to lose our business, Papa, but I will also make sure Skinny knows he can't talk to me that way." He stepped up into the seat of the wagon and drove out to the bean fields. He was there in less than ten minutes and the Saunders boys were waiting for him.

"Let's spread these baskets around first, and then we'll start picking. What we pick today and tomorrow will go to the markets in Salem City and then the next crop will go to Oregon City."

Sam jumped in the back of the wagon and started heaving the baskets out as Hiram drove the team slowly along the rows of beans. Skinny spread the baskets so there would always be baskets available in the rows. By the time Skinny had the rows filled with empty baskets and the wagon was empty, all three boys were covered in sweat.

There were leather belts on the baskets that could be slung around the neck and hung at the side, to be filled walking the rows. It was hard labor and the day was hot.

Hiram parked the team about halfway between the

line of rows on the other end and walked back to the line of baskets. "I put a barrel of fresh water in the wagon for us," he said. He slipped a belt over his head and set the basket for his first row. "You can offer that apology anytime between now and when we finish today, Skinny, but know this, you will apologize." He walked off into his first row of beans, picking bottom to top on the left row, then bottom to top on the right side as he came to each plant.

"When your basket is full, just leave it in the row. We'll pick them up when we're through picking," he hollered.

"We did good, guys," Hiram said, later. "I'll bring the wagon along the line of rows, and Sam, you and Skinny bring the baskets out. I'll stack them in the back of the wagon. Salem City is going to be floating in a sea of green beans, I think." He snickered and found Sam laughing right along with him.

"Can I talk to you for a minute before we start, Hi?" Sam asked. Hiram saw a look of concern in the young boy's face and nodded. "I don't think Skinny is strong enough to hoist one of these bushel baskets into the back of the wagon, Hiram. How about if you and I haul them and let him do the stacking?"

"You care a lot for your brother, don't you?" Hiram got a nod and little grin back, and called Skinny over. "Here's a better plan. Skinny, you hop in the wagon and do the stacking and Sam and I will bring the baskets to you. Don't pile them any more than three baskets high, and get 'em nice and tight. Okay?"

Sam smiled and Skinny, still frowning, jumped in the

wagon. The tailgate was down and Sam and Hi started the long hard process of bringing the full and heavy baskets to the wagon. *With one more man this process would be faster. We could bring the full baskets to the ends of the rows as we picked and that man could load. I need to talk to Papa about that. With the corn crop getting ready to pick, we'll need that.*

THE SUN WAS SLOWLY SETTLING into the blue haze of the mountains far to the west as Hi drove the team into the barn. Skinny and Sam jumped off the wagon and started working to unhitch while Hiram got his notebook out and tore out the page with the day's activities and numbers of bushels picked and stacked. Zeke stepped into the cool shade of the barn and looked inside the wagon.

"Looks like you guys set a new Oregon Territory record for bean pickin'," he said. "Good work. We'll fill that second wagon tomorrow, and then the next day we'll head for Salem City and make our deliveries. You boys will be able to spend a little time with your Mama, also."

Sam and Skinny smiled at that thought, and then a cloud came over Skinny's face. He looked Hiram straight in the face and said, "I don't think I have anything to apologize for, Hiram. He ain't your pa, and you're just a half-breed tryin' to be somethin' you ain't."

"Listen to me carefully, Skinny, before you make things worse than they are," Hiram said. Zeke stood at the side of the wagon, knowing that his son was about to either still be a little boy or become a man in the next few seconds.

Hiram's voice was calm, quiet even, but his fists were clenched and his shoulders were ready for whatever might happen. "I told you I am half- Shoshone, and I told you that Zeke adopted me. He is my Papa." He took a step toward Skinny and said "Do you even know who your pa is?

"You see, Skinny, you tried very hard to hurt me, and you did it because you don't have a pa. You think hurting me will make you feel better, but it didn't, did it? All you've done is make me angry, and now, I've lashed out and made you feel bad. Here's the deal, and I'm only saying it once.

"I'm sorry I said what I did. Now, Skinny, you say the same thing back, we'll shake hands, and it will be forgotten."

Skinny stood stock still, shuffled his feet some, looked long and hard at the barn floor, and got a big nudge from his brother Sam. "Say it, Skinny. Hiram's a good guy. We have good jobs. Mama would want you to, I want you to."

It was a long moment or two and finally, Skinny took a step forward, and quietly said, "I'm sorry, Hi." He stuck his hand out and Hi took it immediately, and then did something that Zeke was almost shocked by. He took Skinny in his arms and hugged him tight, messing up his hair with a big paw, stepped back, and punched him lightly in the shoulder. Both boys were holding back tears as best they could as they left the barn.

"I'VE NEVER BEEN prouder of you, son." Zeke and the family were at supper. "You and the Saunders boys finish with those beans tomorrow, and then I want all you boys to ride with me when we distribute the bushel baskets.

"What happened between you and Skinny turned you

into a man, Hi. A man and son that your Mama and I are very proud of."

Supper was a mish-mash of whatever Zeke and Hi could put together after a very long day. The twins were faced with bowls of leftover vegetables, warmed biscuits, some sweet rolls left from breakfast. Zeke and Hi warmed some salted meat they found, vegetables, and the remains of a pie. Sarah and young Travis slept through the event.

"Will I get to see my new brother in the morning?" Hi had been upset that Zeke didn't want to disturb Sarah. "I know it's best if Mama gets her rest, but I really want to see him."

"I'm sure we'll all get to see him, son," Zeke said. "It's going to be a busy time for your mother for the next many weeks and months, with the twins and now a new baby. You and I will have to be on our best behavior, help with everything around the house as much as possible. Susanne and Joanne will be walking soon and that will create even more chaos around here."

"I heard Mama say she wished grandma was here. Is she going to come out and help?"

"I know Sarah would like that, but nothing has been determined that I know of. Let's get the girls tucked in bed and we can sit by the fire for a while and talk about corn, beans, wheat, and hops. I don't think having the Saunders boys is going to be enough. Our crops are likely going to be ready for harvest at about the same times, and the four of us won't be able to keep up.

"I may send you hightailing it to Oregon City and Portland to bring two or three more hands down."

"I'd like that," Hi said.

15

"THAT'S THE LAST OF IT, HI." ZEKE WIPED HIS SWEATY FACE and head, helping Hiram unhitch the mules after a grueling week bringing in the corn crop. "We have the wheat and corn done for this year. Thank all the gods of Rome and Greece for allowing you to hire those extra hands in Oregon City.

"They were a rough lot but they got the job done. I don't want you using any of their language around this place." They had to laugh at that, remembering that even the mules didn't much care for their actions. "We'll keep Skinny and Sam on permanent, and I'll pay the others off in the morning and send them back north."

"Maybe you should send them to Salem City to work for Mr. Sullivan," Hiram said. "They'd have that brewery finished in a heartbeat. I kinda like old Pepper, though. He sure knew a lot about corn, and he was good at keeping the equipment in working order."

"Pepper was a good hand, but as we talked the other night, Hi, he was a confirmed drunk. He told us that right from the beginning, and it surprised me that he lasted as long as he did. George Willis did his job but he wasn't going to last much longer, either. That's the problem facing our territory, son. The population of single men with a frontier attitude. We need a workforce of men who have responsibilities."

Hi looked at him, almost questioning what Zeke was saying. "Men who are married and have children are what we need," Zeke said. "Men like Pepper and old Willis are good hands for a short time, but you can't depend on them. A married man with children would have a sense of personal responsibility that you could count on."

"What are we going to do about the hops, Papa? Mr. Sullivan said his brewery won't be ready for weeks to come. They'll rot."

"We'll harvest just like we planned, and they do have to dry some before they can be used, so we'll put them in that drying shed we built and hope that Sullivan gets his buildings up and running. At least we know we kept our end of the contract, and we know that we can grow hops."

Doubts about Sullivan's real desire to finish his brewery had been building in Zeke's mind for more than a month, and he worried that the man might not honor that contract they had. Hiram had traveled to Oregon City and Portland and brought back four hands immediately, but Sullivan kept telling Zeke he couldn't find workers.

I'm going to have to have a chat with the man when I'm in Salem City next week. I'm wondering if he's afraid of finishing his project, afraid that the product might not be up to his standards or be accepted. He is a government worker, after all, and they rarely have to think about such things.

Zeke and Hiram were smiling and laughing as they headed for the big house and a late supper on a warm early fall night. "We'll spend the next few weeks cleaning up the messes we've made on this big old farm and get the fields ready for winter. All our equipment will need lots of work, some will need to be completely rebuilt."

"Won't you be having to attend meetings too?" Hiram was fascinated by the entire legislative process and had been reading everything he could get his hands on about how government worked. "I saw those letters that came and the committees that you have been appointed to. That one letter from the governor said the legislature would meet starting in December."

"That's right," Zeke said. "I have the information that was handed me when I won the election, and it explains how the legislature works, the two houses of representatives, various committees, and the relationship with the governor and the courts." Zeke got a big smile on his face, giving Hiram a nudge on the shoulder.

"Your job, son, is to read all that and make sure you fully understand what it all means. You'll be spending some time with me during the session." Sarah had told Zeke that Hiram wanted to be able to spend time with his father during the session and Zeke had just made him one happy boy.

"Just look at that table, Papa!" Hi said as the came into the kitchen. Susanne and Joanne were sitting in their own little chairs pulled right up to the table, baby Travis was in a crib sucking on a bottle, and Sarah was putting a large pork shoulder roast on the table.

"About time you boys came in. Mr. O'Brien dropped off this beautiful roast for us. He couldn't wait until you came in from the fields, though. Go see him tomorrow, Zeke, he has some ideas for you and wants to buy corn and hay for winter feed."

"Good, I'll do that. Hi and I will separate what we'll need for winter feed and make the rest available for sale. It was a good crop, Sarah. A very good crop. The fresh beans we sold brought us good cash money, and we have a stock of dried beans to sell all winter, too. The fresh corn sold well, and the dried will too, and the wheat crop has been excellent.

"For our first year, I'm more than satisfied. Hiram and I will make a few adjustments during the rest of the fall and winter, and we should be able to increase our harvests next year. Most of the ditches we put in worked fine, but some need work. The way I understand the legislative sessions, I won't be spending great amounts of time in Salem City, as we first thought."

"I'm glad of that. I have a question, though," she said. She was trying to smile, but it wasn't a real Sarah-type smile, so Zeke nodded for her to go on. "I'm running out of energy, Zeke. Between the girls, little Travis, and cooking three full meals a day for our help and us, I'm very tired. I think we need to think about some hired help in the house as well as the fields."

"Hiram and I talked about that just yesterday, little Mama," he smiled. "Did you have someone in mind?"

"Edith Petersen, Joshua's wife, suggested Rebecca Williams, and I have sent for the girl. She'll be here tomorrow and we can talk with her. She's the eldest daughter of the grocery clerk in Salem City. Edith thinks she's eighteen or nineteen. She was married to a man who was killed in a logging accident two years ago."

"I'm glad we planned well ahead when we built this house." Zeke was chuckling, remembering the arguments they'd had when she wanted more bedrooms and he didn't. "Let's see if my arithmetic is still with me. One bedroom for us, one for Hiram, one for the twins, one for little Travis, and one for Rebecca Williams. That comes to five bedrooms, which is exactly what you insisted on when we built.

"I agree that you need help, and I'll let you make the decision on who that help is. She will have to live with us, and we'll have to make certain rules that must be followed. You know what you need. With Hiram rapidly becoming a man and with the young Saunders boys here, we'll have to set certain firm rules."

"I can handle those little problems. Are you going to Salem City soon?"

"I was planning on going tomorrow, but I'll hold off a day or two. You said O'Brien wants to see me, and if Rebecca will be here tomorrow, I'll make sure I'm around. Also, I have asked Hiram to study as much as he can about Oregon Territory Legislative rules and laws, and want him to work with me during the session.

"We'll both need something more than our farm clothes." He winked at Hi, and laughed. "After all, we will be representing some fine upstanding citizens while we're in the capital. I'll talk to Barbara about suiting us up."

Hiram went to bed and simply could not fall asleep. Visions of things he had no concept of danced about, thoughts of discussions with the governor, other representatives, and judges were impossible to understand, and it surprised him when little Joanne came into his room and told him he was going to miss breakfast if he didn't get up. *I don't think I got any sleep last night.*

"I THINK I can supply just about all you'll need for the winter, Mike. These aren't the winters I remember back in the Ohio Valley or in Missouri. Most of the pastures and fields I've seen since coming to the Willamette Valley grow all year."

"They do, Zeke," Obrien said. "There is always the outside chance of that rare severe winter storm, and the grasses aren't as healthy as summer grass. I want as much corn and hay as you can offer. I expanded my herd considerably this year and it's paying off. The northern market is good and the southern market is good."

"I've found the same thing. I'm off to Salem tomorrow to see some people in the capital and to talk with Sullivan. I'm worried that he's not going to finish that brewery. I could have built it myself in the time that he's wasted."

"I like Sully a lot," O'Brien said. "He's a whirlwind supporting Oregon Territory but he isn't sure of himself. He can promote and believe in Oregon, he can't believe in himself. To be honest, he needs a manager. He's looking for carpenters, he says, but what he needs to look for is a manager."

"I think you just drove that nail in solid, O'Brien. You're right about that and I'll be the one to tell him so. He wants a brewery and a distillery, and what he needs is a strong manager. Sullivan is a promoter not a builder."

O'Brien poured each a hefty mug of hot coffee and laced each with some fine bourbon, and they settled other issues that faced the territory and their farms. "I better get back," Zeke said. "Sarah has a girl coming in that she wants to hire for help. Four children and three of them still considered babies, and she needs help."

It was a quick ride back to the farm and Hiram was in the barn waiting for him when he rode up. "Better come quick, Papa. Mama's talking with that girl."

"I PUT you on the committee that will discuss the possibility of Oregon statehood, Zeke, because you have done so much to understand the process." Zeke was in Zebulon Bishop's office in downtown Salem City. Zeb Bishop was the speaker of the house for the 1853 session of the legislature, and a well-known attorney in the territory. "Along with the statehood questions, the slavery issue will be an active discussion during this session."

"Thank you for the appointment, Zeb. I rather doubt that a constitutional convention would be feasible this session, but this is a good time to start discussions on the many questions that will surround the effort. Racial questions will definitely be discussed.

"Oregon Territory is not as open to racial equality as many of the other frontier territories and areas. The exclusion law denying residence to Negros and mulattos needs to be repealed, and these questions about mixed race marriages have to be resolved. The idea of statehood cannot be discussed until those questions are answered."

A group from the northern areas of the territory were behind an effort to make it illegal for mixed race marriage in the territory. Zeke was flabbergasted when he heard about it the first time. "My entire family, from my wife's father to my youngest son would be affected by such a law. What would such a law be based on? There's even talk about denying citizenship to those of mixed races. Disgusting, is what I say."

"I'm afraid there are many who don't agree with you, Zeke." Bishop was not one of them, but the governor was. Some of the animosity toward Indians stemmed all the way back to the massacre following the disease disaster along the Columbia River, and some simply from ignorance. "There are those that strongly believe that the territory should embrace slavery when it becomes a state."

"I doubt Washington would embrace Oregon as a slave state," Hawthorne said. The conversation continued for another hour, and included education and transportation along with developing a strong work force.

"It's been a pleasure, Mr. Speaker. We have a full plate, I believe, and I'm anxious to be a part of Oregon's growth into statehood." The two shook hands and Zeke left Bishop's office for the short walk to Sullivan's brewery and more talking. *I'd rather be doing it than talking about it,* he snickered, remembering what O'Brien had said about Sullivan and his lack of progress on the brewery. *I'm gonna give that raving optimist a good kick in the seat of his pants.* He was chuckling with each step he took on his way.

"Mr. Sullivan, I think your good friend Mike O'Brien may have the answer to getting your brewery up and running." Zeke had a broad smile across his face when he barged into Sullivan's territorial land office. "Will you join me for a cold beer and some conversation at Sadie's?"

They walked to Sadie's Clams and Salmon on Commercial Street, found a table and ordered a platter of fried fish and mugs of beer. "So, what did that Irish rancher have to say about my brewery, Zeke?"

"Why don't you tell me again why it isn't up and running? The real reason, Sullivan."

"The only reason is because I can't find the help necessary to get it built. Does O'Brien think it's something else?"

"Yes, and so do I," Zeke said. "Your brewery will be a success because you're the finest promoter I've ever met in my life, but what O'Brien and I both believe is, you are not the best manager that has ever attempted to go into business. You have the right idea, the right product, the ability to bring it to the attention of those who would buy it, but you don't have the ability to follow through and produce that product." Zeke gave the man a gentle smile. "O'Brien hit the nail solidly, my friend. You need to hire a manager and let him build your brewery."

Sullivan sat, quiet as a mouse for the longest minute, staring into the empty air before letting a smile form slowly. "'Tis a fine thing that Irish rancher has proposed, Mr. Hawthorne, a fine thing indeed." He looked long and hard at the ceiling in Sadie's restaurant, enjoying the aroma of cooking fish, and let his mind absorb the thought of having a manager see to it that his ideas came to fruition.

"I think Mr. O'Brien is a genius, Zeke." He was laughing when Sadie brought their platter of fried fish, and gave her a gentle little pat on her ample bottom. "I'm going to hire a manager, Sadie, but before I do, would you bring us another mug of beer?"

16

"WHAT AN INCREDIBLE NOISE THAT MONSTER MAKES. THE
entire building is shaking and my ears hurt. How can you
work around this all day?" Tiny, Barbara Travis was
almost hidden, standing between her huge brother Moose
and the equally large Angus Whitell, watching the big
Rumely steam engine as it powered all the equipment at
the lumber mill. It whumped and it gasped, it clanged and
it belched, with one man feeding the firebox and another
watching various gauges. "I'll never complain about the
little noises that come from my treadle sewing machine."

It was a lovely early December morning and she had
decided it was time to pay her brother's lumber mill a
visit and maybe, just possibly, get to know that big man
from Boston a little better. *I have already made that man's
shirts and mended his coats, I should know him better,* she
mused. The ride up Mill Creek Road on her saddle horse
was pleasant, the trees had already dropped their flaming
leaves, but there hadn't been any rain for almost a week.

There was no subterfuge in her plans, she didn't bring

an extra shirt for Moose or a box of cookies for the crew, simply showed up late in the morning for a tour of the facility. There were generous smiles aimed at Angus, and Moose knew his sister well enough to know exactly why she was there.

"It would take a work force of ten to twelve men to do one shift and this machine doesn't stop for lunch, doesn't take breaks, and works around the clock," Moose said. "This is real progress, Barbara, just like your sewing machine. I'm going to let Angus show you around. I have to check on why the logs aren't coming down the creek like they should. We might have to build those flumes we talked about, Angus." He was snickering to himself as he strode from the mill building.

Whitell smiled, said goodbye, and motioned Barbara to follow him. *Now I'm in trouble*, he chuckled to himself. *I've spent many minutes wanting to be alone with the lovely lady, and now that I am, I'm helpless. Just a big, dumb, land-locked sailor. My heavens but she is beautiful.*

"We have timber cutters up in the mountains and they send the logs down the creek to us," Angus stammered, "but there are places the logs get beached, and the timber crew isn't always on the job. Here is where the big logs are turned into workable lumber." He showed her where the huge racks the logs were rolled onto and moved toward the whirling saws.

"I've never even thought of anything like this," she said. Her eyes were wide and she had definite color in the cheeks as she watched a log four feet thick slowly being sliced. "I remember how hard Papa and Moose had to work to cut a tree down and then split it over and over again to get slabs of wood. This is incredible."

"That log will end up being two inches by twelve inches, and about ten feet long pieces of lumber on someone's building, come spring," Angus said. He explained how one man could operate the equipment with all the power provided by that monster steam engine.

They spent an hour walking through the mill, seeing stacks of lumber in racks that towered over them. "The drying racks are needed to keep the wood from warping. We'll be putting in some heating kilns over the next several months that will hasten the drying process. The mill is truly state of the art, Barbara. This is modern technology at work, right in front of you."

Whitell steered them toward the mess hall and introduced her to Beulah McCarthy. "So, you're the Mooseman's sister, eh?" she said. Barbara fell in love with the lady's smile and her Irish way of talking. "Well, darlin', sit yourself and we'll have us a chat and a bite or two. Like some tea? Or are you a coffee girl?"

"Coffee would be fine, Mrs. McCarthy."

"Off with that stuff, It's Beulah, my lady."

"That it will be," Barbara laughed. "This is quite a kitchen you have to work with. I guess wood for the stove is never hard to get." She was still laughing when she sat down at the long dining table.

"The wood's always available," Beulah said, "but the boys don't always remember to bring it in." She waved her forefinger at Angus saying that, and he snickered, walked out the back door immediately and brought in an armload of stove wood.

"This woman's a task master, Barbara. Like a first mate on a three-masted whaler, but she can cook like she was preparing for the queen herself." He walked to the table and stood behind Barbara. "This lovely lady spent several years in Boston, Beulah, but we didn't run with the same crowd."

"I should hope not," Beulah said. "My goodness, this is a lady, Mr. Whitell."

The conversation was light and warm through a generous luncheon and Barbara said that it was best if she got back to Salem City and her little shop. "Would you mind if I rode part way with you?" Angus wasn't willing to let her get away that fast. "I could show you where I'm going to build my little farm. It's just a mile or two off the Mill Creek Road."

I want to ride with you for a long time, Mr. Angus Whitell, and I'm also terrified of you. You've been around the world, probably known many women, and I've kissed just once in all my twenty years. I'm half Shoshone and you're a Boston whaler and we're together in Oregon.

All those thoughts rolling through her mind and finally she said, "I think I'd like that, Angus. This must be quite a change for you, from being on ships for all those years, and now working high in the mountains."

The next two hours were awkward and anxious for both of them, but Angus found talking with Barbara easier and easier, and she found herself more than enjoying his company. "That slightly, well, almost level area there is where I'll build my cabin," he said.

They rode toward a stand of tall white fir trees, almost a copse set in place to frame the coming cabin, "A few of these trees will have to come down to make room for the house, but the wood will surely be put to good use. I have the design in my head and Moose is helping me to lay it out on paper."

"I'd like to see that," Barbara said. "Will it be a big house?"

"Big enough for me and my wife and children," he said.

"You have a wife and children?" Barbara was set to flee, run with her horse as fast as she could. *No!* She screamed to herself. *He's deceived me, cheated and lied.* She jumped on her horse and took up the reins, ready to race back to Salem City. Tears had already started when Angus responded.

"No, of course I don't," he said. "I'm talking about the future. I want a warm home, a loving wife, and too many children. I want to raise all our own food, hunt our wild game and catch our fish. I've been at sea all my young life, Barbara, and I want to be a simple lubber, a clod buster, and most of all, a father."

She jumped off the horse, ran the few steps to the large man and flung herself at him, sobbing, burying her face in his chest. "That's what I want, Angus," she said, so quietly he almost couldn't hear the words. "Oh, my..." she said. *I didn't mean to say that right out loud.* "Oh, my."

Angus took her by the hand and they walked toward a small stand of lodge pole pine trees and settled into a bed of pine needles, sitting across from each other. "I have half a day Saturday and all day Sunday off," Angus said, "So it will take a while to build the house."

"It will give us time to get to know each other." She said it before she even thought, and then said, again, "Oh, my."

They laughed and talked for another hour, understanding they had reached an agreement without ever saying the words. They would spend the weekends together in that stand of white fir, building their future.

"We're all having Christmas at Zeke and Sarah's, Angus, will you join us? I'm planning on being there for two days."

He had his arms around her, holding her close, and looked down into those beautiful brown eyes. He simply nodded yes. They rode together back to Mill Creek Road and he turned to the mill, she to Salem City, both with wild and wonderful thoughts cascading through their minds.

"HAWTHORNE IS GOING to be difficult to work with, I'm afraid. The statehood question will end up as a fully debated issue if he has anything to say about it." The governor was hosting a dinner for several members of the legislature, just a week before the session was to begin. "We can't begin to discuss statehood until the general population is ready to move Oregon into the slave state sector of the country."

"That debate will stymie statehood for several years. I personally don't think Oregon should be part of the slave state group, Mr. Governor." John Bradley had come to the territory twelve years ago as a member of the Hudson's Bay Company and later, the American Fur Company. He was a small man, wiry, and some said, as strong as an ox. He led more than one company into the Yellowstone and called Bridger, Bent, and Carson friends.

"I do agree with you that it will take several years to move the territory into statehood. The word from Washington is that the Snake River area will become a separate territory as will that section we call the Green River area… Wyoming and Idaho. Look what's happening with the area north of Fort Vancouver." Bradley was a fine speaker, was well informed of any issue that might come up, and was willing to take a stand on what he believed in.

"Personally, I'm against the whole idea of Oregon becoming a state." Phil Mason was a Salem City attorney who had come north from California just two years earlier.

"I can remember the fights, the anger, and the bitterness from those original settlers in California when it became a state. The war with the Mexicans was bad enough, but then to have Washington shoved down our throats was too much." He glared about the room and went on. "I don't give a damn about slaves. I don't own any myself, but I'm dead set against statehood. Those fools back east think they have the answer to any and every question that's ever been asked."

"From where I stand," Harold Meir spoke up, "we weren't even given a choice on what territory we would be in." Meir lived along the Columbia River, near where the Snake River joins. "I've felt strongly about being in Oregon Territory, and I would like to see it become a state, but we have to be very careful in how we put together a constitutional convention."

The huge Oregon Territory had several different factions, for and against statehood and, for and against slavery. Many in the Snake River area and along the western front of the Rocky Mountains wanted to break away from Oregon and create their own territories.

"Frankly though, I don't see that happening for at least two more sessions of the legislature." Meir settled back in his chair. "I want to work with Hawthorne. He's a good man, has good ideas, and with his background- he's from the Ohio Valley originally- I think he understands the problems that come with statehood."

The governor looked over to Nate Bishop. "You haven't said much, Nate. What are your feelings on this?"

"I'm going to remain on top of the fence," he laughed. "I'm not taking a fall on either side, just yet. There are some very valid reasons for the territory to become a state, and some negative reasons as well. I'm dead-set against slavery. It's vile, ugly, and certainly not anything I could ever support. Like Hal Meir, I'm looking forward to working with Hawthorne."

"I'm not," Mason said. "That was an ugly campaign he ran. He said some nasty things about people I respect, and besides that, he's married to an Indian. He flaunts that squaw like she's something special, like an angel or a saint. Bah!"

It got quiet in that stately room, the governor gave a long, sour look at Mason, and the others spent long moments contemplating what, if anything, they might say. It was John Bradley who broke the spell. He slowly got to his feet and walked to one of the windows before turning to the group.

"I know many a fur trapper that's married to Indians, Mr. Mason, and they are fine gentlemen. Mrs. Hawthorne is the daughter of Jeremiah Travis, and I've spent many a winter at Fort Bridger with the Travis family. Travis's son Moose is not only a partner, but has done an excellent job building that Donaldson Lumber Mill up Mill Creek, and Travis has his Salem City Trading Post humming." Hew scowled down at Mason. "You're wrong, sir, about Hawthorne, his wife, and his wife's family."

Mason bristled at the comment and it was the

governor who managed to take the edge off. "I think this will be a most interesting legislative session, gentlemen!" he interrupted pointedly. "I hate to break this up, but I *do* have other appointments today. Thank you for your ideas and comments. We'll meet again during the week between Christmas and the New Year."

As the group left the conference room, Bradley walked with Bishop. "This is a strange set-up by the governor, Nate. We're not a regular committee of either house, yet the governor has appointed us to work with him on the question of statehood."

"I'm going to be much more interested in how Hawthorne thinks than I ever would how Mason might believe. In my opinion, the question of Oregon coming into the union as a slave state is not even open for discussion."

"One thing is certain, it's too early for a constitutional convention, and there are too many questions that haven't been answered. Let's visit Zeke Hawthorne before the session begins."

"I'M SO GLAD WE HIRED REBECCA, ZEKE. SHE'S BEEN A God-send around here." Sarah and Zeke were sitting at the kitchen table nursing cups of coffee and nibbling on some sweet rolls. It was a bright day in the first week of December, sun pouring in the windows. The remains of the first winter storm of the season were drying out around the farm.

The high mountains that surround the Willamette Valley were sparkling in the crystal-clear air. A new coat of snow glistened, and plumes were thrown up from the high-altitude winds. "All of that up there will be growing corn and wheat down here come spring," Zeke said. He left the large window and came back to sit at the table.

Sarah held young Travis and the twins were in their playroom making as much noise as possible. "Christmas is right around the corner and the whole family will be here, Zeke. The legislative session gets underway next week, for heaven's sake. I wouldn't be able to handle it all without Rebecca."

"The girls like her, Hiram thinks she's almost as pretty as Barbara, and she's good with the baby, so I guess we must be doing something right. We've come some ways, Mrs. Hawthorne," he said with a smile. "You had your little schoolhouse and I had my two mules at Fort Bridger and now we have four children, a large farm, and three full-time employees."

"I like having Sam and Skinny working for us," Sarah said. "It gives Hiram a chance to be around a couple of boys close to his age, gives him a chance to learn leadership, which is so important for a man, and gives you a lot of help that you need. Will Skinny ever build the strength he'll need?"

"I don't think so. Mary said he was very sickly as a baby, was often sick growing up, and just doesn't have much strength. Sam takes good care of him, though, and he can hold his own on most jobs. Hiram gets along with him now that they got their problems worked out."

Zeke got up and walked to the stove for the coffee pot, filled their cups and stood by the kitchen window for a minute, gazing at nature's beauty.

"I received a note from Nate Bishop saying he and John Bradley wanted to come by for a long talk. They'll be here later this morning, Sarah. We are on a couple of committees this session, so we'll probably be seeing more of them. I'll try to keep out of your way later."

"I know you built that room off the great room just for these meetings," she said, "but I also know just how comfortable you and your friends are here in the kitchen. You just gather around this big old table and eat all my biscuits and drink all the coffee you want," she laughed.

Then sobering, she asked, "How does this session work? You'll meet before Christmas, but then what?"

"We'll meet starting next week. Many bills will be introduced, committee assignments will be finalized, and then we'll recess for the holidays and come back into session the first Monday in January. We should be finished with all our work by the first week of February, unless there is some kind of emergency. I'll only be gone two or three days at a time, I think." Zeke sat thinking for a moment and added, "I had a long talk with Hiram and the Saunders boys, and I'm sure everyone knows what to do while I'm away. Hiram is the boss in my absence and he will see to it that you have plenty of wood for all the stoves and fireplaces, plenty of water, and will take care of all the animals. Life will go on just as if I were here. I'll be working very hard on the education bill that you helped me write, and I'll be fighting a couple of bills that would simply be wrong for Oregon."

"What would those be, Zeke?" She hadn't heard anything about the bills he was upset with, only the ones he fully supported.

"There's one dealing with who can and cannot own land, and that one is just wrong. Phil Mason wants a law to prevent anyone of mixed race from having citizenship, and I'll fight that as hard as anything. He wants to include in that law that a person of mixed race would be prevented from owning land. Sullivan is screaming about that one, demanding that I do something. As if I could…"

Sarah saw the anger flashing in Zeke's eyes, his mouth grim, and remembered the times at Bridger when his anger came to a head. "I know you could and I know you'll try. A law like that would affect our entire family, Zeke. That's wrong."

"What's frightening," he said, standing up quickly. "Sarah, it could pass." He paced around the warm kitchen, poured more coffee, and finally sat back down. "I've heard some strange comments in recent trips to Salem. I'm going to be talking with Bradley and Bishop about that today." Frustration was written all over the big man's face and Sarah found herself unable to ease the burden.

She stood up and walked over to the window, looking out across their broad plain, seeing corn and wheat stubble, trees that hadn't been there just a year ago, and had to smile. "We are very lucky indeed, Sharp Knife." She handed him little Travis and sat down, looking into his bright eyes. "I love you, Zeke Hawthorne."

Zeke got a little boy's grin on his face, tickled his baby son, and spoke as an orator might, chuckling as he did. "On an entirely different subject, Sarah, what can Hiram and I do to help you get prepared for our family Christmas? We've pretty much got a couple of trees picked out that we'll cut and bring in."

"I guess a big fat buffalo is out of the question," she laughed. "Oh, that would be so nice. Remember your first buffalo hunt? I can almost taste a big chunk of buffalo hump roasted over open fire. Shoshone people eat meat, Zeke. Bring me meat," and they laughed, with little Travis joining in the gaiety.

"If you and Hi go out and find a nice fat elk and some ducks and geese, that would be very nice. Rebecca will stay with us over the holiday and I've asked Sam and Skinny if they want to stay, but they want to spend Christmas in Salem City with their mother."

"She raised a couple of fine boys, Sarah. I'm glad they feel as they do about her. Hi and I will start filling your menu request next week. Don't want to get the meat too early, it's not like Bridger where you simply set it outside to freeze and it stays good. I saw you out picking apples and peaches. I hope they'll be for pies."

"Pies and jam. Have you given any thought to raising some hogs? The meat that Mr. O'Brien brings over occasionally is sure good. He keeps it in a salt barrel."

"Hiram and I were just talking about that yesterday. I'm glad you're in favor because we are too. We'll get started on that right away, and the same with some lambs. As much as we love the wild game, we do need to provide more of our own meat around here. But not cattle, we'll leave that to O'Brien and Petersen."

FOLLOWING the visit by Bradley and Bishop, Zeke and Hiram, along with the Saunders boys, saddled their horses for a ride down to the Willamette River to see if they could put some swans and geese in the game bags. They ran into a small group of wagons headed for Salem City, led by an old trapper Zeke remembered from his days at Bridger.

"Fornier, you scalawag, how are you?" Zeke grabbed the man and they gave each other bear hugs, dancing in the road mud. "So, now you're a wagon master, are you?"

"Aye, Zeke, that I am. I have four families I'm bringing in from Salt Lake. Hard working and with happy children." Zeke was sure that Jacque Fornier was wearing the same buckskins he had on the last time they met. He still carried a long rifle, not a Hawkins, and the scabbard that held his knife was as ornate as anything Zeke had seen in some time.

One of the men climbed off his mule and walked up. "This is Mr. Winthrop, Jesse Winthrop," Fornier said. "He's comin' to the territory from Missouri, just as you did."

"Winthrop, let me welcome you to Oregon Territory. There's some fine land available, as you have already seen, and friendly people to live and work with. Were you from somewhere around the licks?" They shook hands and Zeke saw a tall, rangy man with broad shoulders, a full red beard, and big hands. "What kind of work are you familiar with?"

"Mostly hard work," the man laughed. "I know the licks, but I wasn't around there. Before leaving out for this country, I ran a small company that built any type of building that needed building. I like to work with iron, wood, bricks, rock, anything to build with."

"Then here's what I want you to do, sir," Zeke said. His eyes were dancing with pleasure, knowing that he just found the man that would get that brewery finally built in Salem City.

"When you get to Salem, you find Mr. Roland Sullivan and you tell him exactly what you just told me. Tell him I told you to find him. You'll be working day after tomorrow if I'm not mistaken."

The conversations went on for a few more minutes. Zeke had everyone's attention, talking about Sullivan's brewery, about the legislative session just getting under-way, and about acquiring land. Then the caravan was on its way. *Old Sully will be dancing in the streets tomorrow,*

Zeke thought as he and the boys continued down toward the river.

This is what it will take to bring this territory into the union. Wagonloads of families headed by men trained in a craft, families with children that can be educated and continue to build into the future, and a great desire to succeed.

They were making their way back to the farm a couple of hours later and Zeke had to ride some back from the boys, they were talking and laughing so loud. Hiram was the main topic. "I thought all that talk about bows and arrows was just talk," Sam said. "You really did get two swans with your arrows. Me and Skinny missed both our shots and you got two swans."

The laughter and chatter didn't let up until they were all the way into the barn to put up their animals. "You gotta teach me how to shoot an arrow like that," Sam said, pretending to pull the bowstring back and let an arrow fly at a target. "And you really can shoot fish that way, too? Damn," he said.

Zeke and Hi were laughing as they carried the birds up to the house. Sarah came running out. "I've got the big pot heating now, boys. I saw you coming and put the fire under it, over by the live oak tree. Save as much of the down as you can, please, and I'll be out shortly to help."

"All we need now is that fat elk and we're set for Christmas dinner, Papa. I'll go find him while you're in Salem City, if that's okay."

"It's fine with me, Hi, but take your rifle along as well as your bow and arrows, just in case. There are bears and lions in this country." *And some mean, ugly men once in a while,* he thought but didn't say aloud.

GEORGE BELKNAP RENTED A LARGE, frontier-style home just south of Salem City for the legislative sessions, and was hosting a pre-session dinner party for those of his political persuasion. Rain was pelting the roof, driven by gale force winds, and thunder rolled through the surrounding forest. "I hope this isn't a precursor of the session," he laughed. "The fire is hot, the rum is of the finest vintage, and we'll eat Belknap beef for supper, gentlemen. Welcome."

Along with Belknap's friends, Geoff McCaskill and Peter Flowers, was Assemblyman Phil Mason and teamster Clive Newton. All were supporters of Oregon being proslavery, with or without statehood. Except for Clive Newton all those present were well-educated, with strong southern roots. Newton was a friend of Phil Mason who had issued the invitation.

"Phil, you and I are going to have to carry the load during this session. We must stop Hawthorne by every political means necessary, and we must insist that Oregon go forward as a proslavery territory and later a state."

"I agree, George, but the man is persuasive. He has made many friends in the legislature, and our job will be difficult. He has his position because of some unfortunate activities by others and we'll have to live with that."

The dinner progressed through several hours, breaking up late in the evening. "Looks like you gentlemen will be heading home in a raging storm, I'm afraid," Belknap said. "I'm glad we're agreed on our agenda. The committee appointments have been made in our favor, I believe. We'll need lots of help from you, Geoff, Peter, and Clive.

"You'll be able to mingle with all the legislators and

press the issue constantly. The exclusion law, keeping negroes from owning land is important. The mixed-race law, denying citizenship to those of mixed races is important and, of course, we'll be getting help from our congressional representative.

"Thank you for being here and we'll see you at the opening of the session."

The amount of work involved in being a member of the Oregon Territory Assembly surprised Zeke as the two weeks of the first session developed into a whirlwind of activity. He spent far more time in Salem City than he anticipated, and had far less time to work on territorial problems. "This is maddening, Mr. Sullivan. I'm finding men who have no idea what or who an Indian might be willing to kill or maim on sight.

"One assemblyman from up on the Columbia River district actually put in the record that all Indians in the territory should either be killed or banished! There are three of us in the assembly that are married to Indian women and were present when he said that. Between those feelings and the desire of some to have Oregon be a slave owning state, has ended any hopes I might have had of the question of statehood coming forth this session. What might happen following the holiday break is anyone's guess." His shoulders heaved in a great sigh. "I find myself being ashamed to be in the company of some of these men, and would certainly never let them darken my doorstep."

"You've been here a week and I haven't had a chance to spend any time with you, Zeke, or even thank you for sending that gentleman from Missouri my way. Jesse Winthrop is now the general manager of Willamette

Valley Brewery. That is one go-getter, Zeke, and does he know how to run a crew of workers. We'll be putting gallons of beer in hundreds of kegs sometime in January."

Zeke had to laugh, and said, "That's mighty big talk for a man who spent months not getting anything built."

"You and O'Brien were right. I needed a manager, and I have one now." He was almost bouncing he was so happy, and then calmed down and got back to the subject of the legislative session. "What happens after the holidays, when you go back in session? If you think the question of statehood is out, what about our other programs?"

"Creating a territorial education department is meeting with favor, Sully, and I think that part of my program is safe. It will include basic education for children and trade and craft schools for older children and young adults. That Methodist group has been very helpful, along with Slick Snyder. There's another go-getter for you.

"John Bradley and Nate Bishop are working with me to get the so-called exclusion law repealed, but I don't think we'll make it this session. Too many people believe that Negros should be slaves, and unless they are, they shouldn't be allowed to live in Oregon. We'll have to wait for the 1854-55 session to get that repealed."

Staring out the window for a moment, he added, "I'm really worried about this mixed-race law that's being touted. It's so wrong in so many ways, and will hurt so many people; not just now, but way into the future. There's just too many people saying things that aren't true. They won't take the time to learn the truth, and they're too ignorant to even realize how stupid they are." He had to laugh when he realized what he'd just said.

"Well, you know what I mean." He got up from his chair and walked to Sullivan's big office windows and looked out over the capital. "I could really enjoy a cold beer right about now, Sullivan." They spent the rest of the afternoon at Molly's eating fried fish and drinking cold beer.

"We didn't solve any problems, Mr. Hawthorne," Sullivan said, "but we sure brought them all to the table."

"There's the entire second half of the session coming up, Sully, and I have to say that I'm very glad all you fine upstanding citizens forced me to run. I have a whole new respect for how this country of ours operates. I'm not really sure I approve, though," he laughed.

18

PHIL MASON WAS VISITING HENRY FOOTE, A CLOSE FRIEND from their days in the fur trade. "We have to find a way to shut down this Hawthorne, Henry, or Oregon will fail to become a slave state. This mixing of bloods is wrong in so many ways. Indians are not equal to whites, and the Africans are even less so. You have two slaves right now, and Hawthorne plans to outlaw slave owning in the territory."

"That savage loving fool will have to face me, Mason. Those two blacks are bought and paid for and are mine to do with as I please. Hawthorne, that squaw of his, and those bastard children might find themselves out of a home if he keeps it up. I've killed me more than one red-skinned savage and have the scalps to prove it."

Mason stepped back quickly. "No, Henry, that's not what I'm talking about. No, we can't make the man a martyr."

Foote's hair, white, stringy, and long was swirling around his head as he stormed about the room. He was not very big, thin to be sure and showed every year of his fifty some. His nose, long and thin, protruded over a mouth that hadn't smiled in years. Henry Foote had never been a success at anything he tried and blamed anyone and everyone for his problems, was more than willing to kill for what he believed in, and had a hatred for anyone who would oppose his position on any subject.

Foote came west from New Orleans in about 1830 with the two slaves, and ran independent trading posts, the ones not connected to one of the fur companies, not part of the rendezvous. He traded in whiskey to the Indians and was known as an Indian hater. The man stood about five feet ten, weighed no more than one thirty, and spent too many hours drinking whiskey and hating the world. The scalps he flaunted cost him two bottles of Virginia rum.

When the fur trade came to an end, Foote moved into California and helped round up run-aways from the California missions. He sat comfortably under shade trees and paid men to do the hunting of Indian slaves, sometimes saving back a young girl or two before returning them to their masters.

"Hawthorne has to be stopped, Foote," Mason said, "but I'm not willing to burn the man out or kill his family. That's more than I would be able to do. No, he simply needs to understand our position on slavery and the mixing of races." Mason was horrified when he realized what Foote was contemplating. He was a politician not a murderer, and now feared what Foote might actually do.

"Hah!" Foote shouted. "To stop that man will take far more than words. His father in law, that foul Travis should have been burned out of Fort Bridger, and now look, his bastard son is part owner of the lumber mill, his bastard daughter flaunts her women's fashions in a sewing shop, and Hawthorne displays his bastard children in the Capitol itself."

Foote was right on that last point. Zeke had Hiram with him for the opening sessions, and introduced him from the floor. Hiram sat in on several committee meetings and many found him a joy to talk with in the halls and offices. More than one legislator was heard to comment that the boy asked the right questions and actually listened to the answers given.

"Burn him out, Mason, and those like him will run like the cowards they are. That fool Sullivan giving away Oregon land to anyone who asks for it, supporting men like Hawthorne. Sullivan needs to understand that this territory should be run by those of us who were here first."

Foote always claimed to be among those that helped settle the territory before it became a United States possession, but he wasn't. He moved from hunting runaways to operating miserable trading posts along the Sierra Nevada gold country, making his way into Oregon just two years ago. His stories of knowing Bridger and Bent, riding with Carson, or killing Indians simply didn't hold up under a good light.

He may have been in the Rocky Mountains, he did run some vile trading posts, but he didn't run with the likes of Carson, Bridger, or Bent. Foote's name was never mentioned among the real trappers that worked those mountains.

Mason had come to Foote to get help and left the meeting a frightened man. He rode from the small patch of weeds that Foote called a farm to find another member of the governor's committee, Harold Meir. *My God, I've made a terrible mistake. I thought Foote would understand that we need to change Hawthorne's mind, not kill the man and his family. Now, I fear, I have given him the idea to do that.*

"ARE you sure you can't come to Zeke's for Christmas? It would mean a lot to me." Barbara Travis was wrapped in a wool point blanket, sitting on a buffalo robe under a white fir tree watching where Angus Whitell was laying the foundation for their home. "The whole family will be there, and after all, sailor-man, you're almost family." Her little giggle tinkled across the open grass, making Angus laugh right out.

"That I am, my lady, that I am, and sure you know, I want to be with you for the celebration, but I promised Beulah and Moose that I would watch the mill, feed the crew that's staying, and keep steam up in old Ironsides. That's what we're calling the engine now." He was chuckling, his eyes dancing with mirth, and walked over and plopped down next to Barbara.

"The next party I want to go to will be the one celebrating our marriage, dear lady. I'll have walls, floors, and a roof on this home of ours well before spring, and we'll have our celebration right here." He took her in his arms and held her. They kissed, gently, because they understood their passions and knew things could explode quickly if they let them.

"There have been some dreadful things said about Zeke and our family, Angus. I don't know what to think of some of the people I've met or heard about."

"Their ignorance leads them, Barb. Falling in love with you, working with Moose, and knowing Zeke gives me a wonderful perspective, and of course, with my Boston background, I have an open mind when it comes to the various races. Those with closed minds and little ability to think, will always be loud and stupid, and in some ways, you're right to have some fear of them.

"My travels have taken me to the four corners of the compass, dear lady. I've met people of every imaginable color, praying to gods whose names I can't even pronounce, and believing in things that only bring wonder to my mind. And, dear lady, I've discovered that we all have one thing in common. We're humans," he laughed.

"What I've read in the paper, and what I've learned from talking with Zeke and Moose, I think Zeke's doing the right thing, working to make Oregon one of the free states, and abolishing the exclusion laws, but there are some strong forces opposing him. I rather doubt that they will be violent. More political debate than violence, I hope."

The afternoon began to chill and Angus helped Barbara wrap her blankets and robes and get settled in her buggy for the ride back to Salem City. "I'm going to stay here for another hour or so before heading back to the mill. You have a good ride home, little darling," Angus said. He gave her a warm kiss and hug and watched her drive the team off the property and back toward Mill Creek Road.

I'm sorry now that I promised Beulah and Moose that I would stay at the mill over Christmas. Someone must, though.

Moose asked, and I said yes, so I will, but I wish she had asked first.

Barbara was cold by the time she drove the team to her shop, and looked forward to building a good fire and making a pot of strong coffee. As she pulled the team to a stop, a man stepped out from behind a tree, shaking his fist at her.

"Heathen savage," he stormed. "Bastard half-breed," he screamed, and held his walking stick as if to strike the girl. Barbara was too fast for the old man and she turned the team and swatted their butts into a fast trot away from the area. She kept the horses at a trot all the way to the sheriff's office. Panting, shaking with fright, she pulled the team up fast, jumped out of the buggy, and ran into the office.

"Barbara, my God, girl, what's wrong?" Sheriff Fred Sharp came around from behind his battered old desk as Barbara tried to blubber out her story, crying, talking, sobbing all at the same time. "Josh, get this girl a chair and a cup of coffee," He hollered at his chief deputy and held Barbara so she wouldn't collapse.

"Slow down, girl, and tell me what happened." He eased her into a bent cane chair that Josh brought over. "Are you hurt?"

"No, only scared," she cried, trying to wipe her nose with her coat sleeve. "I drove the team up to the front of my store and this man, a horrible man, jumped out at me. He was swinging a club of some kind, and screamed at me. Sheriff, he wanted to kill me."

"Did you recognize him? Was he someone you've seen before?" Sharp remembered the incident with the ugly posters that had been pinned to Barbara's shop during the election.

"I don't think I've seen him before. I'd remember that face," she said, feeling a shiver run up her back. "He was skinny, long scraggly hair, a sharp pointed nose, and older, I think. He called me horrible names, said something bad about Zeke Hawthorne, and about my Papa."

"Sounds a lot like old Henry Foote," Josh said. "Here's some hot coffee, Barbara. Sip it slow."

"It certainly does," Sharp said. "Why don't you take a ride around and through that part of town, Josh and see what you can find." Josh left immediately, slipping into a heavy coat on the way out. "I'll escort you back to your place after you have some coffee and calm down a bit," the sheriff said to Barbara.

"Other than tonight and the problem with those awful posters, has anything else been said to you recently? Anyone threatened you or acted aggressively? I don't know where all this is coming from... I really don't." Sharp had come to Oregon Territory by way of the fur trade, also. Not as a trapper but as a representative of the Hudson's Bay Company. He came in from the Minnesota country and the upper Mississippi trapping areas.

"I've worked with people of every imaginable color and background, and I've found some really ugly, nasty types of people. People you wouldn't save if they were drowning and you knew you could. And I've found some fun, loving, warm and friendly kinds. We're all different from each other, for God's sake," he said, pouring more coffee and storming around the little office. "You can't hate somebody 'cuz they be different."

He wound up behind his desk, plopped down in a

well-worn chair, found a cigar butt in a saucer and lit it up. "Was there anyone with that man, Barbara! Maybe hanging off to one side or the other, or back behind in the shadows?"

"I didn't see anyone, Sheriff. I was too scared, I think, to even look. He was swinging that big stick and screaming at me and I just whipped those horses into action and raced here."

She's so tiny, and so damn good-looking. What kind of man would insult such a lady? Most of the men I know would start a war to defend her honor. "Do you feel comfortable enough to stay at home? I'm sure Mrs. Sharp would be glad for some company tonight."

"No, I'll be fine, Sheriff. Papa taught me how to shoot when I was young, back at Fort Bridger."

"Maybe it might be best if you carry a weapon," he said. "I'll escort you home, and we'll keep a close eye on your neighborhood. You keep your weapon loaded and don't be afraid to use it should someone bother you again."

The ride back to her shop was much slower, and as Barbara thought about it, a little more dignified. *My skirts must have been blowing around and I'm sure I was wearing a hat earlier today.* She was chuckling as she opened the door to the living quarters of her shop. Sheriff Sharp had helped her put up the team and stood by as she unlocked the back door and slipped into her home.

"Thank you, Sheriff. I feel better now," she said. He nodded and mounted his horse, then rode back onto the street for a ride around the neighborhood. Barbara got some lamps lit, built a big fire in her cook stove and put a pot on for coffee. "What a stupid way to end a beautiful day," she murmured.

Heathen, he called me. Bastard and half-breed, he called me. Well, mister bad mouth, she thought, *I will be carrying that little pistol Papa gave me, and that big knife Moose made for me and you'd better not call me names again. Ever.*

JOSH SIMPSON CAME west with a pioneer group into California with the idea of becoming a rich landowner and farmer. California was part of Mexico in those days and Simpson found himself an enemy of a local Alcalde and headed north and out of danger quickly. Alcaldes were the lords of the land, made the rules, and saw to it their rules were followed.

Mexican law was interpreted by those that owned the vast Spanish land grants. The benediction could be kind or it could be fierce. Simpson was facing a fierce and angry man by the name of Don Pedro Benitez Castro Vallejo, and the vaqueros and charros that rode for him had already picked out the live oak tree Simpson should hang from. Simpson has often told the story of his horse being able to run more than one hundred miles per hour as it made its way to the Oregon country and safety.

Simpson took up some land near the Willamette River and found he simply wasn't a farmer. He'd tried his hand at fishing and failed, at building and failed, and when old Scotty Belanger offered him a deputy's badge up in Oregon City, he found his calling. "I can wander around town all day and all night, talk to as many people as I want to talk to, and get paid to do it. Somebody does something stupid, I can bash and thrash 'em as much as I want, and get a thankee from the sheriff, and still get paid."

On top of all that, Josh Simpson discovered that many lovely young ladies enjoyed being seen out with a man wearing a shiny tin star. "There is no reason for any man to talk filthy like that man did to Miss Travis," he muttered, walking his horse slowly up and down the streets of Salem City. "If it *was* Henry Foote, I'll see to it that he pays dearly for his actions."

He rode down toward Commercial Street hoping to find Molly still open and get a cup of coffee and some fried clams, and saw a figure duck down an alleyway. He tied his horse off and strode toward the dark passage, easing himself into the shadows. The figure was trying to hide behind some barrels and trash about ten feet into the alley.

"Stand up so I can see you," Simpson said. "I'm Deputy Simpson, stand up now." He snarled it out this time, and pulled a big knife from his belt. Simpson didn't carry a firearm, just the knife and what he called, his war club, a cudgel that would cave a man's head with one blow.

The figure of a man slowly stood up and came into view. "I ain't done nothin', deputy. You ain't got no call to pull no knife on me." He was whimpering some, and took a step back, giving Simpson the idea he was about to bolt.

"You try to run from me, I'll whup you into Sunday, mister. Now walk toward me nice and slow and we'll step out into the street there. Come on now, before I git myself all riled up and angry." Simpson was looking at a man about thirty or so in years, and filthy in body and clothing.

"You were told to leave Salem City several months ago,

Johnny Loper, what are you doing back in town? Doesn't look like you've been out of those clothes in all this time, either. What were you doing sneaking around back there?" Simpson demanded.

"S'posed to meet a man about some work," Loper said.

"Sunday night, couple of days before Christmas, and you're tellin' me a story like that? March yourself in front of my horse back to the jail, Loper and work on a better story for me when we get there." He mounted his horse, made Loper walk in front of him down the middle of the street back to the sheriff's office.

"Look what I found, Sheriff!" he said, bringing the filthy Loper into the office. "Sneaking around in an alley off Commercial Street. Isn't that where you shot him?"

"That's right," Sharp said. "You some sort of stupid, Loper? Why'd you come back where you ain't wanted?"

"Said he was meeting someone about a job," Simpson snickered. The deputy walked to the stove, threw some chunks of wood in, and poured coffee for the three of them. "Warm yourself, Loper, and tell us about this man who wants to hire a known criminal."

Loper took the offered coffee and was giving an eye to the door before he started to answer. Simpson saw it, smiled slightly and said, "Go ahead, fool. Sheriff Sharp hasn't shot anyone since the last time he shot you." He smiled all the way to the door and slammed the bolt into place. "He is a fool, sheriff."

"Who were you lookin' to meet?" Sharp asked again.

"Only name he gave me was Henry. Don't know if that's first or last. Been without food or fire for a week, sheriff. He offered me gold coins and a horse if I'd do a special job for him."

177

"What was that job, Loper? Seems to me that half the town businesses have job openings. They did when you tried to steal food, if I remember right. What kind of job did this Henry offer you?"

"He didn't say what it was, just that it was worth some gold coins and a horse."

"What did this Henry feller look like?" Simpson asked.

"It was dark when we talked, so I don't know."

Sheriff Sharp cocked his eyebrow some, looked at Simpson, then at Loper. "Mr. Simpson, why don't you take an amble along Commercial Street and see if you can locate this Henry feller. See if any of the restaurants might be open and bring something back for our friend here.

"Mr. Loper, you were told to leave Salem City and not return, so I'm going to lock you up and then tomorrow or the next day, we'll see what the judge has to say about your lack of respect for the law around these parts." He wore a smile the whole time he escorted Loper back into the cell area and locked him in one.

SIMPSON MADE arrangements for supper to be delivered to the jail and walked to the Willamette House Hotel and Gambling Parlor. There was a fair Sunday evening crowd enjoying some piano and banjo music, a few gentlemen at the faro tables, and four or five men standing at the long bar. Crystal chandeliers were glittering in candlelight, lamps burned behind the bar, and the barman, Wild Willie Williams was telling yet another story.

"Evening Willie," Simpson said. "Looks like you're enjoying a Sunday's evening. Any strangers in tonight?"

"Not so far, Josh. I think I know everyone that's here," he said. "Looking for someone in particular?"

"I got two things on my mind tonight and they just might be connected somehow. I'm looking for an older, skinny man with long scraggly hair."

Wild Willie laughed. "Sounds like that old Henry Foote, Josh, but he don't come in here. He can't start a conversation without gittin' all riled up and startin' trouble. I just won't let him in anymore."

"Where does old Henry drink these days?"

"Try the River Inn. They don't seem to mind a rowdy crowd from time to time, and if Henry Foote's around, it will get rowdy."

The River Inn was the next block up and Simpson headed that way, passing only a couple of people out on the cold night. *If Loper was looking for Henry Foote just what kind of job would Foote be offering that fool? Loper's just a second-class thief with a bad mouth.*

The River Inn's name had far more class than the place itself, and Simpson checked to make sure his knife and cudgel were handy before he walked through the swinging batwing doors. The crowd was smaller but noisier, the lamps were grimy and dim, and the piano man was drunk. Other than that, no difference between the two saloons, Simpson snickered to himself.

"Hello Ted," he said. "How about a big cup of hot coffee and some talk?"

"Evening Josh. Looks to be a cold one tonight." Ted Martin owned the River Inn and got Simpson's coffee right away. "Something on your mind?"

"Yup, 'fraid so. Looking for an older man, skinny, and with scraggly long hair. Goes by the name of Henry."

"You talking about Henry Foote?"

"Don't know for sure, Ted, but he does fit the description I was given by two people. Seen someone around like that this evening?"

"Foote was in a couple of hours ago, had two quick shots of whiskey and left in a hurry. Said something about getting back home fast."

That makes sense to me, Simpson thought. *Put some terror in the life of Miss Travis and then run away like a coward. But then, would he forget about his meeting with Loper? Or maybe Loper wasn't meeting Foote.*

"Anybody else around that might fit that description?"

"Naw, just locals around tonight. Christmas kind of slows down the bar business," he laughed. "You want something a little extra in the coffee?"

"Better not, Ted, I think I'm in for a long night."

"THAT FIRE better be hot when I come in that door or that boy is gonna get knocked around some," Foote said riding his horse hard up to the hitching rail in front of his cabin. There was light in the window and smoke curling from the chimney, all coupled with continued anger from the old man.

"Bring me hot coffee with whiskey in it and some supper," he said. The house was warm and the black man helped Foote from his heavy coat. "Put my horse up and if anyone asks, I've been here all night. You got that?"

"Yes, sir," the man said. He walked to the kitchen to get the coffee and Foote walked over to stand in front of the fire, warming his hands and feeling the warmth. "I've got pork chops and fried potatoes for your supper. Will you eat in the kitchen or out here?"

"Here in front of the fire," Foote said. "Hurry up, will you? I'm hungry. Where's Willard?"

"He still be cuttin' wood, sir. Should I get him?"

"No. Tell him what I told you about me being right here all evening. Anybody visit?"

No, sir," the tall, thin black man said. "Been quiet around here all day. Willard and me got most of that wood all cut and maybe 'bout half split. You should be getting' corn seed soon, Mistah Foote. That wheat we put in will be fine come spring, but we got no corn seed."

"I know that," he snarled. "Don't be gittin' uppity on me, Mack, just cuz you git to work in the house some."

"No, sir, no, I won't." Mack walked back into the kitchen and fixed a plate of pork chops and fried potatoes and brought them to a table set up next to the fireplace. "Your dinner, Mistah Foote."

Mack and Willard were bought by Foote as children in New Orleans, traveled along the Santa Fe Trail with him, all through California, and were with him in Oregon. Mack was the older of the two by about a year, and they believed they were brothers, at least they thought they shared a mother. There were the barest of recollections of a past life, and they rarely talked about it.

"Bring me my bottle," Foote snapped. "Clean the kitchen and you and Willard go to your quarters. Take care of my horse and don't forget what I said." Foote had a building with a cook stove and heating stove built for the slaves. There was a table, two chairs, and two rope beds for them. One kerosene lamp was all the light they had.

He finished his supper and filled his glass with

whiskey again and again, waiting for a knock on the door. *That woman should never have been able to run away from me. I should have waited until she stepped off the carriage. Damn stupid of me. I won't be stupid when I burn her out, and I won't be stupid when I burn that trading post down, either.* He let his ugly thoughts roam through his head until he fell fast asleep, his head down on the table.

The knock on the door never came.

19

"WILL YOU HURRY UP, JUST A LITTLE BIT?" TRAVIS WAS trying not to get in a twit, but Elaine and Barbara were taking forever to get all their packages, carpetbags, boxes, and bundles out of the big house and into the wagon for the trip to Zeke's for Christmas. "We're only going to be there three days, for heaven's sake," he laughed. "Just look at that pile, woman."

After all her years with the man, Elaine just smiled at him, gave Barbara that look, and the women continued bringing boxes to the wagon. Moose rode up about then, trailing a mule that was heavily packed. "You look like you're headed back to Green River," Travis said.

"Our family is rather large, Papa," he said. "Zeke and Sarah have four children, I have two crazy sisters, and there are others that may be expecting something from old Moose." He laughed, stepping off his horse to catch his sister in mid-air as she flung herself at him. "Someday, dear sister Barbara, I might not catch you." He spun her around a time or two, laughing with her. "Angus sent a special hug along with me. Are we ready?"

"I want to make a fast stop at the store," Travis said. "Only take a minute and then no stops until we arrive at Zeke's." Travis led the train on his new fancy stud horse. Elaine drove the wagon with Barbara sitting alongside, Moose and his mule trailed behind. It was a short ride to the Salem Trading Post, and Travis tied his horse off and went inside.

"Whatcha cookin' Mr. Snyder?" Travis didn't want any of it, whatever it was.

"Not cookin', Travis. I don't know what that smell is. Coming from the back of the store, I think."

Travis walked through the maze of shelves and racks toward his office and found the odor stronger with each step. Then he saw the smoke. "Fire!" He screamed it out, raced back through the store and around to the back of the building, yelling fire with every step.

Moose was off his horse in an instant and joined his father's foot race where they found a stack of brush piled against the wooden back wall of the building, blazing away. Travis and Moose started pulling the burning brush away, and had most of the fire knocked down in minutes, quickly joined by Snyder and Barbara. Moose was stomping the fire from some brush when he saw just a shadow of a man trying to move through the trees and brush without being seen.

In an instant, he was back in the mountains of the Green River Valley, once again a Shoshone warrior trailing an elk, or maybe a Crow warrior, as quiet as any Shoshone warrior could ever be. He had the man down and unconscious within two minutes' flat.

"Anybody know this fool?" He dragged a skinny man with long white scraggly hair into the clearing at the back of the store.

"I do," Barbara said. "That's the man that called me those horrid names and tried to kill me the other night. Kill him, Moose, kill him." She was shaking with anger, fear, and more- anger. She walked up and kicked him in the head.

Moose took her in his arms and walked back toward the group. "Hold on to her, Papa, and I'll have a chat with this man. Is the fire all the way out?"

"It's out. Snyder just left to find the sheriff. Don't kill him, Moose, but he might benefit from a little terror." Moose smiled as he picked the man up and dragged him to the back wall of the trading post, flopping him down in some hot coals. He moved him off from those and had him sitting with his back to the wall.

"The sheriff said he thought the man's name that attacked me was Henry Foote." Barbara was calmed down some and had her arms wrapped around Travis. "He was going to burn the building down, Papa. He said he was going to kill me." She couldn't control the tears, and Travis walked her around the building and got her up into the wagon, next to Elaine.

"We're going to be here for a while, Elaine. Why don't you and Barbara go ahead and start off. Moose and I will catch up to you on the trail. There's trail food in that sack near your feet, so you'll have something to eat along the way."

Elaine didn't argue at all, but wrapped a blanket around Barbara's shoulders and twitched the reins enough to get the team started. "Try to hurry, Travis. We'll be fine."

PHIL MASON SAT in a rocker near the fire in his living room, staring at the flames, wondering just how much damage he might have caused. "Never in my life would I have expected that kind of reaction from old Henry Foote," he said. His wife, Abigail was getting irritated.

"Alright, Mr. Mason. I've heard that more than ten times now. If you're so concerned, you need to alert someone. I'm sure Mr. Foote didn't really mean that he would try to kill those half-breed children or burn out the families. It's just his way. I can't imagine any man wanting to live with a filthy savage, myself, but I don't think they should be burned out."

"I'm a member of the Oregon Territory Legislature, Mrs. Mason. Think what this would do to my reputation if it should be discovered that I might be partially responsible for Foote's actions. I'm solidly against Hawthorne and everything he stands for, but I don't want his children killed or his family burned out of their home."

"If you're so worried about that, and I don't think you should be," the frail Mrs. Mason said, "then go see Sheriff Sharp and tell him; let him decide whether or not Foote should be considered dangerous. Pshaw!" She wiped her hands on her starched apron and walked back into the kitchen talking a blue streak.

"You're a legislator, Mr. Mason. That means you should have some idea how to make a decision, should have some concept of right and wrong! That Hawthorne fool is as wrong as a man can get, fornicating with a savage. But, just sitting in the front of the fire moping like a child isn't what duly elected members of the territorial legislature do.

"While you're out, stop at that new brewery and pick up a small keg, eh?"

She heard him snicker a, 'yes dear' as he fumbled his way into a greatcoat for the short trip into Salem City. The Mason farm was about two miles south of the town on the road to California. It took just minutes to harness the team and drive out onto the main road.

"Henry has always been angry, at everything." He had to chuckle at the thought. "Maybe I'm the one who's over-reacting, thinking that Henry would really try to harm those children or try to burn the family out. It's simply wrong for the races to mix, they are separate for a reason. God must have had a reason for making the races different, and it's wrong to go against God's will.

It's a proven fact! he thought. *I read somewhere, that the Indian race is inferior to the white race, and it's a known fact that negroes are even more inferior. Slavery is right, it works very well in the southern plantations and it would be an asset to Oregon, should we become a state.*

Mason spent the entire two-mile trip into Salem convincing himself that he was right, and drew the team up in front of the sheriff's office. "Howdy, Josh," he said. "Fred around this morning? I need to talk with him."

"He's out on a call, Mr. Mason, should be back in half an hour or so. Want some coffee?"

"No, thanks. I'll go down to the clam shack and watch for him. Merry Christmas."

"Thank you. Hope you and the Mrs. have a wonderful Christmas as well."

"WHAT HAVE WE GOT HERE, Travis? Hello Moose, you're lookin' good." Sheriff Fred Sharp made the ride up Mill Creek Road to the trading post at a gentle lope, after hearing the building might be on fire. He thought Mrs. Travis and Snyder might have been a little over wrought in their telling of it, but he hurried anyway.

"Mornin' sheriff. Caught this fool trying to burn my building down," Travis said, jerking Henry Foote to his feet. Foote was still woozy from the beating Moose had given him, and Travis had to hold him up. "Damn fool had that brush there all piled up along the wall and burnin' fierce when we smelled it and got it stomped out.

"Barbara said he's the same man that threatened her t'other night. You know about that?"

"Yup." Sheriff Sharp stepped up to Foote and slapped him hard across the face. Travis let go of him at the same time, and Sharp and Travis stood and watched the skinny little man fall back to the ground. "Let's truss him up some and get him down to the office. Looks like he'll be singin' Jingle Bells in his cell this year." Sharp had to laugh knowing Foote had never even said merry Christmas once in his life.

On the ride down, Foote strapped across the top of the load on Moose's mule, Fred Sharp told Barbara's story, first about the posters and lastly, about the physical attack and threat. "We've been lookin' for Foote for two days, Travis. Those slaves of his swear he hasn't been off his farm, but we know better.

"Good thing you caught him and found that fire in

time. Well, here we are. Let's tie off and get him inside. We'll see what the fool has to say for himself."

"You keep squirming like that and I'm gonna make these ropes tighter, not looser," Moose said. He got the knots loose, let the man fall to the ground, jerked him to his feet, and herded him into the warm jailhouse. "Howdy, Josh, got some company for you."

Chief Deputy Simpson got Foote settled in a chair, got some coffee poured for everyone, and Sheriff Sharp asked Foote just what he thought he was doing. "Me and Mason are gonna see to it that these savage-lovin' people get out of Oregon Territory." He looked over at Travis, spit on the floor, and continued.

"Ain't no reason for decent folk to have to live near these savage lovin'-fools and their bastard children." Moose took a step forward and Simpson stepped in front of him.

"Don't make this worse, Moose. Back off now and let Sheriff Sharp handle it." Moose did, his eyes didn't. He was glaring at the puny man, fists balled, thinking of that big knife under his buffalo robe coat.

"You said 'you and Mason,' Foote. Are you talking about Phil Mason, the assemblyman?" Sharp was amazed by the comment. He eased Moose and Simpson away from the prisoner, and got right into his face. "Phil Mason, the assemblyman?" He snarled the question and Foote recoiled from the attack.

"That's what I said. We was gonna get these vermin out of Oregon one way or t'other. You just ask him."

"I plan to," Sharp said. "Get this fool in a cell before I turn Moose loose on him, and get the doc down here, too, Josh, just in case he's been hurt tryin' to start them fires."

Travis and Moose filled out a couple of forms and signed some complaints. An hour later they mounted up for the ride to the Hawthorne farm. "Damn fool," Moose muttered. "Josh should have let me have him. No man has the right to talk about my family that way. No wonder Barbara wanted to me to kill him. I shoulda." He and Travis had to laugh at that.

"Well never catch up with those women," Travis said. He pulled a flask of rum from his great coat, took a long swig and offered the flask to Moose.

"Better not, Papa. I think if I got a good belly of rum I'd turn this horse around, destroy that jail and kill that fool." There was an ironic chuckle, and then he went ahead and took the flask for a quick drink. "Okay, just good thoughts from now through Christmas. Me and Hiram are gonna shoot a deer and call it a Foote."

The big men were quiet for a spell, enjoying a winter's ride along the Willamette River, deep in their private thoughts. It was Moose that broke the reverie. "It's men like Henry Foote that'er going to make it easy for me to leave the mill and return to the tribe. I keep reading in the papers about Indian uprising this and Indian uprising that, but that isn't the case at all." He shook his head back and forth, watched a large swan lift easily from the waters of the river.

It's the white settlers moving through Indian lands without any respect for those lands or the people that live on them. That Foote called me a savage and it was he that attacked Barbara, it was he that tried to burn the trading post down. The mentality of an aggressive savage fits Mr. Foote, not this fine Shoshone warrior." He wanted to laugh and found he couldn't.

"You're an incredibly astute young man, Mr. Moose Travis," Travis said. "I'm one mighty proud father right at this moment. I wonder, though, if you might be of more benefit to the Shoshone Nation by doing what you've been doing, and saying in public some of the things you say to me, Zeke, Hiram, and Angus."

"Oh, Papa," Moose said. "Now that's something that would frighten me, just a bit. But, on the other hand, I do remember reading in those same newspapers about you preaching to a rowdy crowd in Oregon City just a few months ago." *I wonder if he's right, and if I would even be able to do such a thing. I know what I want to say to those fools who are making so much trouble but it isn't them who will have to make the changes.*

Papa is right. Too many people aren't making the connection, they don't see that it is hurting mothers and babies when animals are killed for the thrill of the kill, taking food right out of their mouths. Oh, Papa, what have you done? What will I do? He realized that after saying his piece, Travis just let Moose sit on it. *He calls me astute and look what he's done.* He had a grand smile on his face, looking over at Travis.

The two men were laughing and joshing each other for several more miles down the river, finally turning into the pathway that led to the Hawthorne farm. "I might have to spend a lot of time thinking about that idea of yours, Papa. You may very well be right."

20

PHIL MASON WAS FINISHING A PLATTER OF FRIED CLAMS and watching Travis and Moose ride out of town. *That must have been who I saw ride in with the sheriff. I better get down there before he leaves again. I wonder what brought those two down?* Mason drained his beer mug, wiped a napkin across his chin, laid some coins on the table and headed up the street to the sheriff's office.

"Mornin' again, Josh. Did I see the sheriff ride in?"

"He's in the back with a prisoner, and I think he's looking forward to having a little talk with you. Have a seat. Can I get you some coffee?"

"Just had a platter of fried clams, Josh, don't want to ruin that taste with your bitter coffee." He didn't notice that Josh Simpson wasn't laughing at his joke. He slipped out of his winter coat and pulled a chair near the potbelly stove and took a seat. "Who's the new prisoner?"

Sheriff Fred Sharp walked in and simply said, "Henry Foote." He poured a cup of coffee, sat behind his desk and lit a cheroot. He stared long and hard at Phil Mason, Assemblyman, Oregon Territory.

Mason stiffened at the name, which Sharp saw immediately, and braced himself for what had become his worst fear. *Foote has done something and has implicated me. My God, all I wanted was to change Hawthorne's mind. What has that fool done?* "What has Henry done now, sheriff?" He tried his best to remain calm but even he could hear the fear in his voice.

"Seems as though he physically threatened Barbara Travis. Was going to beat her with his cane." Mason started to stand and say something, but Josh pushed him back into his chair. "You just shush, Mason," the sheriff said. He nodded his thanks to Josh Simpson and continued. "Your friend then spent some time this morning trying to burn the Salem Trading Post down. Mr. Travis brought him to me and he spent some time telling me how the two of you were involved in this plan to run those people out of Oregon and that if they did not run, maybe kill them."

He glared ferociously, and continued, "Those are pretty serious charges, Assemblyman Mason. Damn serious. Ornery Jim Briggs, that feisty reporter from the *Oregon Statesman* is already nosing around because of the commotion at the trading post. What exactly are you and Henry Foote trying to do? Start a race war? Don't get me riled any more than I already am, Mason. Tell me your story right now."

He slammed his fist on the desk, almost chewed his little cigar in half, and glowered at Mason. "There are things I'll tolerate around this fine community because of our frontier background, but I will not stand for open murder or arson, particularly in the name of some damned thought that many others don't believe."

Mason stumbled through a long, disjointed effort at trying to explain what he and Foote had talked about. The more he tried to justify his feelings about people of various races the less sense he made, and Sharp just let him ramble on for almost half an hour. Mason never reached a conclusion, and his story just became a pathetic rant about the white race being superior to all others and that others should learn their place.

Sheriff Sharp was writing furiously as Mason spoke, but he finally put his quill down and shook his head. "I'm going to ask you to sit here, Mason," he pointed at the chair next to his desk, "and write out your statement as best you can. I want you to sign it, and Deputy Simpson, I want you to sign it as witness. When that is done, *you* will join Mr. Foote in one of the cells back there." He pointed to the door that led back into the jail.

"You can't arrest me, sheriff. I haven't done anything!"

"You've planned! That is, conspired, aided, and abetted two serious crimes, assemblyman. You're under arrest. Those charges will be brought before a territorial court immediately following the Christmas holidays. Sit, write, and shut your stupid mouth."

Sharp paced about the small office while Mason wrote his statement. He poured more coffee, stuffed wood in the stove, smoked two more cheroots, and found that his anger seemed to grow instead of dissipate. "Put our fine representative in a separate cell from Foote and Loper. I'd rather they not be together. I'll finish up all this paperwork and then I want you to take everything to the prosecutor, Josh."

"Was Loper looking for Foote? Was he the man who was gonna hire him?" Simpson was sure of that but wanted to hear it.

"Loper popped right out with it when he saw Foote. He jumped up and pointed at him and said, that's the man. Foote squalled at him to shut up, but it was too late." He was chuckling.

"I'm finding it so hard to accept Mason getting involved in something so ugly as threatening a young lady and burning out a business. I don't understand his feelings about people of different races and backgrounds, but even so, I would not have believed him capable of this level of violence."

"I've never known Mason to be the least bit violent, sheriff." Josh Simpson had sat through both tirades, Foote's and Mason's, and had trouble equating the two men. "Henry Foote has been angry from the time he arrived in this country, but not Phil Mason. Maybe it will all come out in court."

WHEN WORD SPREAD through Salem City that Phil Mason, that fine territorial representative had been arrested for attempting to harm Barbara Travis and burn down the Salem Trading Post, it was John Bradley who paid a visit to the jail. "If it's possible, Sheriff, I'd like a word with Mason. We sit on a committee appointed by the governor and this is most annoying. The governor will want an answer."

"I'm sure he will, Mr. Bradley," Sharp snickered. "Mason will have a hearing before Judge Brown on Tuesday, and I'm sure you realize these charges are more than just serious, they're damning. Foote was planning to burn out or kill those of different or mixed races, in the territory. In my opinion, Foote is mad, and I can't for the life of me understand Mason being involved."

"I wasn't aware the charges against Foote included Mason? My God."

"As near as I can figure this out," Sharp said, "Mason wanted Foote's help in changing Hawthorne's mind on the slavery issue and on the statehood issue. Foote interpreted that to mean wipe out the Travis/Hawthorne families and businesses and Mason, in turn, didn't attempt to correct him. I believe Mason and Foote were conspiring to do what Foote believed.

"I'll let you read what Mason wrote in the statement that will be entered into the court record come Tuesday morning. You're an attorney, Mr. Bradley, I think you'll see what I'm seeing."

"I'm representing the governor, so I can't represent Mason on this, but I would like to see that statement. I'll contact John McDonald to represent Mason." Sharp handed the sheaf of hand written papers to Bradley and went into the back to bring Mason out. Bradley poured a cup of coffee and sat at the sheriff's desk to read the statement.

THE RIDER BALED off his horse before it stopped and raced to the top of the stairs to pound on the front door. "Belknap, it Toby Klein, let me in."

Belknap opened the door and before he could even say hello, Klein continued. "They've arrested Phil Mason and Henry Foote. Sheriff says the two tried to burn down the

Travis Trading Post and was plannin' to kill Hawthorne and his family. You gotta do something, George. This is what we were trying to keep from happening."

"Mason? Phil Mason was working with that fool Henry Foote? No, Klein, you must be mistaken. Mason would never do that."

"It's true, George, I was at the jail. Josh Simpson told me the whole story and I rode as fast and hard as I could to tell you." Toby Klein was one of those men who could fix, build, or repair just about anything and worked off and on for George Belknap and dozens of others. He was on a first name basis with half of Salem City.

"Well, then, Toby, here's what I want you to do." He wrote half a dozen names on a scrap of paper and handed it to Klein. "Ride to each of these men and tell them what you told me. Tell them to be here this evening and we'll see we what we can do to put out this fire." *What on earth was Mason thinking? My God we just talked about this, made a commitment not to engage in this kind of stupidity.*

"I TELL YOU, Abigail, Phil is in trouble." John Bradley rode to Mason's home to tell Abigail. "I read his statement, listened to him, and already contacted John McDonald to represent him in court. The governor is beside himself, and I'm not sure that Phil won't be coming home for some time. These are very serious charges."

Bradley spent an hour with Abigail Mason, tried to give her a little comfort at least, and beat a hasty retreat when he couldn't slow her crying down. "I've got to report back to the governor, Abigail. I'll check in on you. Would you like an escort to court on Tuesday?"

"Thank you, John," she blubbered. "I'll be fine."

"In all my years, I've never considered what I've heard about in just these last few hours." Bradley muttered to himself as he drove his high-wheeled cart and matched pair of grays to meet with Governor John P. Gaines. "Gaines is gonna have a heart attack when he finds out what this is all about. Joe Lane will simply accept what happened and let it go, but not Gaines. I need to talk with Zeke Hawthorne, too."

The meeting with the governor was chaotic and loud and lasted far longer than Bradley anticipated. "You see to it that Mr. Mason gets the finest representation possible, Mr. Bradley. I will not believe that Mason is guilty of such behavior. Straighten this out, Bradley, and do it before the legislature reconvenes in January."

Bradley knew that there was nothing he could do other than make sure that John McDonald understood the governor's feelings. "This will be an incredible session when we reconvene," he mused. "Tomorrow, Sunday, is Christmas, Mason's in jail, court is Tuesday, and I need to talk to Zeke." He flicked the reins getting his grays into a nice rhythmic trot and high-stepped his way home.

"I think the rest of today and tomorrow will be just mine. I'll sit before the fire, nip a sip of rum, and enjoy the holiday because the entire world will explode when the rest of the legislators hear about this mess." He wanted to chuckle but just couldn't do it.

21

"JUST LOOK AT THAT FEAST." TRAVIS WAS IN HEAVEN. ELAINE couldn't help smiling remembering how many feasts Travis had put on at Fort Bridger, how many hundreds of people had been fed at his fires, and how much pleasure these parties gave the big man. "Just look at that table, Mrs. Travis. I see venison, salmon, swan, pork, lamb, and beef. Where's the buffalo?"

"Me and Hiram couldn't find any, Papa," Moose laughed. "We trailed a herd that must have numbered in the hundreds, but we couldn't catch up."

Hi joined the fun. "I almost got a shot at one, but he was just too fast for me, Grandpa. We'll have to settle for what we have."

Christmas dinner started around one that afternoon and it was well after seven when the family retired to the living room and gathered around the roaring fireplace for the distribution of gifts.

It was the following morning, while the women, including Elaine, Barbara, Sarah, and Rebecca, were involved in cleaning that the men took a long walk along the creek that ran through the farm. It was Travis's idea and no one was willing to argue with that man. He was solemn as he began. "There are some ugly and mean people in this territory, Zeke, and it will be up to the Travis clan to clean things up."

"Obviously, something has happened to bring that kind of talk, Travis." Zeke hadn't heard about Foote's escapades, the attack on Barbara or the fire at the trading post. Travis and Moose had conspired to keep it quiet until after the festivities. "Tell me what's on your mind."

"Before I do," Travis said, "there's something you need to hear from me. From the day I met you, I saw something special. You have a way about you that I like. Your honesty is part of it, you value responsibility well beyond what most would call normal, and you will defend your loved ones with your life. I'm very proud that you're the husband of my daughter."

He smiled fondly, and continued. "You're a born leader, and so is my son Moose. There are problems in this territory that will erupt into dangerous conditions and it will take your kind of leadership to keep that from happening. We can't change people, but we can educate the young, and those that we can't change need to be kept from positions of leadership."

Zeke started to say something and Travis cut him off. "Not yet, Zeke. I'm not through." Zeke could almost see the huge mountain man conducting some kind of discussion around a large rendezvous fire. "There was a problem in Salem as we were leaving, a problem that started a few days before when a foul man named Henry Foote attacked Barbara. No, no, Zeke, she wasn't hurt, just scared. But later, that same man tried to burn the trading post down. It was the morning we were leaving to come here. Moose caught him and I'm sure he still has aches and pains from that little meeting." Everyone chuckled, but there was too much serious in the air to last long.

"Other than Foote, no one has been hurt?" Zeke asked, looking at Travis then Moose. "Is the trading post okay? I've not met Henry Foote but I'm certainly aware of his activities. He's a slave owner, belongs to the Firsters, and hates people like you and me, Travis."

"There's more, I'm afraid," Travis said. "The store is fine. We got the fire out before it could do any real damage, but it appears that Foote may have had a partner, a co-conspirator. Do you know an assemblyman by the name of Phil Mason?"

"Mason? My God, Travis. Mason helped Foote? I know Phil Mason's in favor of slavery, doesn't favor statehood, and is against inter-racial marriage, but I didn't think he would stoop so low as to burn you out or hurt your daughter. My God!"

Incidents like this had worried Zeke from his first encounter with that fool Farnsworth and his hatred. "I wonder, Travis," he said, trying to calm himself, and get his thoughts in order. "Maybe I was wrong in bringing us all to Oregon country. I was only thinking of myself, and having a good farm and raising a fine family. All I saw was a wonderful family full of love and warmth, you, Elaine and your children," he exclaimed.

Taking a deep breath, he went on. "The ramifications of the family being interracial never entered my mind. I don't understand that kind of hatred. It must be driven by small minds and ignorance." He put his arm around

Hiram and hugged him tight. Moose and Travis saw Zeke tighten up, stand just a bit taller, and square around in front of Hiram.

"No, I wasn't wrong. Most of the people in Oregon Territory are not like Henry Foote or Farnsworth, and by damn, I'll tell you right now, I'm going to see to it that those of Foote's ilk in this country will not prevail. I will help bring Oregon into the union and it will not be a slave state." If those that opposed Zeke Hawthorne could see the set of his shoulders or the glare in his eyes, they would back down immediately.

They made their way slowly back to the farmhouse, looking for a late breakfast. "Because of what I saw and heard, I had just about made up my mind to return to the tribe," Moose said. "Papa and I talked a lot on the ride out the other day and he has me convinced that I can do our people more good working against the ignorance and hatred right here in Oregon."

"It will take far more than anything you or I could ever accomplish, I'm afraid." Zeke was remembering his talk with congressional representative Joe Lane and how the government itself was encouraging hatred of Indians, encouraging the killing off of buffalo herds, and sanctioning the taking of native lands. During the last five minutes of their walk back, Zeke spelled it out, almost word-for-word, as he'd heard it from Lane.

"It's 1852 Moose, and it will take twenty-five years or more, but the government will subdue the natives, will isolate them on reserves, and will give away their most precious land. There will be hundreds of millions of people in this nation in the next hundred years, and far fewer Indians. All the white Americans have come here from Europe, and in Europe today, there are only white people.

"If there are people other than white, they are either slaves or indentured in some way. That culture is what dominates this country now, and it is the natives who were here first that will suffer the most. No one, Moose, is going to change that. All we can do is our best to work toward the concept of freedom for all, to offer education for all, and to offer economic opportunity for all. Unfortunately, the Indian nations may not be included in any of that."

"That's a sad commentary, my friend," Travis said.

THE OREGON TERRITORIAL LEGISLATURE reconvened the first Tuesday in January without benefit of Phil Mason's attendance. Groups of elected representatives debated among themselves what it meant, why it happened, and what might be done about it. Zeke was prominent in those discussions, on the floor of the assembly and in committee meetings. He held forth at any and every opportunity to promote statehood, to promote the building of a territorial education system, and to condemn slavery and hatred. His strength came from his family and from his oldest Oregon friend, good old Sullivan.

"I think it's your brewery that keeps me going, Sully. You do offer a fine ale my friend. What's the word on the street? Does anyone even give a damn what we're trying to do?"

"Ah, Mr. Hawthorne, sir, that they do. Foote and Mason are being held in high contempt by most people I meet. I believe the slavery issue is more favored by newcomers rather than those who have been here for a while. On the issue of statehood, many seem to wonder about the rush. Personally, and I guess you don't mind hearing my opinion, I think the question of statehood needs to be fully debated, more so than is being done."

"You mean maybe the next legislative session?" Hawthorne asked with a sly smile.

"Or the one after that, possibly. As this spring wears on, we'll have many wagon trains coming across the Oregon Trail, and we are already seeing many pilgrims making the trek from the empty California gold fields to Oregon's fine climate and good soil."

"Ever the salesman, Sully," Zeke laughed. "Those hundreds of wagon trains bother me as well, because of what Joe Lane told me. Our own government working to wipe out the native people of this land. Maybe statehood isn't the right answer. Maybe we should be a free and independent nation, like Texas did. Join with California and become the Western States of America."

"Don't get yourself in a twit, Zeke, worrying about something you have no control over. Statehood, slave free, is the answer for Oregon and you know it. And education is the driving force to make Oregon an economic haven for those willing to put their shoulder to the wheel." Brightening, he changed the topic and asked, "I heard the most wonderful bit of gossip yesterday while up at the Salem Trading Post. Travis said that his daughter Barbara is going to be married. Did you know that and not let me in?"

"Well, well, well," Zeke said. "Barbara told us all about

Angus Whitell over Christmas and I knew they had plans for the future, but does this mean they have set a date?"

"Travis said March twenty-first. A new beginning at the spring equinox, how about that?"

* * *

THE LEGISLATURE CLOSED at the end of January, a short session according to the old-timers, and the question of statehood did not make it to the floor. Zeke found considerable support for the issue from representatives up and down the Willamette Valley, but those in the eastern counties weren't supportive.

"Oregon is a huge territory, Zeke, and what it would take to govern it is best left to the federal government." Zeke was talking with Nate Bishop, one of his supporters and a member of the governor's committee on statehood. Bishop represented an area near where the Snake River and Columbia merged. "This territory extends east into the Rocky Mountains and north through the Yellowstone. Vast areas with little or no law enforcement, no education facilities, no infrastructure at all," he said, adding, "Along with that, we have that snake-oil question of slavery. Those of us that support statehood and abhor slavery have our work cut out, Zeke, and it might take another session or two to work out the problems.

He sat back in his chair with a thoughtful expression. "One thing I see is our territory breaking up into smaller areas. Oregon is huge and there are some that see the area most known as Wyoming becoming a separate territory. There are many folks who see the Snake River area as a separate territory. Right now, Oregon Territory is just too big and unwieldy to be considered a state."

"I know you're right, Nate. I know it in my heart, but I do want to see Oregon in the union. Thank you for your support of my education programs. Those will be operational before the end of summer. We'll have a school system that includes higher education and trade schools."

"I would like to see a small group of us that support statehood spend time traveling to the various towns, villages, and outposts in the territory. We could hold open meetings in each area and openly discuss the pros and cons of the issue. Would you be able to break away from that farm of yours from time to time and participate?"

"You couldn't keep me away." They laughed at his comment and walked out of the temporary Capitol Building, into a cold north wind belching rain and sleet. "Sullivan never talks about this kind of weather," Zeke joshed.

"That may be, but one thing you can say, he never stops talking." They chuckled all the way down to Sullivan's brewery for a late lunch and a cold beer. "I supported your stand on having our congressional representative Joe Lane take a position opposing the government's handling of Indian lands and territories, but do you think he really will?"

Nate Bishop's district was home to Bannok, Shoshone, Paiute, and Crow tribes and all of them were riled by the way the immigrant wagon trains behaved while moving through.

"Not for a minute, Nate. This government of ours will have the buffalo wiped out within ten years and have the Indian tribes sanctuaried on miserable land within twenty-five, you mark my words. There's a tidal wave of people coming at us Nate, the natives are now aware of this, and we have to be ready."

"I see what many of the people in my area of the territory are clamoring for, too. Many want to see the Wyoming area as a territory or state, and the Idaho and Snake River region as a separate territory. I think that will happen soon, particularly if all those people you envision actually show up."

"I'm sure I would be in favor of that, Nate, but it would mean losing you as support in the legislature."

"True, I would stay in my Snake River home, I would, I would! Most beautiful country in the west, Zeke."

"Now, sir, we're going to get into a bit of a scrap. Just look around you at this Willamette Valley."

The two argued loud and long all through their late lunch, through more than a couple of pints of ale, and finally, called the debate a draw and went their merry ways, to the small apartments they kept during the session. Zeke was planning a quick visit with Travis in the morning and then a quiet ride back to the farm afterward.

IV

BOOK EIGHT: IDAHO
TERRITORY, THEN
WYOMING TERRITORY

22

"THESE LATE WINTER RAINS HAVE SLOWED ME DOWN, Barbara. I was sure I would have our home ready well before March 21, but right now, I'm not so sure." Angus Whitell's frustration was written deep in his Irish mug as he walked Barbara Travis through what would be their home. "It's a fine floor and walls I've managed to get stood, and our roof will not leak, but I can't get my wagons in with all the finish lumber that I've on hand at the mill."

"It's beautiful, Angus." She had watched since just after Christmas as this amazing sailor man, rarely getting any kind of help, had moved so many wagons filled with timber and built the house. It had a porch all the way around, there was a fireplace in the living room, a cook stove in the kitchen, and fireplaces in each of the two bedrooms.

"Just look at you, Mr. Whitell. You're a stonemason, you're a carpenter, and apparently, a glazier too. You've done an incredible job, and I'm going to be so happy living here, raising our children in this fine home." Her little speech almost brought tears to her eyes and she flung herself at Angus, blubbering.

"You're a gem, little lady. I want you to help me stake out where we'll have the barn and corrals, and then we'll need to stake out where you'll want your kitchen garden. We'll need to get seeds in the ground about the time we get married, I think."

They spent the rest of the day plotting out the barns and corrals, getting stakes in the ground, and Angus making notes about where ground might have to be leveled, and where drainage might need to be cut. They wanted to keep as many of the trees as possible, but marked a few that would need to be cut. "We'll need them for firewood anyway," Angus said.

The kitchen garden was an easy choice, along the south wall of the home, getting all that early spring and late fall sunshine. "I want some chickens, too," Barbara said. "We'll have fresh eggs and raise young ones for meat, and we need to figure out where the lambs will be."

"You've done all this, my lady, whilst I was out floundering in the seven seas. Okay then," he said, "chickens and lambs it'll be." They walked toward where the barn would be and Barbara took over the staking.

"Pigs can get out of anything," she said. "They either dig under the fence, climb over the fence, or just knock the thing down, meaning, our pigs will need to be in very sturdy pens. Lambs can get rambunctious as well, and their pens need strength. With all this land we have, why not put the sheep and lambs in a well fenced pasture instead of pens?"

"Our milk cow could be in the same pasture?"

"No, she should have a pasture of her own, and close to the barn so she can come in to be milked twice a day. This is wonderful, Angus. Wonderful!" She flung herself at him again, and they twirled and danced some in the mud and grass.

It was about time for Barbara to drive her team back into Salem City and Angus to ride his horse back to Donaldson's Mill. "Have there been any more threats to you or to Travis since Christmas?" Angus had mentioned several times over the last few weeks that he should escort her back to the town and she insisted it wasn't necessary.

"No, nothing, Angus. Don't start on that again." She remembered, though, just how scared she was the night Henry Foote tried to hit her with his cane, screaming those horrible words at her. "Papa taught me well and my cap lock pistol is always handy when I'm out. I'll shoot 'em first and then use the buggy whip." She wanted to put up a fierce front and Angus got a kick out of it, laughing, feigning being whipped and chased, but they also knew how serious the conversation really was.

"If anyone attacked you and I wasn't there, I'd die," Angus said, many times. "I still can't believe people think the way they do, and I'll never allow anyone to hurt you. I'll tear a mountain down to protect you, pretty lady."

It was a long ride back to the mill and new rains started while he was still a couple of miles out. "That creek will be raging again, and those logs coming down from the cutting area will be all jammed up. I hope old Snickers has kept the fires up in the Rumely." He was soaked to the bones when he put his horse up and made his way to the bunkhouse.

Beulah waved him to the cook shack on the way.

"Moose wants to see you at his cabin before supper." She yelled through the wind and rain, and Angus hurried over to Moose's cabin.

"No sense getting into dry clothes just so I can walk through the rain to get here," he said to Moose, trying to get out of his slicker. "Have a good Sunday, did you?"

"I did. Mill Creek is a river right now, Angus. I sent word up the mountain to not send any logs for the time being. We'll cut what we have in stock, and do some finish cutting on other timber. How's my little sister?"

"Barbara's just full of vinegar, Moose. We spent the day staking out enough work to keep me out of mischief for weeks to come. Ah, I almost forgot." He reached inside his shirt and pulled some newspapers out. "She sent these up for you. Said something about you not bothering to visit her or your folks. She was smiling though." He grinned at his boss- and friend. "There's quite a bit in there about Hawthorne and the end of the legislative session. Looks like we won't be the State of Oregon for a while." He took the cup of coffee offered by Moose and looked around the cabin. "This furniture is beautiful. I didn't know chairs and sofas of this quality were available here. This is what you see in Boston and Europe."

"Ah, Angus Whitell, my friend," Moose said. "You forget that Ezekiel Hawthorne is a journeyman cabinet maker. He made all of this and is teaching Hiram right now. Wood or iron, Zeke can make anything you want or need. It's just that he prefers being a dirt farmer! Why don't you go put some dry clothes on and I'll join you at the mess-hall? Beulah just happens to have an elk tenderloin in the oven and is brewing up a pot of mushroom gravy to drown it in. I think I can taste it already."

"AFTER THE WEDDING and after I get the crops in and established, Nate Bishop and I are going to take a tour of this grand territory of ours. I will see to it that you and the children will be well provisioned, and that Hiram understands he is the man of the family ready to take care of the farm. We'll be gone for several weeks."

"You sound so solemn, Zeke. Are you anticipating problems?" Sarah and Zeke had talked about this before and he had not indicated any concerns.

"No, just the opposite, I think. If Wyoming and the Snake River districts of the territory break away, it will be much easier for Oregon to become a state. West of the Snake River to the Pacific Ocean and from the mighty Columbia south to California is almost natural borders for our, soon to be, state," he smiled.

"I think Nate and I will learn a lot from this little trip. Most of the objections to statehood reflect the feelings of those in the outlying districts and counties. Those along the Columbia River still have a fear and hatred of the Indians stemming from that unfortunate massacre so many years ago. The fear and hatred must be eliminated if we're going to progress as a people."

Sarah stood behind Zeke while he sat at the kitchen table sipping his coffee. She rubbed his strong shoulders, tousled his hair, and enjoyed listening to him talk about their future. "I'm a very lucky woman, Sharp Knife. I have two daughters, two sons, and the finest man any woman could ever hope for.

"I'll think about you, miss you, every day that you're gone, and all of us will work to keep the farm in excellent condition for your return. And if you get into the high meadows of the Rocky Mountain, and stumble onto a herd of buffalo, kill one and bring me the meat."

They rocked in laughter for several minutes over that and Zeke promised he would do exactly that. "I better get out there and help Hiram and the Saunders boys. We'll be busy for long hours right up to my departure, getting it all planted. Hiram told me that we have twelve little piggies running around this morning. Miss Peggy, as he calls her, brought us her first litter."

It was warm and drying out this first week of March and Zeke pulled his old floppy hat on and headed out to the barn. He saw high, bright cumulous clouds sparkling in the sunshine, could almost hear the creek as it roiled its way down to the Willamette River. He watched a covey of quail, trailing fifty or more babies scatter into the brush and found himself almost singing as he walked.

"Hey there, boy, it's a beautiful day," he said. Hiram was hitching one team to a four-bottom plow for Skinny and Sam to take up to the northern most cornfields. "Looks like you and the boys are just about set up. Any problems?"

"Not a one, Papa. Sam and Skinny will work the north corn, I'll work the south corn for the next few days, and then we'll get into the bean fields. I'm sure glad we hired them."

Zeke chuckled at that, and helped hitch the team to the double tree on the plows. Hiram raised the plows and set his braces before walking them out of the barn. Zeke watched him hand over the reins to Sam Saunders and clap Skinny on the shoulder. *That's one fine boy. Sarah didn't go far enough. We're both very lucky to have the family we have.*

It was a good morning to get contemplative, and Zeke took full advantage of the situation. He walked through the stands of hops thinking good thoughts of Sullivan, had a gentle conversation with Elizabeth, which he had continued from the day she passed on. *It looks, dear girl, that I am the leader you always said I was. It's that word itself that always frightened me. Leader and leadership, the ability to direct men's minds in specific direction, and believe you're right in doing so.*

Some men believe leadership is loud voices and screaming obscenities while the real leaders quietly go about leading, usually by example.

He had to stop and chuckle, thinking about what he had just thought and relating that to Sullivan and his brewery. *If Sully hadn't realized what he needed at that exact moment, we'd still be hearing stories of no labor and worst of all, no brewery!*

He settled in at his desk in the living room extension he'd built for himself and started composing what he wanted to say when he and Nate Bishop made their journey through the territory. "Freedom is what Oregon is all about, should be all about. A man should be able to raise his family without fear of the state, without fear of his neighbors, nor fear from those who were here before us.

"Freedom, a strong economy, and excellent opportunities for education are what I'm going to pound on during these next few weeks." He was just putting his quill away when Sarah slipped quietly into his little office.

"I've brought a friend," she whispered, handing the baby across the desk.

"And good morning to you, Master Travis Hawthorne. Are we going to spend the rest of the day fishing or are you just going to sleep through it?" He poked and prodded while talking, getting back just what he wanted, squeals of delight, and laughter to fill the room.

"He had a huge lunch, Zeke, so I'm sure a long nap is in order. Are you taking food out to the boys today? It's ready if you are. If not, I'll send Rebecca."

"No, no." He said quickly, handing Travis back to his mother. "I like to spend time with the three big guys out there. Hiram is a natural leader and it's interesting to watch the interplay among them."

23

"ANGUS, MY SON, YOU HAVE HAD THE FIRST DANCE WITH MY daughter, and it's a father's prerogative to demand his turn on the floor. Mrs. Whitell, may I have the honor?" Travis was beside himself with happiness this first day of spring, 1853. As he wheeled his youngest child about the dance floor, he was amazed at the number of people in attendance. *Who are these people and where did they all come from? The governor is here as are many from the halls of government. There's Mr. Sullivan and our banker Obediah Sinclair.*

"This is something different, I think," Barbara Whitell, formerly Travis, said. "I've not known the fearless mountain man Jeremiah Travis to be so quiet? Are you well, Papa?"

"Oh, little Barbara, I'll howl with the wolves a little later this evening, you can place your bet on that." They spun around the outside dance floor that Ezekiel and Moose built for the party. Many were standing around open fires burning late into the night. The Saunders' boys gave up their quarters to the governor and his wife, and many planned on raising tents and lean-tos for the evening.

"This is a splendid wedding," he said. "I just wish that some of the old people from the tribe could have been here for you. Bridger and Broken Hand should be here kicking up their heels, too.

"These Oregon people are our new family, but there are times, dear daughter, that I truly miss my old family.

"I think Moose spoke for the tribe when he approached Angus and pulled that beautiful knife of his and offered it to his new brother. I loved the look on poor Angus's face when Moose pulled that knife."

Travis returned Barbara to her husband and asked about the house. "Oh, my," Angus said. "I may have to expand those walls some. Zeke made some incredible furniture for us and delivered it too. What an amazing man he is.

"But to answer your question, the roof doesn't leak, the walls are sturdy, the floors only squeak in a few places, and it stays warm. We'll not see nor'easters in these parts, but if we did, she'd stay square to."

"Are you spending the weekend here?" Travis asked, getting a scowl from Barbara. "Oops," he chuckled.

"We're secreting ourselves in a little valley not far from here. I have the tent up and the fishing rods rigged, and we'll not say one word to another person for the next several days."

GOVERNOR JOHN GAINES found Zeke and Nate Bishop in deep conversation and barged right in. "I was just talking with Speaker of the House, Zebulon Bishop, and Council President Ralph Wilcox about your plans to travel through the territory and speak to Oregon statehood. I'm in favor of this type of involvement. We are elected leaders and we should make it a point to talk to those that elected us. Might just find out something interesting, eh?" He maneuvered them into a copse of trees with some chairs already planted and waiting. A beautiful fire was blazing its warmth into the spring air as the gentlemen settled in.

"Give me a solid run-down of your plans. Would it be possible for Mr. Bishop and Mr. Wilcox to join this little traveling medicine show? There will be a big push in the next two sessions for the Wyoming country to ask for territorial status, and the Snake River area-they're calling it Idaho-to do the same.

"This would give us, in what would be left of Oregon Territory, a good idea of where we would be in terms of area, economy, and what infrastructure might be called for."

"I agree, Governor," Zeke said. "That is a part of our itinerary along with the opportunity for face-to-face meetings. Oregon Territory is huge, from the Yellowstone to Utah, from the Pacific Ocean to the Continental Divide. It's amazing, really, that you are able to even consider governing such an area."

The fire was stoked several times, the bottle of rum was passed around, and the business of Oregon Territory was taken care of, the meeting coming to a close when Mrs. Gaines suggested it might be an early morning ride back to Salem City.

"This was a wonderful opportunity to get things out in

the open, Mrs. Gaines," the governor chuckled, allowing her to lead him into the bunkhouse. "Those four gentlemen will lead this territory, Wyoming, and Idaho into the future, all because a little half-breed beauty got married to a Boston immigrant."

Zeb Bishop and Nate Bishop wandered off toward their tents, discussing the upcoming tour of the territory while Ralph Wilcox and Zeke settled back into their chairs by the fire. "You're a strong-willed man, Hawthorne, with a sound head and deep feelings. It's one of the reasons I put you on some of those special committees. Don't let your temper get the better of you.

"Your ideas are right, what you believe in is proper, but sometimes you simply have to step back and accept that other people may not think the same way, and may have just as strong beliefs."

Wilcox had come to Oregon country on that first large group that Broken Hand Fitzpatrick led and became a successful farmer. Unlike some, he welcomed newcomers that produced and barely tolerated the bummers. "I see nothing but prosperity for this country and our people, Zeke. Our timber resources are equal to anything in New England, and our agriculture potential is immense.

"Oregon will reach statehood, but we need to make sure that what we bring to the union is what will be best for the union. I see terrible problems in the future, for the planters of the south, for the native populations that must give way to the settlers, and to those that won't allow themselves to be educated."

Wilcox found himself standing in front of the fire surrounded by many of the wedding party merry-makers.

"You running for governor or president?" Sullivan asked. "You got my vote either way."

Banker Sinclair piped up with, "No new taxes, Mr. Governor."

Wilcox chuckled, poured the last couple of drops of rum into his cup, and looked around at all the people. "Oregon could use a strong president, you know. And with that, I bid thee good night." He set his cup down and with a little help from Mrs. Wilcox, found his way to his tent.

"TRAVIS FORCED me to drink the whole keg," Zeke complained, trying to find his way out from under covers and blankets, the sun streaming through the morning air. "I've never slept this late in my life." He looked around and realized he was talking to himself. "Those animals will be angry with me this morning." He managed to get into pants, shirt, and sweater and make his way downstairs into a busy and full kitchen.

"Well, now, Mr. Hawthorne. Nice of you to join us," Travis boomed from near the hot stove. "You just missed saying goodbye to the governor and his wife, and you'll be glad to know that my son and your son are doing your chores."

He wanted to smack Travis and it was all he could do to get that little boy grin on his mug, find the coffee pot, and plop down in his chair. "I have twin daughters that will be doing this in fifteen years or so. My God."

Nate Bishop handed a platter of scrambled eggs and a slab of ham to him, and little Joanne teetered across the floor to hug his leg. He picked her up and squeezed her, making her laugh. "You will run away and get married; do you hear me?" He chuckled and let her sit on his lap. "I take it there are no bodies lying about the farm, that all are accounted for?"

Elaine snatched Joanne from Zeke and hustled her off somewhere. Sarah dashed by holding Suzanne, and somebody had hold of little Travis, clearing some of the chaos from the kitchen. Hiram, Moose, Skinny, and Sam rumbled into the melee, all wanting more coffee and biscuits.

Rebecca came back from the nursery and got yet another large pot brewing. She pulled more biscuits from the oven and had Hiram bring another tub of butter in from the springhouse. "My goodness, you people do like to eat," she said.

It was well into the afternoon before any semblance of calm existed on the Hawthorne farm. Almost everyone had packed and left and Sarah took a quick count to see who would still be around for supper. "Looks like just family, Mama," Hiram said. "Mr. Sullivan was the last to leave. Grandma and Grandpa, Uncle Moose, Skinny and Sam, and us is all that's left."

"I don't know if there's even any food left," Sarah said. "How many people came to that wedding? Did we invite that many or did they just show up?" She was laughing, doing a little two step dance around the table, and started singing the Shoshone wedding song. Elaine moved right in with her, and Hiram to started dancing and chanting.

"This is why I'm the happiest man in Oregon," Zeke said, walking in on the show with Travis and Moose. Moose didn't miss a beat and fell into line with the others. The dancing and chanting continued for a full fifteen minutes. "I wish Barbara was here to see this," Zeke mused.

Moose, Travis, and Zeke had spent the past hour walking through where the corn had been planted discussing farming, Oregon, Indians, and settlers. "Barbara has told me of the east, of the millions of people, of the potential for this tremendous migration west, and I think I'm more than aware of the significance its impact will have on my people." Moose was more contemplative than Zeke had seen him in months.

"I'm not going to leave the Donaldson Mill. It's my future, I know that, but I'm going to make a journey back to Green River and talk with the elders. The Shoshone people have been friends of the white man almost from the first encounters, and I don't want to see that end."

"What exactly do you think you would be able to do that the elders couldn't do on their own?" Travis still had it in the back of his mind that if Moose left he would not be coming back.

"I can be a bridge, Papa. I am, after all, half-white, and I think I will hate myself forever if I don't at least try. The white men I know or have known, I get along with pretty well, for the most part. Those coming west I don't know and right now, don't understand, but I know I have to try to help the people."

"You're a deep man, Moose Travis. I'm very proud to be a part of your family." Zeke whopped the big man across the shoulders, ducked a feigned left hook, and the two shook hands and hugged each other tight. "You'll do well. Will you leave Angus to run the mill?"

"He's the best thing that's ever happened to Donaldson's Mill, Zeke. He'll do fine and I'll only be gone for a few short months."

AFTER A LATE AFTERNOON supper of pork shoulder and corn, with early greens from the kitchen garden, the Travis's headed back to Salem City and Zeke and Sarah found themselves alone for the first time in three days.

"What were you and Moose so interested in?" She poured yet another cup of coffee and put a piece of warm apple pie in front of Zeke. "You two wandered off for an hour or more."

"Moose will be leaving soon for Green River, but he'll be back. He feels a great obligation to your people, Sarah, and yet he's fully aware that his future is right here in Oregon."

"I bet he comes home with a wife." She was giggling, teasing a little, and was ready to dance some more. "We'll have another great wedding."

After all the planting was done, Zeke and the legislative committee began their pilgrimage through the territory. Following the heavy spring run-off, Moose began his journey back to Green River and Angus took over as interim manager of Donaldson's Mill. It was a quiet time at the Hawthorne farm.

"How long will Papa be gone?" Hiram and Sarah were enjoying a last cup of coffee following supper. The twins and little Travis were in bed, Rebecca had the kitchen put back together and it was just the two of them.

"He said it would be a fast swing through the Snake River country, along the western front of the Rockies, probably through Green River country, across the Yellowstone, and back along the Columbia River. Probably at least six weeks or more. He wants to try to visit as many districts of the territory as he can."

"I put together an itinerary of what I want to accomplish while he's gone, besides managing this old farm of ours." Hiram pulled a couple of sheets of paper from his shirt pocket and opened them up. "I'm going to build a writing table for my room. Papa's spent more than a year teaching me wood working and I think I can do it."

Hi handed Sarah a working drawing, to scale, of the table. "I didn't know you could do this kind of work! This is beautiful."

"I helped Papa make the furniture that we gave to Barbara and Angus, too. The farm will come first, of course, but I might spend many evenings in the shop after supper." He got a little boy grin across his face when he said, "And I won't forget to do my studies, either, Mama."

Sarah was a stickler for studies, and Hiram was busy reading the classics and learning Latin. Working with numbers, angles, circles, and concepts kept him busy most evenings. Critical thinking and learning how to ask questions were a big part of his education, and what he learned was put to use on the farm regularly, whether building something, repairing something, or designing something.

All the fields were laid out on paper first, irrigation ditches were designed to flow naturally, using the lay of the land to their benefit. Zeke was firm in his idea that the farm and its fields were laid out as a geometric gem. There had been very little soil loss from run-off because of their planning, the creek was maintained so that spring flooding was at a minimum, and the main path leading to the farm from the Willamette River Road was such that run-off did not create deep ditches.

"Do you think Rebecca is too old for me?" Hiram asked out of the clear blue sky and Sarah didn't know whether to chuckle, cry, or smack him across the back of the shoulders. "She's a very nice girl. I've been teaching her to read."

Sarah gave him a kiss on top of the head. "I think it's bedtime, son," is all she could manage to say.

IT WAS a good spring up and down the big valley and everyone was anticipating a large harvest down the line. Hiram made a couple of adjustments in the wheat fields and the hops, based on orders from Sullivan's brewery. "It seems, young Mr. Hawthorne," Sullivan said one day, "that a brew that is strong in hops doesn't have the staying power that allows for good distribution.

"What I need then is more wheat or barley in my brewing and less hops. Will that be a problem for you?"

"I don't see a problem, Mr. Sullivan. Your order here is for the same amount of hops as last season and considerably more wheat. Splendid." Hiram had increased the wheat planting as it was, with the large gristmill operating along Mill Creek out of Salem City. "I guess you don't plan on brewing corn beer?" He was joshing the jovial man and Sullivan enjoyed that.

"Ah, my friend, I will be ordering corn, and by the wagon load, as soon as I get that liquor business all put together. My plans for the distillery have been approved and building will start soon. Thank you for this contract and now, it's off to Oregon City and Portland for more."

Sullivan was traveling in a fine buggy drawn by two grays, and he headed out to the main River Road. The further north he drove, the heavier the traffic became. "It appears to me," he murmured, "that the migration has begun. The Oregon Trail will be a busy road this season. I hope to God Almighty that it's a safe road."

"IT'S BEEN A LONG ROAD, and I, for one, can admit that I've learned a considerable amount during these many weeks." Zeke and Nate Bishop were enjoying a summer night in the Yellowstone country, eating elk steaks and wild onions. "This Oregon Territory of ours is magnificent, huge in scope, and filled with opportunity."

A bright blanket of stars spread across an endless sky, the aroma of roasting meat filled the air, and early evening whispers from the great forest could be heard. Wolves were prowling the mountains and valleys, hunger powering their way, and the prey animals were seeking shelter on this crisp summer evening.

"You're starting to sound like Roland Sullivan, Zeke. Better be careful." He was laughing over the comment but had to agree with what Zeke said. "You're right about size and opportunity. We've been travelling through what will probably be Wyoming Territory in the next couple of years, and we've already visited the district I represent, the Snake River country. It is magnificent.

"You said you learned something important. What would that be, sir?"

"I think I've been pressing too hard for statehood, Nate. We've been traveling through open country, barely populated by civilized people. I've been influenced by what I know about the Columbia River and Willamette River districts of the territory. I moved here from Fort Bridger. I knew this area is still very frontier in nature, but didn't take that into account.

"When and if the Snake district and the Wyoming district become distinct territories on their own, then Oregon Territory would be ready for statehood. I've gotten ahead of myself and I was wrong. It will take two or more sessions of the legislature before the question can be raised effectively."

"It takes a mighty big man to say that, Zeke. I think you'll be governor of our territory someday, old man."

"Never, Nate. Never. I'll do my best to help usher this territory into statehood, and then I'll be through with politics. I have a large family and a producing farm that needs all my attention. My God, Nate, two years ago I was a widower alone on the prairie and now I have a wife, two daughters and two sons, and a hundred and sixty acres of Willamette Valley to till."

Laughter rang through the camp and the two talked about the future of the west, their personal futures, and just how fine those elk steaks tasted. They would start the trek south to the Columbia River and in a couple of weeks find themselves back home in that big welcoming valley.

HIRAM AND SKINNY were putting up the mules after a long hot day in the cornfields when a rider came up the drive from the River Road. "You Hiram Hawthorne?" He was a year or two older the Hi, tall and rangy with long flowing blonde hair and bright blue eyes. He wore buckskins, long buckskin leggings, and carried a knife that Hiram immediately appreciated.

"I am," Hiram said. "Step down, if you please. How can I be of service?"

"I have a message from your father." The young man

stepped off his horse and Skinny stepped up to take the reins. "The message is for you and your mother. I'm Buck O'Keefe recently of the Yellowstone country."

"Welcome to the Hawthorne farm, O'Keefe. Come with me and I'll introduce you to my mother. A message from Papa? Is he well?"

"He's fine and looking forward to being back home."

They walked across the wide yard between the barns, sheds, and corrals to the house and onto the mud porch. "Mama, we have a visitor with a message from Papa. This is Buck O'Keefe. Buck, my mother, Sarah Hawthorne. Those two little imps are my sisters, Joanne and Suzanne, the squirmy one is my brother Travis."

"Please, come in, Mr. O'Keefe." Sarah got everyone settled, set coffee and warm biscuits out, and sat down. "Is Zeke well? What is the message?" She was excited and fearful at the same time. It had been well over two months since Zeke left for his trip and there had been no word from him since.

"He's very well, Ma'am. Please, call me Buck." O'Keefe pulled a letter from inside his buckskin tunic and handed it to Sarah. "I've been helping guide the party from the Green River through the Yellowstone. Your man is known by the Shoshone as Sharp Knife, and is well liked.

"I spent a week with your brother, Moose, and he sends his greetings as well."

"Oh, I'm so glad. Thank you." Sarah opened the letter and read it slowly, absorbing every word, almost hearing Zeke say the words. "Your Papa will be home in ten days, children.

"Buck, he wants you to stay and work with Hi and the Saunders boys." She put the letter down and gave Buck

O'Keefe a long hard look. "You've had a bit of a bad time, eh Buck? You'll be welcome here for as long as you want to stay."

"Thank you, Ma'am. It was very hard at first, but I'm strong and I'll survive."

"Hi, take Buck out to the bunkhouse and help him get set up. I'll have supper ready in an hour or so." She watched the two boys walk out and noticed that Hiram, a couple of years younger, was almost as stout if not as tall. *He was a skinny little kid when we got him and he's a strapping young man already. I wonder what the full story on Buck O'Keefe is? You never fail to surprise me, Sharp Knife.*

Hi and Buck walked toward the bunkhouse as Skinny and Sam came out of the barn. "Hey, guys, we have a new member of the company. Meet Buck O'Keefe. Buck, this is Skinny and Sam Saunders. You'll be bunking together."

It took about ten minutes for Hi and Buck to get his limited pack in the bunkhouse and the two took a little walk. "I want to show you around the place and you can tell me about my father's trip." Hi snickered a little. "I also want you to tell me about that knife you're wearing. I'm a knife man myself, and that's one fine piece of steel you have there."

"I saw the knife your father carries, and he told me about your knives as well." O'Keefe spoke with a soft voice that was deep and full. As young as he was, Hiram could feel a history, that Buck O'Keefe was sure of himself.

"I lost my parents a year ago to an Indian attack on the Oregon Trail. There were four of them, came at sunrise to our camp and my father foolishly let them come in by the fire.

"They attacked immediately, killed my mother first, then came for me. Father killed two before he went down, and I killed one. The fourth man, injured, ran away, and I took this knife from the one I killed. Your father said it was Sioux that attacked and this knife was probably stolen from another white man. He said it's extremely well made."

"That's a horrible story, Buck. I'm sorry for your loss. Papa would know about the knife. He's a journeyman metal worker and does some fine work. How did you survive by yourself? You must have been half frightened to death."

"I was alone with two mules and a wagon, Hi. I buried Mama and father and cried for two days when an old guy, covered in animal skins and with long hair and a beard, showed up. We traveled together to the Green River where he had a camp. He said his name was Ole and that's all I ever got from him. He was one fine woodsman and I know I'm alive because of him."

"I'm glad you're here, Buck. We work long, hard hours every day, we eat better than most, and we play hard every chance we get. Mama's gonna be ringing that bell soon. We better get back. She's been roasting a huge pork shoulder all day and I know I'm ready."

"To sit at council with the elders and hear Moose speak to the complicated issues faced by, not just the Shoshone nation, but the entire indigenous population of the west, filled my heart with so much love." Zeke was almost crying as he related his time with Moose and Shoshone elder, Washakie.

"Moose visited the nearest army outpost and found his old friend Broken Hand there and related what he had spent days discussing with the tribal elders. Thomas Fitzpatrick is an equally insightful man and he promised to carry Moose's words and thoughts when he spoke with army officials."

"My people have always been friends with him," Sarah said. "Is Moose coming back?" She was as fearful as Travis about Moose not returning.

"He's guiding a large wagon train from the Green River to Oregon as we speak. He will be weeks away but is surely coming back. I learned something new every single day I was on this trip, and I missed you more with every passing day."

"I cried myself to sleep for the first week and then scolded myself, as you would have done, and simply let the time go by, knowing how much I loved you." She was nestled deep into his shoulder. "You're home, Sharp Knife. It's time to make me a happy woman."

It was a joyful kitchen the next morning, with the family back together and all the farm hands crowding around too. "There are ranches along parts of the Snake River where there was nothing just two years ago," Zeke said. "The Columbia River banks are filled with people, and in areas of what the people are calling Wyoming, herds of cattle can be seen regularly.

"I'm glad Nate Bishop and I made that trip, but it will be many years before I leave this farm again."

Zeke and his pack mules had arrived late the night before after finally making it across the hard pass out of Oregon City and hadn't found anyone awake to greet him. It was Buck O'Keefe that had awakened and came to the barn to help him get unloaded. He looked around the long kitchen table, at Hiram and Sarah, the Saunders boys, Rebecca, and Buck O'Keefe. Sarah was holding baby Travis and the twins now were sitting at their own special table.

"What a gang," Zeke laughed. "I'm home! I have no idea whether anything was accomplished by this trip, but I learned many things and feel much more comfortable about what I should work toward in the legislature's next few meetings. Thank you all for keeping this place in order. Let's eat our fill and get to work."

IT WAS the middle of July before Moose arrived back in the Willamette River Valley, and his first stop was the Hawthorne farm. Hiram spotted the huge man walking his horse and trailing a pair of pack mules up the long drive from the River Road. Everyone on the farm could hear Hiram's squalls as he raced down the drive to welcome his uncle. The scene quickly turned to what Barbara would have said. "Looked like when the pack trains arrived at Fort Bridger."

Everyone turned out, from the big house, from the fields, from the barns and shops, to welcome Moose Travis home. "I'm glad to be here, I love you all, but what I really want is a piece of meat this big," and his arms were spread wide, "and a bucket of cold beer this deep."

Hiram took his horse, Buck grabbed the mules, and the entourage made its way up the drive to the big house. Hiram, Buck, and the Saunders boys took care of the animals and Hiram saw to it that everyone was headed back to work. Zeke, Sarah, and the children escorted Moose into the house.

"This man needs food, Rebecca, let's see what we can do about that." Sarah was laughing, almost dancing with joy at Moose's return. "Sit yourself, little brother and tell us all about your trip. Did you bring a bride home?" Her laughter filled the warm kitchen.

"It was a long spring and early summer. I spoke with many people, and saw wagon train after wagon train move through the country. I now know what Barbara and Zeke have been talking about. The Indians that fight this onrush of people will simply be pushed aside, even if they fight back. Our people will work with the white people as long as the white people maintain a bit of dignity."

Zeke saw that Moose didn't really believe what he was saying. "You don't see a bright future for the Shoshone people," Zeke said.

"No, I'm afraid I don't. The white people I met, even those I guided into the territory, don't know one tribe from another, and don't care one way or the other about whether a tribe is friendly or not. All they see is what they've been told. All Indians are the same, are savages wanting to kill, rape, and steal. There's going to be war, Zeke, and the Indians will lose in the long run."

Rebecca slipped a large slab of pork roast with potatoes and green beans in front of Moose. "Biscuits will be out in a minute, and there's more where that came from," she smiled. "You'll have to talk to Zeke about that pail of beer."

"I could drink a pail full of beer right now, but I'll be satisfied with coffee. To answer your other question, dear sister, I did not bring a wife back with me. No Shoshone maiden in her right mind would want to spend the rest of her life with me." Saying that, he tore into a pound of pork and cup after cup of hot coffee.

IT TOOK JUST a couple of weeks for Moose to get back into the swing of things at the Donaldson Lumber Mill. "Does everyone in the territory think it's necessary to come to the mill to welcome me home? When I left, they were fighting over who would be the one to burn me out, now they're fighting over welcoming me home."

He and Angus Whitell were laughing about the number of visitors, but Moose was right about the change in people's attitudes. "I think that trial in Judge Virgil

Brown's court changed a lot of minds, Moose." Angus was talking about the revelations that were brought forth during Henry Foote's trial. The second trial, that for Phil Mason was also alarming for many.

JOHN MCDONALD, at the behest of John Bradley, had represented both Foote and Mason, but it was Henry Foote who spoiled any chance McDonald might have had. Every day during his three-day trial he ranted and raved about slavery, about the mixing of races, about God striking everyone and their dogs down if Oregon became a slave free state.

Judge Brown did what he could to quell the outcries and finally, on the third day, removed Foote from the courtroom. Late in the day the jury came back with a guilty verdict and Brown sent Foote to prison for three years. "You're a vile and ugly man, Mr. Foote, and you have been found guilty of assault and attempted murder. There is no place in today's society for your brand of violence and hatred."

All the hatred Foote spilled onto the courtroom visitors, the judge, the jury, and anyone associated with the Travis and Hawthorne families carried over into the Phil Mason trial, despite the strong objections from McDonald. At every opportunity, the prosecutor quoted Henry Foote and Mason's feeble attempts to deny any association, despite John McDonald's objections, failed miserably. Judge Virgil Brown let it continue.

Several members of the legislature were called on as character witnesses for Mason, but the echoes of Foote's hatred and anger reverberated through the jury's debates.

Mason was found guilty of conspiring with Foote, and was finally given a three-year sentence also.

GEORGE BELKNAP LEFT the courtroom along with Geoff McGaskill following Mason's trial. "Everything we tried to do taken from us by a madman," Belknap said. "How could we have prevented Henry Foote from this atrocity? How will we be able to press our case when, at every twist and turn, Foote's raving will be repeated?"

Belknap was thinking of his position in the legislature and how these convictions would have an impact during debates over statehood. McGaskill was a businessman and had his thoughts more on how those convictions might affect his business. "I think we need to accept the fact that we have lost, Belknap. I believe now that because of those courtroom circuses, the people of Oregon will not support Oregon becoming a pro-slavery state.

"Because of what we saw from Foote and Mason, our fight was lost by way of the uneducated. We're capable of thinking an issue through, but Foote and people like him only react. They've never been taught the art of critical thinking, as we have. Worse yet, there are more just like him and they make more noise." He heaved a great sigh.

"No, Mr. Belknap, sir, I think it's time to fold our cards and take our losses. Our job now is to make Oregon an economic gem and bring the old girl to statehood with as much dignity as we can exert."

George Belknap wanted to object but knew that McGaskill was right. "Pragmatic to the end, eh Geoff? Well, I must admit that you're probably right. I'll stand for re-election, yes I will, but our fight is over."

"I THINK IT'S TIME FOR YOU TO COME CLEAN, MR. MOOSE Travis." Beulah was standing in the middle of the lumber mill's kitchen, a carving knife in one hand and a venison back strap on the carving table in front of her. "Just what have you been doing these evenings and where have you been going?"

An astute person might have caught just a touch of redness to Moose's neck. "I just like to get out into the forest in the evening, dear lady." His smile tried to fend off more questions, but Beulah wasn't having any of it.

"Out in the forest were ye?" She chuckled, pointed that big knife at him. "Sure, ya were, laddy-buck. Dressed in clean trousers and starched shirt. Boots polished to a sheen, you were traipsing among the fir and pine.

"Now, Mr. Travis, once again. Who is she?" She had him and he was thankful that it was only the two of them in the kitchen, and that Angus and the crew were still hard at work. Beulah had a wide smile on her face, set the knife on the cutting board and let the sound of her tapping toe continue the question.

"You've heard me talk about Thaddeus Chapman and his family?" he asked. Beulah had heard many stories about Chappie and Moose on the trail from the Rockies to Oregon. She heard about the hunting trips, the fishing ventures, the wrestling contests, but not a word about a daughter.

"Are you saying that this Chappie feller has a daughter? Or are you saying that you dress up to visit Chappie and talk late into the evening?" She had him again and Moose decided the best bet was to come clean with the astute Irish lady.

"Chappie has a daughter, Beulah. Her name is Clementine but I call her Clemmie. She's seventeen years old, and she's from an eastern tribe. Chappie and his wife took her in as a baby when she was abandoned. They adopted her. She's never known anything other than being raised by a white family.

"I've been instructing her in the ways of the Shoshone."

Beulah couldn't stop laughing, had her arms tightly wrapped around herself, shaking with mighty guffaws. "I bet you have," she finally blurted, wiping tears from her eyes, trying her best to get back under control. "Will we be hearing Elaine, Sarah, and Barbara chanting the Shoshone wedding song soon?"

Moose walked over to the large cast iron stove and poured a mug of coffee, took a long sip and set it down on the table. He stepped up to Beulah and slipped an arm around her ample waist. "There is the possibility that drums may beat, feet may dance, and my mother and sisters may sing, dear lady, but not for many months to come. I promised Chappie that I would build a fine house on a piece land that could be worked.

"I'll be filing on property near Angus's place this week, and Clemmie and I will design and build our home. I call her my Iroquois Princess, if you must know."

"Thank you, Moose," Beulah said. "You know I just had to know. Will we get to meet this lovely lady?

"Soon," he said, finished his coffee and fled the kitchen amid gales of laughter. *That woman is too wise for her own good*, he chuckled. *I guess the entire camp will know within hours, and if Angus knows then Barbara will, then Mama and Papa, and then Zeke and his whole family.* His thoughts entering the mill were that he might just bring Clemmie up for supper with the crew one evening soon.

"IT'LL BE A FINE HARVEST, I think," Zeke said. He and Hiram were walking through one of the cornfields late in the summer. "You've done a fine job, Hi. There aren't too many lads your age that run a crew of three, maintain most of the equipment and still have time to do your studies. I'm mighty proud of you, son."

Hiram reddened some and was glad that Buck and the Saunders boys weren't there. "You taught me well, Papa. We'll need to hire people again for the harvest. Those two we had last year were good, but we'll need at least four this year, I'm sure. We have two large fields of sweet corn, so we'll need to get that to the southern and northern markets, probably using Mr. Johnson's wagons.

"The same with the beans. We'll have green beans for Oregon City, Portland, and the northern market, and for

Salem City and south. Then, later, we'll have the dried or feed corn and the dried beans. And we haven't even begun to talk about wheat, barley, and hops."

"This is a big farm, Hiram. Are you comfortable with this much responsibility? You're almost as big as Sam and Buck, strong as any of our mules, but are you okay with all this?" He and the whole crew had been at it from before sunrise to after sunset most of the summer with little time off for fishing, swimming, and just knocking around.

"I feel good, Papa. I love this farm, and I can sneak off sometimes once I get everyone on the job. With Buck, Sam, and Skinny, I can get a lot done in a day, and if we hire four more for harvest, we'll be fine."

Changing the subject, Hi asked, "When will all your legislative business start? You were pretty busy last year."

"Part of the being so busy last year was the election, but I'll start getting busy again with committee work and writing bills sometime in October. Hopefully, it won't interfere with harvest."

"Or hunting," Hiram joshed. "Buck and I have already made plans to fill that smoke house we built."

"Along with a couple of deer and an elk or two, remember we have those hogs coming up for slaughter. That smoke house will be full to the brim, I think." Zeke whacked Hiram across the shoulders and the two feigned, jabbed, and joked their way back to the barn. "Who's that riding up the trail?" Zeke was pointing at a wagon coming toward the big house.

"Mr. Johnson," Zeke hailed. "Welcome. We were just

talking about you. I'm sure there's coffee and there are always biscuits. Is this a business trip?"

Johnson climbed down from the high seat and clasped Zeke's hand, then Hi's. "Business and pleasure, Zeke. More pleasure than business." Hi took the wagon and teams toward the barn and Zeke and Johnson went into the house.

"Look who's here, Sarah. All the way from Portland just for some of your coffee."

"Rebecca just took sweet rolls from the oven, Mr. Johnson. Is that what made you turn into our little farm?" She was all smiles and they hugged hello. "Coffee's always hot around here. Sit yourself, sir, and I'll get you all set up."

"I bring good news from Travis," he said. "It seems Moose has found himself a young lady."

"Oh, lord," Zeke exclaimed. "I hope that doesn't mean another huge wedding." Sarah gave him a scowl, halfway in jest. "Who is the lucky girl? He told us he didn't bring a bride from his visit to the home country." Zeke poured himself some more coffee, thinking also about how much more furniture he would be building.

"He calls her Clemmie," Johnson said. "Clementine Chapman, came in on the wagon train he guided. Moose and her father, Thaddeus-he calls himself Ted-became good friends on the journey. Moose has found a piece of ground he likes, staked it out and is drawing plans for building."

"Sounds pretty serious to me," Zeke said. "Have you seen her? If Moose picked her out, she's got to be attractive. Probably gorgeous." He smiled up at Sarah and got one back. "Old man Travis will find all his children married off, and have half a score of grandchildren to pamper, eh, Sarah love?"

"I'm so happy for him," she replied. Then she gathered up the twins, picked up little Travis, and headed out the door toward her kitchen garden.

"We need to talk contracts, Johnson," Zeke said. "My harvest will be considerably larger than last year and I'll need wagons, drivers, and teams to get this bounty to market. Better get your notebook out and I'll give you the details. Also, can you provide me with four good men during harvest? Maybe even five."

"I already have you penciled in for the wagons and drivers, Zeke, so that won't be a problem, but for harvest help, I'll have to work on that. There are always people not working but that doesn't mean they want to work," and he laughed with a definite sardonic flavor to it. "It is getting better, though. Most of my teamsters and lead men in the warehouse have been with me for a while, but casual labor sometimes is hard to come by. I'll surely do my best, sir."

They spent a couple of hours working out the contracts for corn, wheat, beans, and hops, minus, of course, the actual dates, which would be put in as harvest time came closer. Johnson had his mid-day meal with the family and Sarah fixed him a large basket of food to take along with him.

"There's a special place along the River Road where I can get back into the forest and make a camp for the night. This basket will make my day complete, dear lady." Hiram brought the teams and wagon up and Johnson climbed aboard. "Come to Portland and visit this old man," he said. He tapped the lead horses with the reins and they were off in a cloud of dust, everyone waving and hollering their goodbyes.

"I'm going into Salem City tomorrow, Hi, and I want you and Sam to come with me. We have some work to do." Zeke clapped his son on the shoulder and they walked off toward the shop buildings. "We'll ride horses instead of taking the wagon."

"You sound worried, Papa. What's wrong?"

"I've seen what you were saying about our coming harvest. I know just how big it's going to be and how many people we'll need to get it in. Johnson just told me he may not be able to provide field workers this year, so I want you and Sam to scour Salem and come up with five good men for us. I'll be meeting with Nate Bishop and won't be able to help you."

"You figure Sam Saunders might know some people that would be looking for work? We'll talk with some of his friends, and his mother might have some ideas. Skinny and Buck can continue working the fields, or if you want, Papa, we can give them the day off, too. They deserve it."

"That's a good idea. We'll take off as soon as the morning chores are done."

27

"THOSE BOOKS THAT JOE GAINES PROMISED ME CAME IN ON that last mail schooner, Nate, and I've had a chance to study them well." Zeke and Nate Bishop were in Bishop's Salem City apartment, having coffee and sweet rolls. "He included a long letter discussing his feeling about statehood and I'm pretty much in agreement with his ideas."

"I have some ideas as well, Zeke, that's why I suggested this meeting. This thing we call Oregon Territory needs some serious adjustments and it may be up to us, with Joe Gaines' backing to get it done."

The two men were at the forefront of some major changes in how Oregon Territory was going to change over the next several years. Partly because of the long trip through what would become Wyoming and Idaho and partly because of feedback from the people of the territory, the two were discussing changes many felt were late in coming.

"I think Oregon's natural eastern border ought to be somewhat along the Snake River's northern journey. The northern border is pretty much in place, what with the British and the Columbia River, the Pacific Ocean determines the west, and California lines out the southern border." Zeke hade a large map spread on Bishop's desk, and was pointing out the obvious.

"It's here, along the Snake that Idaho Territory could be formed." Zeke ran his fingers along the river, remembering just how beautiful that valley was. "You could lead the faction that would ask that Idaho break away from Oregon Territory, become an unorganized territory, as Gaines described the move."

Bishop was looking at the map closely. "That California border extends across Utah Territory and is in place. Along this longitude then," and he let his finger move from the south to north on the map, mostly following the Snake River, "would be the border between Oregon Territory and Idaho. Would breaking away be legal? Would Idaho have any legal standing?"

"According to Joe Gaines, that's what I'll find in these books he sent. According to everything I've read and studied, the process is long and involved. It will take more than what we've discussed in the legislature. We need to hold a constitutional convention, make the decisions on Idaho becoming a territory, and petition the government for statehood.

"It's the convention and the Idaho questions that will determine whether we become a state of the union. I plan to begin the process at our next session, come December." Zeke walked over to the window, looking out across the Willamette River toward the west. "Are we still together on this, Nate?"

"We are, Zeke. Yes sir, we are. I'll be heading back to

Idaho country next week and I'll work my way from Fort Boise to every community in that vast area, and when you see me next in December, we'll work out position papers and write up the legislation to get this started.

"I think that border between Oregon and Idaho will be more to the west, Zeke. I think the entire Snake River Valley should be in the unorganized Idaho territory." He paused for a minute, but didn't get an immediate reaction from Zeke. "Anyway, we can work those details out easily, and by then, I'll have feedback from those living in the area. My God, I'm excited!"

Zeke was excited, too, by the prospect and shook Nate's hand over and over. "I think a visit to Molly's, some fried clams and cold beer for a celebration lunch is called for," he said. The two were laughing most of the way down to the waterfront restaurant. They were not surprised to find Roland Sullivan at a window table.

"I'm glad you're here, Sully," Zeke said, taking a seat. "We have some news and over the next few months will need someone like you to help spread the word." Lunch extended into the late afternoon with Sullivan promising to spread the word from one end of the Oregon Territory to the other. It was agreed that the three of them would work to get enough support to call for a constitutional convention following the regular session of the legislature. Zeke faced a long ride back to the farm and knew he would still have a smile on his face when he arrived home.

"WHERE WOULD WE START?" Hiram and Sam Saunders had left Zeke when they arrived in Salem City late in the morning. "The important thing is to find at least five people that we can count on," Zeke said, "that are responsible enough to show up and work."

Sam was laughing gently as he commented, "And be strong enough to do the work you demand of us." Zeke had to chuckle right along with him.

"Yes, Sam, I'm a real task-master," he said. "Would you like to stop off and see your mother before we begin this search?"

"She'll be at work, but I want to drop by our house and leave her a message. I also snubbed some stuff from the kitchen garden for her. Your mother took me by the arm, pointed at some squash, beets, and carrots and handed me a canvas bag. It's in my saddle bags." Hiram got a good laugh out of that, picturing Sarah with her hands on her hips.

"I know a couple of families that have boys about mine and Skinny's age that are probably looking for work. We'll start there and see what happens."

The boys had developed a strong relationship even though there were several years separation in their ages. Sam didn't seem to have the least problem working for the younger Hiram, following his directions to the letter. Hiram had learned farming from Zeke and Zeke knew what he was teaching.

Sam had tremendous respect for Zeke and let that filter right on down to Hiram. "We'll find some fine gentlemen that you can spend the rest of the summer and fall harassing, young Mr. Hawthorne," Sam laughed.

Sam led them into a section of Salem that Hi had never visited, a bit south of the city and in the foothills. They rode into the yard of a small farm of about three acres and tied off their horses at a rack in front of a small, slightly neglected cabin. The farm was neat and tidy but showed a few signs of wear. The fences drooped some, the trees hadn't been trimmed recently. Not neglect, as such, just possibly more work than could be done.

"Good morning, Mrs. Brown," Sam said when Lizzie Brown came to the door. "Is Tom home?"

"Well, Sam Saunders," she said. "I haven't seen you for more than a year. Where have been keeping yourself?"

"Mrs. Brown, this is Hiram Hawthorne. Skinny and I work for the Hawthorne farm, north of Salem City." Hiram shook Lizzie's calloused hand and she nodded to him. "It's a big farm and Hiram is hoping to hire extra help for the harvest season. Is Tom around?"

"He should be out with the hogs, Sam. We could sure use some extra money around here."

"Thank you," Sam said, Hiram nodded, and the two walked around behind the old cabin letting their noses direct them to the hog pens. "Tom's a little younger than me, but he's always been a good worker. Old man Brown was a bad drunk and got in a fight with some other drunk one night and didn't live through it. He was one bad apple and Lizzie's had a rough time raising her boy."

They walked around the barn and found Tom Brown fixing some broken boards on one of the hog pens. Hiram saw a tall man, probably seventeen or so, broad shoulders, deep chest, but underweight by quite a bit. "Hey, Sam," Tom hollered when they walked up. "Where you been, boy?"

"Hi, Tom," Sam said, giving the tall man a strong hug. "Say hello to Hiram Hawthorne."

Hiram stuck his big hand out and the two shook. Hi

liked the strong handshake he got back and smiled. "Nice to meet you Tom. Sam's told me a lot about you."

"Hawthorne eh? You related to that guy that's always being written about in the newspaper?"

"That's my father, Ezekiel Hawthorne. We have a farm north of town and it's coming harvest season. Sam and Skinny have been working for us for more than a year now, and we're looking to hire men for the harvest. Would you be in a position to take a full-time job for about two to three months?"

"So that's where you've been hiding out?" Tom Brown put his tools down, pulled a rag from his trousers' pocket and wiped his face. "Been hot this summer." He looked at Hiram, then at Sam. "Got a good crop coming in, eh? I know ma and me could sure use the money. Tell me about what you be offering this strong farm-boy."

It was a half an hour and a pot of coffee later that Sam and Hi rode out from the Brown place. "That wasn't so difficult, was it? One down, four to go," Sam laughed. "Tom's a good hand, and with hard work, and the way your ma feeds us, he'll gain some weight and be strong as your pa."

They rode to what Sam called the Thompson place next. "Sam Thompson is a slob, hasn't done a day's work in ten years that I know of," Sam said. "But his kid, Mike, has worked for many of the little farms around Salem. He's tough as nails and honest as the day is long."

They rode up to a forlorn looking cabin tucked back in some trees and tied off. An old man was leaning against an outside wall. His sagging belly was drooping over a pair of trousers that were tied off with a length of rope, his hair was long, filthy, and mostly gray. His eyes were sullen, and Hi knew they also drooped from an alcohol intake that very morning.

"Mr. Thompson," Sam said. "Is Mike around this morning.?"

"Maybe," Thompson said. "Who's that with you? Don't like strangers just riding up, you know."

"This is Hiram Hawthorne. Skinny and I work for the Hawthorne farm and we're looking for help for the harvest season. Is Mike around?"

Thompson's eyes narrowed some as he squinted at Sam and Hiram. "Hawthorne? The man that's living with a squaw? You one of his bastard kids?" His anger was fierce but Hiram didn't respond, Sam did.

"No call for that kind of talk, Thompson," Sam said. "I'll whack you a good one if you say something like that again."

Hiram said, "No, Sam. No need for that. Mr. Thompson is simply an ignorant fool, too stupid to understand what he's saying. Let's just go on about our business." Hiram had learned much since his encounter with that fool at Travis's trading post. As he and Sam started to mount up, Mike Thompson came out of the cabin.

He was in stark contrast to his father, standing about as tall, but in excellent physical condition. He wore his hair long and it curled around his ears. Hiram saw bright green eyes, broad shoulders, and strong arms. "Sam Saunders, you old son of a gun. Where you been hiding?"

"Hi, Mike," Sam said. "You got time to take a short ride with us? Grab your pony and meet us out on the main road."

"You bet, Sam. Damn, it's been more than a year." He

didn't even acknowledge that his father was angry, tensed, and wanting to start a fracas. Mike Thompson ran to the barn to saddle up and Sam and Hiram mounted and rode off the property.

"I don't know, Hi," Sam said. "I think I would have throttled old man Thompson for what he said."

"Papa has showed me that sometimes it's just best to ignore those that are so stupid. If he had been aggressive, I would have beat him to the ground, but all he is is a bag full of manure with a mouth. An ignorant and stupid man, and I won't lower myself to his standards."

"I'm glad I work for you, Hiram. I'm glad I can call you a friend."

They rode their horses into a little grove of fir trees to wait for Mike Thompson. "I hope Mike isn't like his father," Hiram said. "That would be unfortunate."

"I've known him for many years, Hi. He's a good worker, I know that, but until today I didn't know how bad his father is. I'd still like to go back and beat some sense into that old man."

Mike Thompson rode up on a rather thin mare and the three stepped out of the saddle, tied off, and settled down under the trees. "So," young Thompson said, "where have you been, what have you been doing, and who's your friend?"

"Mike, say hello to Hiram Hawthorne. Skinny and I have been working for the Hawthorne farm for more than a year now. Hi is looking to hire a good crew for the harvest season coming up, and I brought him here to talk to you."

"Hawthorne? My pa sure doesn't like him. I've read about what some people say, but don't understand why Pa is so angry about it. Your pa is married to an Indian?" Mike said it as a straight-forward question, not as an insult.

"My mother is half Shoshone as I am, yes. Papa and Mama took me in when my parents couldn't take care of me any longer. I'm half Shoshone also and adopted by the Hawthorne's. Your father doesn't approve and has said some ugly things to me this morning. I understand it's simply a case of ignorance and hope that if you're looking for good honest work, you don't feel the same."

Mike Thompson had a grave look on his face, looking back and forth between Sam and Hi, finally taking a deep breath. "Interesting way to start the day," he said, with no smile on his face. "To be honest, I've never met an Indian before. I've certainly never been offered a job by one, and I do know how much my father hates Indians. I've never known why." He sat very still for a few minutes, deep in thought.

"My ma died a few years ago and I promised her that I would take care of Pa, and it's been very hard," Thompson said. "I do all the work on our place. Pa doesn't do anything but drink and cause trouble with the neighbors. I've wanted to leave so many times, but I promised. If I leave, the old man will die. Our place would rot away just like he would." Tears filled the young man's eyes but he wiped them away and muttered, "Damn, Sam, what can I do?"

Sam and Hi could see the anguish in Mike's face and knew they couldn't answer his question. Mike Thompson got up and paced around the little area and finally sat back down.

"Mama always said that Pa is the way he is because he

never grew up, always had someone else to do his work. She pounded it in to me to grow up, be a man, and take responsibility for my life. I guess today is the day she always talked about." He looked over to Hiram, then to Sam. "Tell me where I need to be, when I need to be there, and," he paused letting a smile slowly spread across his face, "how much money I might make."

His smile brightened and he added, "You know, Sam, now that I think about it, Toby and Brian Stockridge have been hurtin' some these last few months since their ma and pa died with the flu. I know they'd jump at the chance for a few months of good work."

"They're good boys, Hi," Sam said. "Couldn't do better."

"Tell them what I told you, Mike, and if they agree, you get the word to me as soon as possible." Mike nodded his head and the three spent a few minutes going over everything that Mike needed to know and to pass along to the Stockridge boys.

Half an hour later Hi and Sam rode into town and stopped in front of a home that didn't sit on farmland. It was right in town. "This is where Tom and Edith Wilson live," Sam said. "Their son Rich needs to break away. He's sixteen years old and I know his pa and ma want him to start finding his own way in the world."

They tied off their horses and walked toward the front door of the home. An elderly lady answered the door. She was rail thin, the skin on her face pulled taught over the bone structure. Her eyes were bright blue and her long white hair was pulled back and tied with a bow.

"Sam Saunders as I live," she exclaimed, throwing her arms around the big man. "What a wonderful surprise.

Your mother told me you've been working at a big farm north of here. Skinny too," she said.

"Hi, Mrs. Wilson. Been working at the Hawthorne farm. This is Hiram Hawthorne and we're here to talk to Rich if he's around." Hi and Mrs. Wilson shook hands and she ushered the two into the house.

Hiram found a cozy, warm home, immaculately clean and tidy. Mrs. Wilson had the boys sit in comfortable chairs that Hiram noticed were well built. "I have fresh coffee if you'd like some, and then I'll go out back and find Rich."

"That would be fine," Sam said.

She scurried into the kitchen, brought coffee, and scurried back out. She wasn't gone two minutes and returned with young Rich Wilson, a small boy, smaller than Hiram, but sturdy, compact, and probably very strong. "So, Sam Saunders is alive," he smiled grabbing Sam by the shoulders.

"Good to see you, Rich. Say hello to Hiram Hawthorne. Skinny and I work for the Hawthorne's at their farm north of here. Hiram's here to hire a crew for the harvest season. It would be two to three months of good hard work and the pay is good too."

"I've read about Ezekiel Hawthorne," Rich said. "Pa and I sat in on a couple of sessions of the legislature… you know how Pa loves his politics. I heard your father speak at one of the sessions. And you're asking if I'd like to go to work for him?" Hiram smiled at the comments and nodded yes.

"Well, you bet I would! I've been all over this town trying to get some kind of work that would challenge my body and muscles, and I know a good corn and wheat harvest would do that." He laughed, hugged his mother, and sat back down. "Tell me all about it."

It was a pair of happy young men that headed back along the River Road late that afternoon. "I'm glad we stopped for the fried clams," Hiram said. "We came to town looking for five good men and got 'em," he laughed. "We'll have nine strong men, that's including me, of course, working those fields this year, Sam. Old Mr. Johnson better be ready to bring those wagons in cuz we're ready to fill 'em up."

2 8

Long hot days in the field during harvest kept Zeke and all the hands busy from near sunrise to sunset. The mid-day meal was a hornet's nest of activity with Sarah and Rebecca feeding the multitude. Cribs were filled and wagons were loaded and cribs were refilled. Fresh green beans and sweet corn headed to markets north and south in the early harvest.

There would a break for the men and boys to savor a little less time in the field and then it was back to bringing in the wheat, barley, late corn, and dried beans. Hops had to be harvested and dried as well. Johnson had wagons moving all fall with produce from the Hawthorne farm and other producers up and down the great valley.

There were other equally busy activities taking place in the territory. George Belknap had formed a committee of pro-slavery supporters who would work with him to defeat any possibility of a constitutional convention that didn't include slavery for Oregon.

Roland Sullivan had also formed a committee of those

looking to separate Idaho country from Oregon Territory to hold a constitutional convention that would bring Oregon into the union as an anti-slavery state. Riders moved between Salem City, Oregon City, Portland and other communities constantly.

"THAT WAS A LONG DAY, HIRAM," Zeke said as they tromped their way onto the mud porch to doff their boots. "Let's see if your mother has any more of that pie and talk about how harvest is coming along." In the evening, it had become a regular routine of eating something light and talking about the day's activities.

"You've grown another two inches at least," Zeke said. "Keep it up and you'll be as big as Moose soon."

They found chairs and had just plopped down as Sarah brought plates filled with large wedges of apple pie and a pot full of hot coffee. She also put a bottle of rum down next to Zeke's coffee cup. "Looks like you boys are almost wiped out tonight. It must have been brutally hot out there. I know you like it when Rebecca and I bring dinner out to you but I wondered if you would be better off to have your dinner under the trees near the bunkhouse? It sure would be cooler."

"It would mean bringing all the animals in, unhitching all the equipment, and extend our dinner time by that much," Zeke said. "It would be nice but it would be considerably more work and time. Just keep the water coming, dear lady, and none of us will die."

Hiram was chuckling at his father's comment. "I thought I would a time or two out there today. Our crews are working out well. With you leading the corn pickers and me taking care of the beans, we're ahead of last year's harvest. Putting Skinny Saunders on the wagon instead of picking is working, too."

"Any problems with any of the boys?"

"I've got Mike Thompson, Rich Wilson, Tom Brown and me picking with Skinny handling the wagon and team. It's working out good. Tom Brown is getting stronger every day and none of them are slackers at all." Hiram was a leader in every sense of the word, and Zeke wondered where it came from.

"I've had one problem with Tom Brown and Skinny Saunders, but I think I got it worked out. Tom, like Skinny, isn't very strong, and I've been giving him plenty of time to get his muscles built up. Skinny, of course, will never be strong and is a perfect fit driving the teams. Tom thought he ought to have time on the wagon. He felt I was being hard on him making him stay in the corn picking."

"What did you do?" Zeke asked.

"I asked him if he had ever driven four up and he said no, but he also said that he had never picked beans before either. I told him that picking beans and doing it wrong was one thing, but driving four up and doing it wrong could jeopardize lives. I told him because Skinny had the most experience with teams that he would have that job.

"I'm getting a lot better at holding my temper, Papa. I took the time to explain how difficult it is to move four mules and a large wagon in tight quarters and just how dangerous it could be if the animals panicked, or if the driver did. Tom gave me a full day's work, and I went out of my way to compliment him on his effort."

Here was this skinny little twelve or thirteen- year- old who was almost an introvert when he came to us and just look at what he has become. His shoulders are broad and strong, his chest deep, and look at the size of those hands.

"What are you thinking about, Papa?" Hiram was fascinated at how Zeke could just sit and look at someone or something. "Are you analyzing something that we need to do?"

"No, old man, I was analyzing you," he laughed. "We don't know for sure whether you're fifteen or sixteen, but right now, you're a man. Just look at him, Sarah. He towers over you, is almost as tall as I am, and was just a skinny little kid a few years ago."

Sarah put her arms around Hiram's shoulders and kissed the top of his head. "You are a leader of men, Hiram Hawthorne, just like you father. With our people in the tribe you would be reaching warrior status, and with our people here, you are a leader and a man."

"Am I too young to have my own place?"

"You mean your own farm?" Zeke asked, cocking his head slightly at the unexpected question.

"No, I mean my own home. I would like you and me to build me my own home, right here on the farm. We have land that can't be tilled, isn't good for orchards or crops, and we have time during the winter months to do it, Papa."

"We do indeed, son. I've wanted to buy that quarter section to our east, a little higher in the foothills and incorporate it into our farm. It's good land, there's fine water, and putting in the irrigation wouldn't be as hard as what we did here. We'll give that some thought.

"Is there some reason you would like your own home?" Zeke looked at Sarah with that question in his eyes. She had the same look and just shrugged. She also remembered Hiram saying how pretty Rebecca was and asking if she was too old for him.

Hiram just smiled at Zeke. "No, no special reason," he said. "I just have this feeling that I should be taking care of myself, have my own home. How old were you when you built your first home, Papa?"

Memories flooded Zeke's mind with that question. *My time with the cabinetmaker and the blacksmith was over. I was considered a journeyman and father wanted me to open my shop. And then I met Elizabeth. My God, I was only eighteen.* Zeke took a long look at Hiram and a smile slowly crept across his face.

"I guess I was about two or three years older than you are right now, Hi. Let's spend some time working on that idea of yours. We will have time come winter. That is, after the legislative session."

Hiram finished his last bite of pie, whopped Zeke across the shoulders, hugged and kissed Sarah, and bounded upstairs with a wide smile. "See you in the morning," he said on the way.

"Something going on I don't know about?" Zeke asked.

"I have no idea," Sarah answered. "He's quite the young man, Sharp Knife. He and Moose are a pair."

"I'm glad you were able to come on such short notice, judge," Sullivan said, welcoming District Judge Virgil Brown to his home. "I think you know Obediah Sinclair and Assemblyman, Nate Bishop. Would you like a sip of my own bourbon, straight from my new distillery?"

"Long in the barrel is best, Mr. Sullivan, but I would like to try yours out. Good evening gentlemen," he said to the others. Sullivan poured each a hefty taste of his bourbon and was about to sit down when there was another knock at the door.

"Ah, Mr. Chapman, welcome," he said. "Gentlemen, meet one of our newest citizens, Thaddeus Chapman, originally of Pennsylvania." There were handshakes all around, and more drinks were poured.

"In just a couple of months the next legislative session will be getting underway," Sullivan said, getting the evening's agenda started. "For statehood to take place, many things must be accomplished at the legislature. Nate Bishop and Zeke Hawthorne have put together the program they would like to see, and Nate is here to outline what they hope to put together this year."

"As young as this whiskey is, Sully, it's quite good," Bishop said.

"I've been working on getting the distillery up and running for some time, Nate. This is actually about four years old,"

"Well, sir, I'll be a customer. Now, about statehood for Oregon," he said. For the next hour, he talked about how there would have to be a separation of the Snake River country from the vast Oregon Territory. "Idaho will become an unorganized territory and that would include what they are calling Wyoming country, as well. It's very safe to believe that the question of a constitutional convention being called for during this session is almost moot.

"However, we believe the big debate will be the slavery question. Assemblyman George Belknap is adamant about Oregon being pro-slavery, and we are just as strongly against the possibility. Oregon must be a free state. That is why Sullivan has invited us here tonight."

"Thank you, Nate," Sullivan said. "I was going to prepare a speech for delivery right about now, but I knew you'd just get up and walk out the door." There was genuine laughter from the group at that comment.

"Despite the good liquor, I would have been the first," Judge Brown quipped.

"Each of us has a bit of influence with various segments of our society and we need to spend the time between now and December spreading the word that Oregon must be a free state."

"What's the feeling of the general membership of the assembly?" Banker Sinclair thought that most folks favored a free state.

"I think most favor a free state, but I don't have the numbers yet," Bishop said. "We need to have as many people as possible contact their representatives and voice their opinion for a free state. If we can separate Idaho from Oregon and have a strong majority for statehood as a free state, I think we could offer a chance at a constitutional convention in the 56-57 session."

"Mr. Chapman, as a newcomer to the territory, how do you feel about what we're doing?"

Chapman was dressed in a city suit with polished boots, a frock coat, and starched shirt. "I'm an insurance representative for a major east coast firm that would probably close our Oregon offices if the territory became pro-slavery. I also have considerable background on Oregon politics because of our trip from the Green River here on the Oregon Trail.

"Our guide was a man I've come to have great respect

for. Moose Travis is a partner in the Donaldson Lumber Mills and guided our wagon train here. We spent many nights listening to him talk about Oregon, talk about his brother-in-law, Assemblyman Ezekiel Hawthorne, and talk about statehood," he paused for a moment and cleared his throat. "He and my daughter, Clementine, have become rather close lately. In fact, I expect him to ask for her hand at any time now. I want my family to live in a free state. I abhor slavery, my company will not support a slave state, and it appears as though grandchildren may be in my future. I want them raised in a free state."

"There's our argument right there," Sullivan said. "Economics and family. Let's get out in the communities and talk to everyone we know."

"We know you will, Sully," Bishop said. Sullivan beamed his pleasure at the remark, filled everyone's cup and raised his.

"To the free state of Oregon!" he said.

"AT EVERY INSTANCE when we thought we were moving forward with our plans, ignorant fools have come forward to thwart our efforts." George Belknap was hosting a party at his lavish home south of Salem City. "I'm disgusted with the Ted Newcombs and Clive Newtons, and most of all, the Henry Footes that we've run into. Their fight is not our fight, yet too many people believe it is.

"We need a new approach, gentlemen. We are educated southerners who have moved into this rich territory and I'm not willing to give up my heritage as we civilize Oregon. Oregon will be to the west what Virginia is to the south."

The group may have had McGaskill and Peter Flowers at the tables, southerners to the core, but a couple of Clive Newton's followers were present as well. Bud Best, a day laborer, and Ole Gunderson who worked in the timber fields when he needed some extra cash, were on hand.

"I'm a friend of Clive Newton," Best said. "He and Henry Foote worked long and hard as Firsters, as Ole and I have. We believe that Oregon's best ground is being given away to these eastern foreigners coming in. And," he said, "like Foote, I believe in slavery."

"We'll not change minds by violence toward those that disagree with us," Belknap said. He raised his voice just a bit, pointed a finger at Bud Best. "What Ted Newcomb and Jonah Smith attempted in Oregon City, and what Clive Newton and Henry Foote attempted in Salem, set our program back at least four years.

"If you are going to work on our behalf," he stormed, "you must be willing to put violence against those that disagree with us, aside. We are an intelligent, civilized, political movement not a rowdy street gang filled with hatred and violence."

Gunderson and Best were quiet for the rest of the meeting, enjoying the fine liquor that was served. Best was planning ways to stop Ezekiel Hawthorne in any way that he could, despite the lecture from Belknap. Gunderson didn't care what happened as long as the immigrants stopped flooding in.

Peter Flowers, the rancher, said he would do what he could talking-up the issue with other ranchers and farmers. The trader, Geoff McCaskill, said he would also talk about the issue with everyone he met. "The new legislative session is just a month or so away," Belknap reminded everyone. "We have our work cut out, and it's on a long, hard, uphill road."

The meeting ended pleasantly enough, but Belknap feared that he was backing a losing cause. He would not return to Virginia, he had a fine farm that was doing well and he enjoyed his position in the legislature. Thoughts of the governor's office or of the U.S. Senate also had room in his mind. *I like Oregon. I like where I am in this old life, but I miss the civilized life of a plantation owner. I would like Oregon to be the Virginia of the west. That's my fight and I must win my fight as a southern gentleman, not as a street fighter with no education.*

V

BOOK NINE: A LONG ROCKY
ROAD TO STATEHOOD

Zeke was surprised one morning in early December when the Salem barber, Paul Pritchett, rode into the farm. "Mr. Pritchett, welcome, sir. Hiram, could you take care of Mr. Pritchett's horse, please?" Zeke couldn't remember talking to the man after his fracas with Clive Newton.

"Come in, please," he said, escorting the gentleman into the warm kitchen. "It's a cold morning to be out for a little ride."

Pritchett sat down as Sarah poured some coffee for the three of them. "My wife, Sarah. Sarah, this is Paul Pritchett, a fine barber and gentleman."

"It's a pleasure, Ma'am," Pritchett said. "I was told by one of those angry old men who call themselves Firsters that George Belknap is going to do everything he can to keep you from being able to call for a constitutional convention. I would like to be able to help you in your fights during the session."

"That's wonderful, Pritchett. Wonderful. I don't think

we could call for that convention this year no matter what Belknap and his people might do. Let me explain what our plans are and then we'll fit you into our program." Zeke had a smile on his face remembering just how ugly the scene had been at the saloon that morning and how Pritchett had reacted. *I doubt this man has ever seen a man pull a knife on another man and actually see that knife used. He has strong convictions but I wonder if he is really a fighter.*

"You got here just in time for some sweet rolls, Mr. Pritchett," Sarah said. She pulled a pan of rolls redolent of cinnamon, poured some rich frosting across the hot buns, and pulled a platter down. "Politics need a bit of sweetening from time to time, don't you think?"

"My goodness that smells good. I may have to become a little more politically involved," he joshed. "I do want to hear your plans, Zeke. I'm in favor of what you've tried to do so far and want to help, if there's some way."

"I'm positive there's some way," Zeke said. For the next hour or so they munched on sweet rolls, drank coffee, and Paul Pritchett learned all about the Idaho country, Wyoming being a part of that, how the territories would separate, and how the question of a constitutional convention would probably not be in the works this session but would be sure to pass in the '56-'57 session.

"You've been more than busy, I believe," Pritchett said. "If I heard you right, what you're looking for right now is to sell the general public on the idea of bringing Oregon into statehood as a free, anti-slavery state and you need people spreading the gospel.

"Well, I can't walk on water and I'm not much of a public speaker, but as a busy barber I talk to many voting age men every week. It certainly won't be difficult to bring up the topic of a free state of Oregon. You say that my friend Sullivan is leading this charge, I'll make sure he knows where I stand."

The little meeting broke up and Pritchett rode out of the Hawthorne farm with a few pounds of fresh green beans in one saddle bag and half a dozen ears of sweet corn in the other. "Of course, I won't eat for two days now," he laughed. "I think I ate three of those sweet rolls. Thank you, Hawthorne," he said, waving goodbye. *That's one fighting legislator. Even his wife calls him Sharp Knife, I don't think Belknap has a chance against this formidable farmer.*

* * *

"THE SESSION STARTS NEXT WEEK, and then it's Christmas again. Where has this year gone?" Zeke was sitting on a sack of corn in the barn talking with Hiram. "Tell me about your crews, about how the harvest went, and whether we should increase or reduce our planting for next year."

As much as he wanted to, Zeke was aware that his government work took him out of the fields too often and the entire burden had fallen on the young shoulders of Hiram. "I will run for reelection next year, Hiram, but that will be my last time. That is, if I win." He heard Hi say there was no doubt about winning despite his laughter. "I want to escort this lady we call Oregon into the union as a free state, Hiram, then all I want is to be with my family running a fine farm. It's all I've ever wanted."

"We have a wonderful farm, Papa, and it's all because of you. The only problems I had were with Tom Brown continually picking on Skinny. Even when I separated them, he kept it up before and after work. I'd rather not have him back next year. Mike Thompson and the Starbridge boys were good workers and got along with Sam and Skinny.

"I'm afraid that Buck O'Keefe will never be a farmer," he laughed. "He's strong as a bear, will try to do anything you ask, but doesn't have his heart in farming."

"Buck is a good man and I think because of his terrible encounters on the trail, when he lost his entire family, then meeting up with an old-time mountain man, that his future is going to be in those majestic Rocky Mountains. I hope that he and Moose can spend lots of time together during our Christmas. I see Buck O'Keefe as a trail guide, with wagon trains or with the army. Maybe both."

"He'd be good," Hi said. He got a little contemplative and Zeke had to nudge him back to reality.

"Something on your mind?"

"Just wondering how it is that things seem to happen. Moose feels and acts more like a Shoshone warrior but is held up to everyone as part owner and manager of a fine lumber mill. Buck O'Keefe is already known as a guide because of his association with you and will be offered things because of that. Does life always make sense?"

"No, old man, life rarely makes sense. We live in turbulent times, Hiram. More people than can be counted are massing for an exodus that will be more than historic, it will be talked about, written about, for centuries. That migration will not just alter their lives but the lives of everyone on this continent.

"You and your sisters and brother will be part of it in ways that can't be imagined. Don't ever stop asking these kinds of questions. It's these kinds of questions that lead to how the greatest philosophers of time have come to their thinking processes, reached their conclusions, asked even more questions."

They spent another half hour discussing some of the Greek thinkers that Ezekiel studied as a boy and that Hiram was studying now. "We certainly do have a way of getting work done around this old farm, don't we?" Zeke and Hi chuckled and Zeke continued. "You were going to tell me about what our plans might be for this next season."

"The grist mills are already talking about needing much more wheat and rye next year. There are thousands of new people in the territory and they need flour. I increased our wheat this year based on what Sullivan ordered, but we need to make some serious changes for next year.

"That new property we bought has excellent ground for wheat and rye, and we will need to build our irrigation ditches, do some leveling, and take out some timber. We can use the timber for my house, probably."

"You really do have a handle on this, Hiram. Damn, but I'm proud of you. Bring me up to date on the corn, if you please."

"Sweet corn sells as fast as we can harvest and move it. Mr. O'Brien said he will want more of our hard corn for his cattle next year. We have room to increase the corn fields. Right now, all our dried beans are gone, our hard corn is gone, and all our hops are gone, too."

"We expanded quite a bit this year and it paid off. Expanding the wheat and rye next year will just about fill out the property we have. Keeping Sam and Skinny on permanent is good, and if Buck stays, that will be good too. If we lose Buck, I think we need to think about one more permanent employee." He paused for a moment. "Maybe two if we could get the Starbridge boys to stay on permanent. With new irrigation ditches, new land to be leveled, we could put them to work with Sam and Skinny year 'round."

"You've had all that bottled up inside just waiting for me to ask, haven't you?" Zeke asked with a smile.

Hiram nodded his head with a chuckle, kicked some dust around, and got a little boy's grin on his mug.

"You would have blown up if I hadn't asked," Zeke laughed. "I'm sure glad I did. Wouldn't want to clean up that mess," and he shot a little shoulder punch into Hiram, getting one back.

"Think we could catch a couple of fish if we tried?" Zeke stood up and started for the shed where they kept their fishing equipment. Hiram was at his side instantly. "Between the legislature and Christmas, we might not have another chance. How are those hogs of yours coming along?"

"I've got one about forty pounds that's ready for a hot fire. I'll be turning him on a spit for Christmas dinner, Papa. Moose sent me a note and he's bringing a venison that we'll cook over open fire, too. All of that depends on what the weather will be, but you can bet we won't go hungry."

The two spent the rest of the day walking, talking, fishing, and joshing. Zeke let his mind rest for the first time in months. *All of this because I was sad, distraught, lost, and ended up packing my mules. The best decision I've ever made and probably ever will make.*

To SAY the opening of the legislature was tumultuous would be less than adequate. Despite all the cajoling done by George Belknap to keep his people from acting like hooligans, they did. Charles Florin, the Oregon City butcher and Ted Newcomb, the Willamette Valley rancher were venomous when Zeke Hawthorne and Nate Bishop arrived for the opening.

"Hey, injun lover, where are your bastard kids?" Newcomb bellowed. That was followed by even more vile comments from Florin, but it was the one-armed Clive Newton who made Belknap the angriest.

"Smells like a pigsty, doesn't it?" He pointed at Hawthorne. "No, must be smellin' the results of sleeping with a squaw!"

Zeke slowed his pace at that, slowly let his fingers grasp the handle of his knife, and felt a gentle tug on his coat sleeve from Nate Bishop. "Not now, Zeke," he whispered. "He just turned most of this crowd against him with that comment."

"I won't use my knife unless he pulls his," Zeke said. He turned to Newton. "If you value the one arm you have left, you might want to shut your ugly mouth. If you even knew what a gentleman was, I'd call you out to the field of honor, but that, again, is a word you might not understand."

The crowd howled their approval, Zeke nodded to them, turned, and he and Bishop entered the building. "Well done," Bishop said. "I guess we have an idea of what might be said during the session and committee meetings. I thought better of George Belknap."

"Belknap is an educated gentleman, Nate, but those he leads are vermin. The dregs of the Firsters movement. When they put Phil Mason and Henry Foote in prison for their part in this program to make Oregon a slave state, they should have included many more."

For the next week, in committee meeting after meeting on the floor of the assembly, and at evening bull sessions, Zeke Hawthorne and Nate Bishop outlined their plans for developing the unorganized Idaho Territory while George Belknap spent an equal amount of time promoting the concept of Oregon coming into the union as a slave state. The two men seldom saw each other and when they did, Zeke went out of his way to be as polite as possible. Belknap did the same. It was on the street where the ugly took place.

"Well, my dignified and dangerous friend," Bishop said one morning when the two found their seats on the assembly floor, "I have joined the ranks of the street fighter." He wore a smile, hindered some by a fat lip and the leavings of a bloody nose.

"Just what have you done, Nate?"

"That nasty feller from Oregon City, Florin, came at me with a cudgel, a stout piece of oak, I believe, with the intent of putting a dent in my skull. He managed to hit me once, as you can see, and the last I saw of him, he was being cared for by Ted Newcomb and a couple of other Firsters.

"I outweigh the gentleman by at least forty pounds, and every one of those pounds to my benefit," he laughed. "I beat him soundly, Zeke. I did. He'll limp and whine for a week." Bishop settled into his cane back chair, reached into the interior pocket of his frock coat and showed the cudgel to Zeke. It measured a solid twelve inches of thick, gnarled oak.

"That's a fine one, Nate. I assume you'll carry that with the necessary dignity that it demands."

Their laughter was cut short when the speaker of the house gaveled the gathering into order for the day's business.

"THIS HAS BEEN A WEEK, Sarah. I'm exhausted." Zeke and Sarah were enjoying the comfort and warmth of their bed on a cold December night. The wind was screaming, flinging gobs of wet snow onto the bedroom window, and there was even a midwinter thunderstorm wreaking havoc with the atmosphere.

"When do you go back for the second session?"

"We're scheduled for the first Tuesday after New Year, and I need this break. We got our bills introduced and they have been assigned to committees, and we are hearing a lot of favorable comments from the members, but it's the vile, filthy, ignorant fools out on the street that make things so difficult." He had to chuckle, and then told Sarah about Nate Bishop beating the tar out of Florin.

"He's so proud of that cudgel, he's having it mounted and is going to hang it on the wall in his den."

"To change the subject, oh mighty warrior husband of mine, do you think this storm is going to have an effect on our Christmas party?"

"If it sticks around another few days it will. With Travis and that gang from Salem City coming and all of us here, if we have to do everything inside these old walls, they might just burst. You'll never keep Travis from having a party, so we'll just have to live with whatever Old Man Winter brings us."

"I have an early Christmas present for you, Sharp Knife," Sarah said. She snuggled deep into his arms and kissed his neck. "We'll have another mouth to feed early in the harvest next year."

GEORGE BELKNAP HADN'T STOPPED PACING FOR TWO DAYS following the legislative recess, and his language, aimed at anything and everyone, was virulent, far more than colorful. His friend and partner in the pro slavery movement, Geoff McGaskill poured each of them some fine Virginia bourbon and settled into a leather chair. "You'll wear out those elegant boots, George. Take a sip of good bourbon and give it up. We should never have allowed those people to become a part of our program.

"We have almost two weeks to do some serious planning before the second session gets underway. I've made inquiries and believe there is no chance for Hawthorne to get a constitutional convention called in this session, but his call for Idaho to break away from Oregon Territory has tremendous support. If he gets that through, the next legislative gathering is sure to call for a convention."

"Hell, Geoff, I'm in favor of Idaho breaking away, and I'll support a convention in '57." He sat down, drained the glass of whiskey and poured another. "Have your inquiries come up with any other little gems for us?"

"There doesn't seem to be a clear majority on either side of the slavery issue. As many people that support slavery, there are as many on the fence. For every supporter of a free state there is another on the fence. I think those without an opinion at this point are in the majority. That means, we have a lot of work in front of us."

"The most important thing we have to do, Geoff, is shut down those ignorant fools who call themselves Firsters. Ted Newcomb is an overgrown schoolyard bully, Clive needs to be put away, and Charles Florin must be stopped. As much as I would be in favor, we can't just shoot the fools."

"It would make it easier," McGaskill chuckled. "If we paid them off they'd just drink it up and be right back to being stupid. I think maybe it would be a good idea to publicly disassociate ourselves from them."

"You might have something there, Geoff," Belknap snapped, standing tall. "That's the best thing you've said in some time." He paced about, letting the idea take a firm hold.

Belknap poured more drinks for the two of them, and for the first time in a week, actually sat back in his chair. "A series of letters to the various newspapers in the territory would be a good start. You, me, maybe Pete Flowers and others we can trust, can stump the territory and speak publicly at every opportunity, disassociating ourselves from the Firsters and promoting Oregon as a slave state.

"Yes sir, Geoff, that might just be our salvation. It

would certainly clear us from the riffraff and make our platform obvious."

"Might just make you a United States Senator, George." McGaskill was very aware that Belknap had strong visions of that coming about. "Maybe a stop in the governor's office on the way, eh?" He got a sideways glance accompanied by the slightest smile back from the arrogant Virginian.

The two men spent the rest of that bottle of fine Virginia bourbon writing out their program for the two-week period between Christmas and the opening of the second session of the legislature.

BARBARA WHITELL finally decided about what to do with her busy shop. She designed fine gowns, was known up and down the valley as the best seamstress available and did not want to close her shop. She and Angus had discussed what to do about it for weeks. These were, thankfully, discussions, not arguments for Angus was proud of his feisty and independent wife.

"I'm not going to close the shop, Angus. I can't do the work from home either. I need people to come to the shop for measurements and to discuss what they need or want. I can't ask them to come out here." There was a rhythm to her toe tapping staccato, and it was gaining speed. "I'll go in for three days a week. Tuesday through Thursday. That will give me four days at home each week, with two of them being weekend days."

"You know I'd rather have you home every day, but since I'm at work five and half days, this will work. Now, dear lady, that settled, it's time to talk Christmas. The rains they keep right on falling, the roads are bogs, and Travis insists that the whole family meets at Zeke's on Christmas Eve or before. At least those drainage ditches we dug are working. We've got quite a stream running toward Mill Creek right now."

"Think we'll get a salmon run in that creek?" Barbara joshed.

"Now you're talking," He said. "Travis says he and Elaine are going up on the twenty-second. And then he said, 'You know, to help some.'"

"Papa's help will be from his mouth, out loud and often, and from the rum bottle. We have the mules, Angus, and the big wagon. I'm sure we'll make it. It's only twenty-five miles, or so.

"Besides, we've already wrapped all the gifts and made pies and puddings and cakes."

"Well, twenty-five miles to a Boston sailor is one thing, but I guess it doesn't mean much to a Shoshone princess who spent her youth dashing through the forest in bare feet fighting off grizzly bears and Crow warriors."

"You got it, white man," she laughed, cuffing him lightly on the shoulder. He reached out and picked her up and carried her into the bedroom. Laughter and giggles slowly turned into quiet sighs for the rest of the night.

A GRAND PROCESSION was seen leaving Salem City on the morning of December 22, consisting of several wagons and buggies along with outriders. Elaine Travis drove a team of grays pulling a spring wagon heaped with boxes, packages, and blanket-wrapped items. Barbara Whitell drove a team of mules ahead of a heavy wagon filled to the top as well, and Thaddeus Chapman and his daughter Clementine were in a surrey driven by a team of dancing ponies.

Travis, Angus, and Moose were on horseback. It was a gray day, heavy wet clouds obliterated any color or brightness, and the wind carried guarantees of more rain. Mud flew in every direction with every step of every animal, but none of this had dampened a single spirit.

Moving slowly through the deep mud, Travis turned in the saddle looking back across the train and started bellowing a Christmas carol. Within moments, everyone was singing and laughing, and the idea of driving twenty-five miles to the Hawthorne farm seemed to be an excellent idea. Everyone had something tucked in the wagon seat or saddlebag to munch on, and the train didn't stop until they made the turn into the farm.

"I love a party with lots of food for everyone," Travis cried out more than once during the journey. "I plan to eat and drink everything in sight for three or four days," he laughed.

Moose rode close to the Chapman surrey during the trip, talking with Thaddeus and Clemmie. "You'll come to love my crazy family," he said. "Remember, we're half wild savages by blood, and all wild savages by design."

Thaddeus liked to be called Tad, and joined the merriment. "I'm afraid we're east coast all the way, Moose, but I'll say, your father certainly does know how to have fun."

"He's the hardest working man I've ever known, Tad, but when it comes time for a party, he's the first one in the door. He put on a feast every year at Fort Bridger, for the tribe, the old-timer mountain men that were still around, and for anyone who happened to be there. He's big, he's loud and boisterous, and the most honest man in Oregon Territory."

"I'm very glad that we're becoming a part of this wild, savage family," Chapman laughed. "When I lost my wife and Clemmie and I decided to come west, we had no idea what to expect. We knew nothing about Oregon other than what we read in the papers, but when my company accepted my offer of coming here to open the west for them, they seemed delighted and so were we."

Moose had been very formal when asking for Clemmie's hand, had spent considerable time discussing just what she would be marrying into, including all his background with the Shoshone nation. He didn't hide anything or try to disguise anything, and Chapman gave his approval at once. He only asked that they be married by a clergyman.

Moose had no problem with that and then told how Zeke and Sarah had been married the mountain man way with Travis doing the honors. "Those old ways are going away, Tad. Old Gabe is an old man now, I haven't heard from Carson in ages. When I saw Broken Hand last summer he said our mountains will be filled with people within a generation.

"I will always be a Shoshone, Tad, you must remember that. Your grandchildren will have tribal blood, and they'll be raised to be proud of that. I will love your daughter forever, sir, and she'll not want of warmth, food, or protection, ever."

Chapman was thinking of that night as he drove the surrey along the muddy River Road. *Just months ago, I sold insurance to men in fine silk suits wearing tall silk or beaver hats, men that raised fine racing horses, built large buildings, and sat at the head of the boardroom tables. And Clementine is about to marry a man who is a respected member of the Shoshone tribe, wears traditional buckskins, is on a first name basis with men I've read about in history books, and is a partner in a successful lumber mill. My God, life can be more than entertaining.*

As the day progressed the weather seemed to lighten up some. The threatened rain did not appear, the clouds thinned, and periods of warm sunshine fell about their shoulders.

"I knew it!" Travis bawled from his lead position. It was a joyous group that drove up the lane to Hawthorne's large farmhouse.

Hiram was the first to spot the caravan and raced down the path to welcome them. Travis put an arm down and Hiram grabbed it to swing up behind his grandfather for the final hundred yards or so. Zeke and Sarah came out onto the wide veranda porch, Sarah holding little Travis and the twins holding her skirts. Buck O'Keefe and the Saunders boys came rolling out of the bunkhouse, and a small city of people gathered to say Merry Christmas.

THE RAINS and cold weather held off and most meals were had outside, those at the tables protected by fire pits placed strategically around the long, rough-hewn table. For three days, what has become known as the Travis Clan in the territory partied, honored the holiday, and ate and drank everything in sight, just as Travis had proclaimed.

"You took quite a beating during the opening session, Zeke. Is it worth it?" Travis had herded Zeke, Moose, and

Hiram out the kitchen door and toward the creek that was still running slightly more than full. "The newspaper seemed to give the impression that those attacking you were numerous."

"Not so," Zeke answered. "Just a small group of ignorant fools, Travis. These are the same idiots we've been fighting from the day we arrived in Oregon City. Inside the chambers things were considerably different."

"I was led to believe that if Oregon gets its statehood that there would be immediate raises in taxes on businesses like mine," Travis said.

"I've heard the same thing," Moose said.

"This is coming from a small group that is against statehood. It's a given that any political entity must have revenue to operate, and that is generated by taxes. The taxes that are in place to run the territory will probably be transferred to the state. I don't see any need to increase or add to what we generate right now."

"When are you going back, Moose?" Hiram asked.

"Tad and Clemmie want to leave tomorrow. You have something in mind?"

"There are fish in that creek, you know. And we haven't had much chance to talk." Hiram wasn't willing to give up his time with his uncle, no matter how his uncle felt about a certain young lady.

Moose turned, whopped Hiram across the shoulders and took off back to the barns as fast as he could go. Hiram was almost ten years younger than the big man and within moments had caught him, whopped him back as he passed, and was waiting at the barn doors for him.

"We won't see them much before sunset," Travis said.

"I swear that boy of yours is going to be as big as Moose. He was just a skinny little kid, Zeke."

"He was that, but he wasn't fed right, and surely didn't work hard. He runs this farm, Travis. He and I are going to build him his own house this winter. Can you imagine that?" They found that their conversation had taken them almost into the gentle rise that led to where Hiram wanted his house.

"Just over that little ridge," Zeke pointed. "The land flattens out some and that's where we'll build his home. I taught him how to make engineering drawings, drawings to scale, and his house is going to be something. All right out of his head. Man's got a knack for visualizing what he wants to build."

"You mean, like his Papa before him?" They laughed loud at that, turned and headed back to the home ranch.

31

"Have you heard what George Belknap has been saying in the newspapers about us?" There was a gathering of some of the old Firsters at Bud Best's shack in the foothills south of Salem City. "Says we're just a bunch of ignorant fools and we are not associated in any way with his programs."

"How do you know that?" Clive Newton pulled on a bottle of whiskey and passed it to Charlie Florin.

"That's what it said in the newspaper."

"You can't read anymore that I can. Can you read, Charlie? Did Belknap really say that?"

"I could make out just what Bud said. Said that we were hooligans and should have been arrested for what we did to old Hawthorne. Hell, Clive, I thought we were doing it because that's what Belknap wanted us to do." Florin took the bottle, tipped it back for a good swallow and handed it off. "Maybe that old southern gentleman needs a good horsewhipping himself."

Heavy footsteps were heard just before the door to the

shack flew open and Ted Newcomb came in. "I heard the word, horsewhip," he said. "Who're we going after, that injun lovin' Hawthorne?"

"Glad you made it, Ted. Have a drink." Bud Best handed the bottle to Newcomb. "We're talking about what George Belknap's been saying about us in the newspapers. He's calling us fools, hooligans, criminals. I thought we were doing what he wanted."

"We were," Newcomb snarled. "Now, he's got himself all riled, turned yeller and squeamish, and is blaming us for his failures. Hell, boys, a horsewhipping might just be what that old man needs. Bring him down from the high horse he rides." He took another long pull on the whiskey and settled in at the table with the others. Newcomb was just as big as his voice and mannerisms, forcing those at the table to adjust for him to take as much room as he wanted.

"What we have to concentrate on is stopping Hawthorne. Belknap has forgotten that, so it's up to us to finish the job. Belknap talks about his Virginia background and education as if that alone will stop a man like Hawthorne. Hawthorne's smarter than Belknap, but he doesn't have the country savvy of men like us.

"Best way to stop him is to hurt his family. He'll turn and run if they're threatened, and I know which member to take. Henry Foote had the right idea, he was just too stupid to know how to do it. He went after that little seamstress with his cane, late at night, when he should have gone after her with a lynch mob at sunrise. That's what we need to do."

The man at the table one would expect to be totally involved, Clive Newton, frowned and slapped the table.

"No! The sheriff, his deputy, and half the damn territory would know it was us the minute something like that happened."

"Clive's right," Bud Best said. "Belknap said in the newspaper that if anything happened to Hawthorne or his family, we would be responsible."

"That bastard set us up," Newcomb snarled. "The legislature opens Tuesday morning for the second session. That gives us two days to come up with something. You got another bottle hidden around here, Bud?"

NATE BISHOP WAS RIDING a fine horse down the River Road, trailing a pack mule that seemed almost overloaded. He'd spent his Christmas and New Year holiday at his home ranch in the Snake River country, north of Fort Boise and up in the foothills east of the river. Bishop was heading for Salem City and the opening of the second session of the legislature. He turned up the lane toward the Hawthorne farm and a visit with Zeke and the family.

"That old mule's gonna collapse, Nate." Zeke and Hiram came out of the barn to welcome Bishop. "Hope you're planning to spend the night, old man."

"Thank you, sir, I was," Bishop laughed. He climbed down from his horse, handing the reins to Hiram. "Quite a bit of what's on that old mule's back is gonna stay right here when I leave out in the morning. Gifts from the unorganized territory of Idaho," he laughed. "Anything exciting go on while I was away?"

"You might put it that way," Zeke said. "Let's find some sweet rolls and coffee and talk some. Sarah will be glad to see you, and be advised, the twins can run, jump, and are sure to spill your coffee at least once."

It was a pot of coffee and several cinnamon rolls later that Zeke and Bishop took a walk out to the barn. "So, Belknap provoked those Firsters into all those attacks and now leaves them hanging like salmon on a stick. They'll simply get angry and act even more stupid, Zeke." He kicked a rock thinking about it. "They'll come after you, sure as hell, my friend."

Bishop undid the pack from the mule and distributed his bounty among the Hawthorne children, holding back one package. "This is for Sarah, Zeke. Wait until I'm gone in the morning before you give it to her."

"I can smell it from here, Nate."

The two men spent the rest of the day and well into the evening talking about the second session coming up starting Tuesday morning. Nate Bishop, with a much lighter pack on his mule left for Salem City early in the morning. "You keep your eyes open, Nate. The session gets underway day after tomorrow, and those fools might try anything to keep us from attending."

"You do the same, Zeke. They are more than treacherous."

Zeke watched him ride down the path to the River Road and walked back to the barn. "I wonder just what he brought that smells so good and it's for Sarah only." He picked up the package, which seemed to weigh at least ten pounds, and walked to the house.

"This is for you, my pretty," he said. "Nate brought this from the Snake River country just for you."

"Oh, that smells good," she said. It took a sharp knife to get the cords off and when she finally got the large package opened she shrieked in pleasure. "Zeke," she cried. "Look." It was about ten pounds of smoked buffalo meat, cut in strips, the Indian way. "It's the hump meat, Zeke. What a wonderful thing to do. Oh, my!"

She reached out for Zeke's knife and cut away a couple of pieces, gave one to him and munched, as noisily as she could on her piece. "I'm in love," she cooed. The family had smoked buffalo hump stew for supper that night, the first time the twins had tasted the delightful meat. Sarah wagged her fingers at the girls and laughed, "Shoshone women eat meat, girls. Never forget that."

ZEKE RODE into town on Monday to prepare for the opening of the legislature the next morning. He maintained a small apartment in the capital city but made his first stop at the sheriff's office. "I just want you to be aware of what might happen during this next session, Fred."

"Do you think Belknap's comments in the paper will stop the Firsters and their attacks on you?"

"I'm afraid of just the opposite," Zeke said. "Belknap has embarrassed those fools, they know now they were used, and they'll take their anger out on those in the legislature that back me and Nate Bishop."

"Do you think Belknap's safe? Seems likely they would go after him as well." Sheriff Fred Sharp got up and stuffed a couple of pieces of hardwood in the stove and poured more coffee for the two of them. "Belknap's a snake, Zeke, and men like Clive Newton and Bud Best are easily led. I'm not sure what I can do. I surely can't put deputies out to protect each member of the legislature."

"I think having deputies about, being seen, would be enough, but they must be ready to act if something starts. In December, you remember, by the time your people arrived on the scene it was too late, and they weren't ready to fight once they got there."

"I've made some changes to take care of that." The embarrassed Sheriff Sharp said. "I'll have two or three deputies on foot patrol around the area, Zeke. Good luck."

Zeke rode to his apartment and got settled in for what he figured would be a two to three week stay. *We're in the middle of the nineteenth century and the human being doesn't seem to have evolved one degree since the time of the Greek philosophers. I wonder if I'm just jousting with windmills or if mankind can accept the concept of a slave free state. Men have put men in chains for hundreds of thousands of years and all I can do or say is; that's wrong.*

TUESDAY MORNING WAS COLD, wet, and stormy. Zeke woke in a foul mood, having been awakened several times by howling winds, massive claps of thunder, and, at least, one tree falling near his second-story window. "These rains will make my crops grow," he said out loud, nursing a fire to life in his kitchen stove. "If I say it often enough, I'll find some way to smile."

With a fire burning hot there was soon a pot of coffee, and Assemblyman Ezekiel Hawthorne was in a better mood. He could see the remains of the tree outside his window and thanked his lucky stars it hadn't come right through the wall. He fried some bacon that Sarah sent with him, poured cup after cup of good coffee, and went through all his notes for today's opening session.

"I'm ready," he murmured. "Bring on the stupid." He tucked everything in a leather case, bundled up and headed out the door for the two-block walk to the capitol building. His eyes darted about as he made the trek, and didn't find anything out of the ordinary. He let his right hand nudge the big knife he always carried and felt good feeling the handle.

Cold rain splashed across the grounds driven by gale force winds, and the few people who were out scurried from point to point, keeping their eyes on the ground for fear of tripping over debris. Many trees had lost branches during the night, and the city's trash was being blown about willy-nilly.

As he turned on to the capitol grounds he found Nate Bishop coming toward him. "Good morning, to you, Nate. Fine weather for our first day, eh?"

"Good morning, Zeke," he said. "You look fit. Just think, in just a few weeks it'll be spring." They laughed and turned toward the steps leading into the building when a shot rang out and Zeke heard the whap as the big lead ball slammed into Nate Bishop's back. The man was flung forward from the bullet's velocity and crashed head-long into the oak doors of the building.

Zeke grabbed his friend and pulled him into the building as two more shots rang out, splintering part of the doors. Legislators, spectators, and others scattered as the gunfire echoed through the early morning storm. Zeke felt for a pulse and found one, and tried to get Bishop's heavy coat off and find the wound. "Easy, old friend. Don't you die on me, now."

The fifty-eight- caliber lead ball had slammed into Bishop's back, tore through his kidneys, nicked his liver, and tore up his intestines. Blood was pouring from the wound and Zeke couldn't even slow it down. Nate Bishop died just as Fred Sharp pushed through the crowd to help Zeke.

"One of my men saw three men with rifles just after hearing the shots and gave chase, knocking Bud Best down and putting him under arrest. The other two got away. Deputy Hank Hawes is sure one of them was Clive Newton."

"This all goes right back to George Belknap, Fred. Best and Newton may have done the shooting, but Belknap is responsible for this man's death."

32

It was a subdued session that lasted for a two long, cold weeks, wrapping up after not being able to come to a positive vote on the question of a constitutional convention to gain statehood for the territory. "The only positive that came out of this session was the separation of Idaho territory from Oregon." Zeke was sitting at Molly's Clam Shack down on the waterfront, talking with Sullivan.

"I'll tell you right now, Sully, because of Nate's murder, Oregon will be a free state following the next legislative session. Belknap's finished. The Firsters have been cleaned out. Bud Best will hang because he was the only one caught, but they tell me Clive Newton has given up his teamster's business, and Ted Newcomb is selling out."

"Nate Bishop was a good man, Zeke. Have you heard from his family?"

"Yes. He has a fine cattle operation in the foothills above the Snake River and they will be fine. His children are old enough to run the ranch. What a miserable person he must be to shoot a man in the back like that. Face to face, man to man, that's fine with me, but to shoot a man in the back and then run away. That's the lowest scum I can think of."

"What happens now, Zeke?"

"I've got a big farm to run, a big family to take care of, and several months to worry about what's next." An ironic grin crossed his face, as he settled back in his chair, and looked out across the Willamette River, in deep contemplation. "This whole issue of statehood has been a frustrating experience, Sully. I will stand for re-election on the free state of Oregon platform and we'll work hard for that convention. Plus, there won't be any Belknaps or Clive Newtons to clutter things up. I'm leaving for home first thing in the morning."

"You've said the right words, though" Sullivan said. "I will begin the process of getting you re-elected, my friend. I've already written several tracts that I'll have printed and ready for distribution."

"You are something, Mr. Sullivan," Zeke laughed. "That's the first time I've been able to laugh for three weeks, sir."

ZEKE HAWTHORNE WAS on the River Road not long after sunrise, driving a surrey with two grays pulling it along at a good clip. *What a horrible time this has been. I've lost an excellent friend, we made little progress toward our goal of statehood, and our new governor, George Law Curry seems on the fence when it comes to statehood.* Zeke got a smile across his face and said right out loud, "I've got a few months to change his mind, though, and by damn, I will."

There are times I wish I were more like Travis. Right about now he'd break out in some rowdy, bawdy mountain man ditty, get the horses riled and into a good gallop, and not have a care in the world. He's the finest man I know.

He was about half way home when he saw two riders approaching, coming at a strong trot. *Now what?* He made sure his rifle was at the ready and he had access to his knife. As the riders got closer, he relaxed and gave a hearty yell of hello to the boys. Hiram and Buck O'Keefe roared their welcome back.

Traffic was effectively stopped on the River Road as everyone dismounted and hugged their howdies and welcome home salutes. The excitement was over within minutes, the boys were mounted and Zeke had the team moving smartly. "It's good to see you two. This must have had this pretty well timed," Zeke said.

"According to our plan, you left Salem City a little later that we thought. Hiram figured we'd run into you much closer to the farm." Buck O'Keefe was wrapped in a buffalo robe and Hiram was wearing one of Moose's old blanket coats to ward off the winter cold.

"You got me there, Buck," Zeke laughed. "Everything okay at home, Hi?"

"Just missing you, Papa. I shot a swan yesterday and Mama's going to roast it for supper for tonight. I kept our feed corn separate from everything in the cribs, and it's a good thing. Mr. O'Brien bought everything we had. Mr. Johnson said that O'Brien is shipping thousands of pounds of hides out of his Portland warehouse."

It was a gay ride home. Despite the storm thrashing about, the river high and roiled, all the three men and boys were filled with good thoughts. Hiram and Buck took over the team when they arrived home, and Zeke had one satchel and one carpet bag in hand when he slipped in to the house through the kitchen door.

A tornado of love and kisses welcomed him. Sarah flung her arms around his neck, Suzanne and Joanne flung their arms around his legs, and little Travis did what he could to crawl across the floor to welcome big Papa home. "I was so worried when we got the news about the shooting," Sarah said. "I almost sent Hiram to make sure you were okay."

"This has been a miserable time, Sarah. I lost a dear friend, we have been frustrated in our efforts at statehood, and ignorant hooligans seem to have won the day. Did the sheriff send a rider to tell you I was fine?"

"Yes, that's how we found out about poor, dear Nate. Are you home for the winter?"

"I am," he said, pulling her in closer and feeling her meld into him. "I missed you so much, dear lady. I told Sully I would stand for re-election, but only this one time. I'll not continue in the world of politics. There is a definite lack of truth and ethics in that game," he chortled.

He managed to free himself from the women, picked up little Travis, and sat down at the kitchen table. Sarah brought him fresh hot coffee, his bottle of rum, and joined him. She spent the first minute just gazing into his eyes, smiling her welcome home.

"You're very tired, Zeke," she said. "Are you sure you want to go through all this again?"

"I'm exhausted," he said. "It would be easy to say no, to quit, just accepting defeat, but you know that's not who I am."

"No," she said. She smiled at him, took his hand, and continued. "My man, Sharp Knife, doesn't quit."

"It'll be spring soon and this old farm is going to need me. According to the Hawthorne farm manager, Hiram Hawthorne, we sold our crops at a profit this year, despite my not being around much, and he has plans for increasing our output this next year.

"I'd best be careful, though... that boy will be shoving me aside soon, assigning me to a rocking chair somewhere." He was laughing as he poured a healthy dose of rum into a fresh cup of coffee. "You haven't said anything about our soon to be new addition, Sarah."

"There's activity in the playroom," she giggled. "I think we'll be looking at late August for the arrival. That will give us five children in four years, oh mighty warrior husband."

"If this child is a boy I'd like to name him Nathaniel. Would that be right?"

"More than right, Zeke. And, if a girl, maybe Natalie? That's a pretty name."

BUCK O'KEEFE ANNOUNCED during supper that he would be leaving the farm in the next week or so, and travelling to Arkansas country to work for the army as a scout and guide. "Moose introduced me to some of the people last spring and I've been accepted. This will make Hiram very happy," he laughed.

"Hiram spent most of this last summer trying to teach me to be a farmer and he'll be the first one to tell you, it didn't work out very well."

"Another season or two and you'd have been fine, Buck," Hiram laughed. "Will you work with the army or be in the army?"

"I'll be a scout and guide attached to an army unit, according to the packet I received." He looked around the table, at the twins, Sarah, Zeke, and let his eyes stop at Hiram. "I'm going to miss this. You've taken me in as one of your own, and I love you all. I'll never forget these times. Ever."

"You'll always be welcome here, Buck O'Keefe," Zeke said. "You've learned considerable from Moose and you would be wise to remember it. There will be difficult times coming, with hundreds of thousands of people streaming through from the east, literally forcing those already there to move aside. There will be hurt, anger, desperation on both sides, and the army will be the instigators of most of the trouble.

"They'll blame the problems on the savages, of course, and you'll often find yourself in the middle. You've a fine head on those shoulders, Buck. You'll have our prayers and good thoughts all your days."

The rest of supper was quiet, everyone deep in their own thoughts. "Buck told me yesterday that he was leaving," Rebecca said. She stood up and crossed to the large cook stove. "I made us something special for the occasion." She opened the oven door and pulled out two large pots, steaming with flavor. "Buck told me his mother made the best peach cobbler in the world, but tonight, he's going to have to put up with second best."

She pulled large soup bowls out of the cupboard and ladled full helpings into each. The twins got smaller bowls, but when everyone was served, both large pots were almost empty. The big surprise came when she sent Hiram out to the springhouse to bring in another big bowl, this one filled with whipped cream she had stashed out there.

"If this doesn't show you our love, nothing will," Zeke laughed. "My God, it's been years since I've had peach cobbler and whipped cream. You'll have to leave more often, Buck, if we're going to get this kind of dessert."

The almost somber atmosphere was lifted and gaiety returned to the table. "It's the nicest party I've ever been to," Buck said. "Rebecca, your cobbler ties with ma's."

* * *

"I WANTED Oregon in the union as a free state and she's not there yet," Zeke said. He and Hiram were walking to the barn to saddle their horses. "As your mother said, I'm not a quitter. We'll make it yet. Tell me about this house we're going to build, young man, and about all these new fields we'll be planting."

Hiram and Zeke spent the rest of the day riding over the new quarter section of land they had purchased. Hiram had the plans for the house drawn up and they spent time plotting its location, even putting some preliminary stakes in. "Will you be comfortable living off our home place? I understand the desire for independence. I've lived with it my entire life," Zeke said. "The first time, though, can be a bit overwhelming."

. "Everything I know, I know because of you and Mama, and Uncle Moose. I read English, Latin, and Greek. I speak English and Shoshone. I'm going to finish my training in cabinetry with you, finish my metal training with you, and become the finest farmer in Oregon because of you.

"Mama has taught me, you have taught me, Uncle Moose has taught me, and I'm ready to put all that to good use. I need a little room, Papa."

"I've never been prouder of anyone in my life, Hiram. You're a man in every sense of the word, and it is time. We'll build you your home. I'll be running for re-election, pal, so the farm will be yours again this next season. Let's spend the next few weeks putting all of this together."

They rode back to the barns across rolling hills, dotted with stands of hardwood, fir, cedar, and pine, grasses thick with what animals need, and it took just a nudge from Hiram to get a full out race for home started. Both men were excellent horsemen, both were riding fine stock, and both knew the country well.

From the porch just outside her kitchen, Sarah watched her two "boys" howl and laugh, charging into the wide area around the barn at a full gallop. "Just like Papa, these boys will never grow up, either," she smiled.

"I almost had you, Papa," Hiram laughed. He jumped off his horse, taking the reins from Zeke. "Almost."

"The old man's still got it, eh son?" Zeke was whopping Hiram on the shoulders and got a good whop back as they led their horses into the corral. "It's gonna be a good year, Hiram. A good year all the way around."

A LOOK AT OREGON STATEHOOD
(EZEKIEL'S JOURNEY BOOK III)

Spring floods, outlaws roaming the Willamette Valley, and men with clubs looking to pound his head will not stop Ezekiel Hawthorne from striving for statehood for his beloved Oregon. Young Hiram takes on a gang of outlaws and Travis enjoys the best Christmas party he's ever thrown.

Moose invites a young lady to spend the rest of her days in his lodge and feisty little Barbara, with the help of a shotgun, tangles with outlaws.

Every journey has a beginning and an end, but statehood is yet another beginning. Zeke is hurt, worn out, and enthralled as 1858 finds another star added to that magnificent starred and striped banner, and he can retire in peace and honor.

AVAILABLE NOW FROM JOHNNY GUNN AND WOLFPACK PUBLISHING

ABOUT THE AUTHOR

Reno, Nevada novelist, Johnny Gunn, is retired from a long career in journalism. He has worked in print, broadcast, and Internet, including a stint as publisher and editor of the Virginia City Legend. These days, Gunn spends most of his time writing novel length fiction, concentrating on the western genre. Or, you can find him down by the Truckee River with a fly rod in hand.

Gunn and his wife, Patty, live on a small hobby farm about twenty miles north of Reno, sharing space with a couple of horses, some meat rabbits, a flock of chickens, and one crazy goat.